Big Bad Betrayal

An Enemies-to-Lovers Wolf Shifter Romance

Werewolves of Wall Street
Book 6

Renee Rose

Lee Savino

Content Warnings:

This book depicts an enemy cult with demeaning sex rites and gender roles for females. The topic is not glorified, but if you find it triggering, we suggest you skip this book in favor of our cozy paranormal series, *Bad Boy Bears* or *Shifter Ops*.

Note from the Authors:

This book features a Deaf character who was taught Total Communication (speaking, ASL, and lip reading). It should be noted that lip reading is only 30% accurate, so Noah catching full sentences is unrealistic. While the signs described in this book are actual ASL signs, in order to ease the reading process, the conversations are not written in true ASL format. In the audiobook, the narrator does not attempt to replicate deaf speech patterns. This decision was made to preserve clarity and respect while telling the story in audio format.

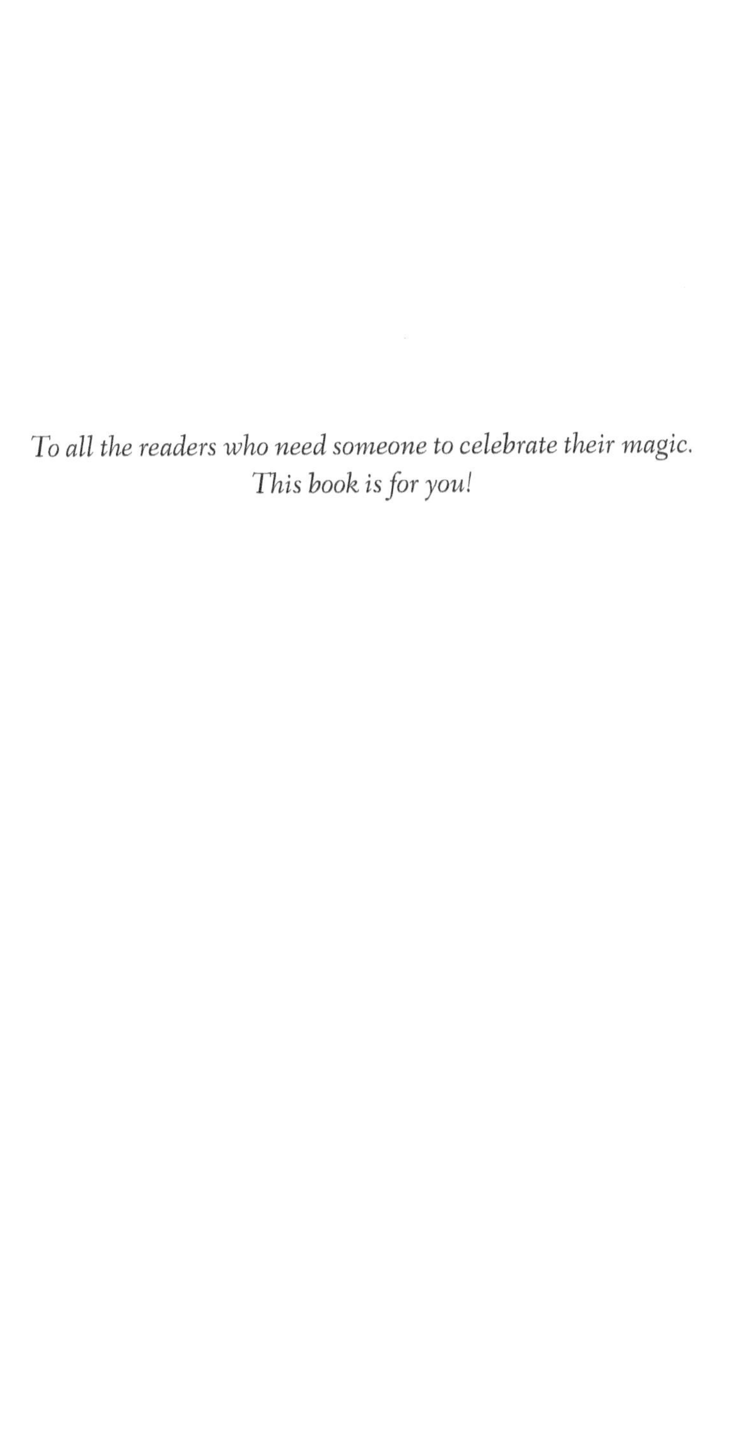

*To all the readers who need someone to celebrate their magic.
This book is for you!*

Want FREE books?

Receive a slew of free Renee Rose books: Go to **http://subscribepage.com/alphastemp** to sign up for Renee Rose's newsletter and receive free books. In addition to the free stories and bonus material, you will also get special pricing, exclusive previews and news of new releases.

Did you know you can buy direct from Renee Rose? Get signed books, special editions, and heavily discounted bundles. Use this coupon for an additional 10% discount on your entire order - READER10

Or go here
https://shop.reneeroseromance.com/discount/READER10

Download a free Lee Savino book from www.leesavino.com

Prologue

ster, 12 Years Old

Oma thinks I'm asleep, which is the only reason I hear her order a child's murder.

As a seeress for the Adalwulf pack, I'm called to use my power for the good of the pack. But on this cold, dark night, I wish I could live as a normal girl. Then I wouldn't be overhearing Oma, the seeress, plot with the high priest of the Moonborn, the Warden.

I'm curled up in an overstuffed armchair in her quarters, where I'd passed out with an aching head after she put me through a grueling afternoon and evening of training. I woke when the Warden entered, my body coming alert, wary in the presence of a predator, but pretended to be asleep, remaining still and keeping my breath slow.

I work hard to make myself invisible here in the Adalwulf castle. It helps me avoid verbal or physical abuse at the hands of Odin or Aiden. They hate anything they can't control—and no one can control the Sight. Deep down, they fear and resent our witch-muddied bloodline, even though Oma and I are prized possessions as their pack's veilwalkers–the Seeresses who can see beyond the veils of reality into the future.

"I had a vision," Oma tells the Warden.

I can't see him, but I can sense his aura. It's grey and thick and oily like putrid smoke. In man form, he's big and burly, a brutal enforcer. He's always in war paint–his ice-blue eyes framed in a band of black. It's supposed to evoke his wolf's distinct markings. I think he looks like a raccoon. His long, white-blond hair worn with a drastic side-part, makes him look like a mad wizard. Right now, he's probably taking Oma's measure. Normally, she would offer her visions up directly to Odin, so the fact that she called the Warden in here and is speaking to him in hushed tones means there's subterfuge going on.

My skin prickles with warning. Knowledge is power, and secrets are the most powerful of all. I learned that early in my seeress training.

"You need to kill the wolf without ears," Oma murmurs.

"What did you see?" The Warden's voice always sounds harsh. Cold and hungry for violence, never sated.

"It is not for you to interpret the visions," Oma says in the authoritative voice she uses when working with the big egos of dangerous wolves. "I am the Seeress."

"And I don't take orders from you." His voice is as cold as his eyes, and I have to stop myself from reflexively curling into a tighter ball.

I hear Oma pace around the small antechamber to her bedroom. Unlike the wolves who prowl this mansion, her movements are loud and uneven. We're in the medieval stone behemoth built in the crook of the Adalwulf pack's pine forest, nestled at the foot of a mountain beside a crystalline lake. There's electricity and hot water, but Oma insists on living in the dark ages, lighting candles and using the fire for heat. She says fire contains magic, so we must keep it close.

I hear the sound of Oma's teapot boiling, and she pours two cups of tea. The scent of lavender and lemon balm nips at my nose. She's stalling. She always pours tea when she's debating her next course of action.

Oma's ancient—she won't tell me exactly how old, but I think it's over one hundred. She and Odin, the alpha of the Adalwulf pack, are magically bound by a powerful spell. Oma draws power from Odin's body, giving her an unnaturally long life. By sharing in his alpha magic, all of her visions are of and for the pack's well-being. She siphons some of his alpha power, as she did from his father before him. He will be the last alpha she serves, though. When he dies, so will she.

The fire pops and crackles in the grate.

"I won't drink your witch's brew," the Warden says.

"I have no reason to poison you." A touch of condescension in Oma's tone. A bluff, a challenge. Oma has plenty of poisons in her apothecary. My first chores revolved around tending, picking, drying, and storing the powerful plant medicine. I wouldn't put it past her to put something in the Warden's tea, to make him more pliable. She's done it to me plenty of times.

Another long silence. This is how you play pack politics: slowly, using silence to shift the power to your side. It's not easy when you're the lone woman among arrogant alphas—cruel wolves who'd rather kill first and never ask questions.

A chair scrapes across the stone, the sound startling me. I stifle my gasp. It's nothing, I tell myself. Just Oma is settling into a seat at her table.

There's so much tension, it's hard for me to breathe.

"I had a vision of a wolf without ears breaking the stone altar. Desecrating the bond of magic shared by the Moonborn and the Adalwulfs. The dais itself cracked in half, and the pup straddled the broken halves. He was bathed in moonlight. He wore the mantle of the Adalwulf alpha."

The clink of china and a slurping sound tell me Oma's sipping her tea.

"You think it's the deaf pup born from the Blood Heir Alpha Rites."

Goosebumps inexplicably race across my skin. Every nerve in my body charges, like I've been asleep for all of my life until this moment.

It takes all my concentration not to bolt upright, wide-eyed and ready.

Everything in the pack revolves around the Adalwulf alpha. His power is propped up by the cult of the Moonborn.

Hundreds of years ago, the Grandmothers' Coven made a pact with the Adalwulfs. The pack provided protection to the coven in the new world, and in exchange, the coven offered up and bound their most powerful veilwalker to the Adalwulf pack to serve as Seeress. Over the years, the veilwalkers and the wolves bred together to become the Moonborn.

The Alpha Rites—the sex ceremony in which the alpha females are stripped naked and blindfolded, bound with vines to the ceremonial stone to be bred by the alpha or several powerful alpha males—ensures the most powerful pup becomes alpha.

Oma's vision means the end to all that. And it all revolves around a deaf pup. Is that why Oma wants to kill him, "the wolf with no ears"?

Pain stabs my head, a return of my headache from

earlier. I hear whispers from beyond the veil. The Grand-mothers speak to me, and they have much to say. Trouble is, they're all clamoring at once–I can't distinguish any message.

"Yes, the one we swapped for Aiden."

Swapped for Aiden! Swapped. For. Aiden.

Oh, sweet moon goddess. This is a revelation. Aiden isn't really Odin's son? The pup he raised as his own? The pup meant to rule the pack?

Suddenly, Oma's vision makes sense. She's taught me how to interpret the visions and signs we receive. The symbols the Moon Goddess uses to make things clear.

The Moonborn leaders didn't want to face Odin's wrath if they presented him with a deaf infant after conducting the Blood Heir Alpha Rites. They must have told him Aiden was the first child born from the rite, swapping out the true firstborn, who was deaf. Now, with the vision of that child being the true heir to the pack, Oma must destroy the threat to Odin's "son" Aiden before her lies are uncovered.

The whispers in my ears grow louder and more tangled.

"You told everyone the boy was dead," the Warden grates.

"And you let his mother bargain for his life. Track him down and destroy the threat."

My stomach clenches into a knot. I hate this part of being a seeress–choosing who lives and who dies. I don't know if I'll be able to do it. I don't know if I'll be able to become as hard and brutal as Oma.

A horrible sound echoes through the room. It takes me a moment to realize it's laughter. The Warden is laughing. "You fucked up," he says to Oma. "You thought you'd cover it up, but it didn't work, and now you want me to fix it, or you'll suffer Odin's wrath."

"We both will," Oma's tone is cool. "Or don't you remember the part you played?"

I strain my ears, wanting to know what the Warden did that makes him fall silent when Oma reminds him, but neither of them explains.

"Find the wolf with no ears and kill him," Oma repeats.

"Again, I don't take orders from you. But I'll kill the pup."

I hear the door open and close, but otherwise, the Warden moves silently.

Oma's cup clinks in the saucer, and she sighs. "How much of that did you hear?"

Keeping secrets from Oma is a game I hope to win one day. Unfortunately, it seems the woman can fish anything out of my head. I sit up and rub my eyes against the candle-light. "All of it."

"You think I'm being too harsh? Ordering the death of a pup?"

Yep, she plucked the thought right out of my head. "I know you see beyond the veil and judge accordingly."

Oma hacks up a laugh. "An evasive answer if I ever heard one. Well done."

She's the one who taught me "seeress speak" or the art of saying nothing yet still sounding wise. I'm good enough to fool most wolves but not her and probably not the most alpha wolves like the Warden or Odin. It's a skill I'll need to master before I'm the seeress for real.

"Ask the spirits then and see for yourself." Her black eyes bore into me. *Ask,* she orders silently, and I hear it like a booming voice in my head. A compulsion.

So I center myself and open up my senses to the

beyond. This is what it means to be a veilwalker, though I'm apparently stronger than most. Lucky me.

Is the boy a threat? I ask in my head.

The answer is immediate. A flood of images that rush through my head too quickly for me to see while every muscle in my body tightens. My breath is stifled like I'm being choked.

He wields destruction. He will bring an end to the Moonborn.

An end to the Moonborn, the cult at the heart of our pack. I am Moonborn. All my life, I've been taught to uphold the sect's traditions. My position as future Seeress, all my training revolves around the Moonborn's service to the Adalwulf pack. Someday I will be bound to Aiden in a bonding ritual the way Oma is bound to Odin.

If the cult is gone, my entire world would be destroyed.

Oma won't allow that to happen.

I gasp when the spirits release me.

Oma is still watching me with her usual piercing stare, but I can sense that she's pleased with me. "Did you see?"

I nod because even though I didn't see the vision clearly, I heard the message, loud and clear.

"Then you know why I summoned the Warden. You may never speak of this night." The look she gives me tells me death would be my reward if I do.

I bow my head. "You know I won't." Even though my head swims with all the secrets. The false heir. The wolf with no ears.

The destruction of the Moonborn and probably our entire pack.

"Good. Go to bed."

I untuck my legs and stand, feeling the pins and needles attack my sleeping feet. I curtsey. "Goodnight, Oma."

She rests her hand on the top of my head, sending a moon blessing down through my crown. "Sleep."

I rush out of the room, running through the dark corridors to reach the stairs to the dim tower where they make me stay.

I crawl into bed without brushing my teeth, trying to ignore the whispering voices warning me of the wolf with no ears who would destroy us all.

Chapter One

10 Years Later

ster

"The alpha requested your presence in the throne room." Aiden's errand boy, Sam, a fifteen-year-old wolf shifter molded into a super-servant, looms on gangly legs in the doorway to my chambers.

I stand to follow as ordered.

The throne room. Eye roll.

Because that's not pretentious.

Aiden uses all the drama and theater of the best cult leaders, following in his father's footsteps. He rarely subjects me to a big show. I've lived in this mansion since I was ten. I am mostly ignored or treated like furniture, which is the way I prefer it.

I drape myself in a white outer robe and go to the mansion's largest room, where Aiden holds court when he wants to invoke the majesty of the alpha.

I can almost hear Oma scoffing, *foolish pup.*

At times like this, I'm reminded that I'm the only one

who knows that Aiden killed his own father. Not only that, I know something he doesn't—that he's not truly the first-born. If I wanted, I could use this knowledge to challenge Aiden's rule.

These are dangerous thoughts, but being pack seeress is a dangerous job.

Secrets are power. Aiden knows this.

That's why he hates me. He doesn't like anyone having power but him.

With its stone floors and arching beams, the throne room is almost medieval. It stinks like blood. As I walk in, my gut twists. Odin used to deal out his worst punishments here, in full view of the top wolves of the pack.

Today, it's only me and Aiden. And the Warden. I walk in just as Aiden's dismissing him. I try not to breathe too deeply, but I still sense his oily gray aura, a putrid fog that stinks like rotting bones. Of all the Adalwulf wolves, his aura is the most tainted. And that's saying something.

Behind him is another wolf, a thin white woman dressed in the robes of an acolyte. I recognize her narrow face and long brown hair from my childhood days in Moonhollow. Vera, I think her name was. She scurries to follow the Warden out a side door, and when I glimpse her aura, it seems just as tainted as his. Who knows how he's used and abused her.

As he's leaving, the Warden pauses to shoot me a disdainful look, and I ignore him. He's not a threat to me right now. I know enough of his secrets to destroy him.

Aiden is another story. He's a very real and present danger.

There was a time when I hoped a new alpha would make our pack better, kinder. But it didn't take long for my childish fantasy to fall away. Aiden is worse than his father.

Aiden isn't needlessly cruel; he's strategic about it. He's the sort who would patiently explain why your life must be forfeit for the good of the pack, then slit your throat and walk away.

He has no conscience, no empathy. While I feel the full weight of what must be done. My pack has been at war with the Blackthroats since before my birth, and in that war, I am the Adalwulf's most powerful weapon.

I'm caught between honoring my gift and my calling–listening to the Grandmothers–and trying to survive. It's like walking a tightrope, blindfolded, over a pool of hungry piranhas.

"Alpha." I clasp my hands and bow my head before Aiden. His aura is a roiling black with red streaks. Heavy, oppressive, weighing down my shoulders.

"Aster." He doesn't call me *Seeress*, which throws me off, since we're clearly doing formality at the moment. "The Warden has called to my attention the fact that you haven't given a credible vision for the pack since the last seeress died."

A tight fist closes in my solar plexus. I'd feared this day would come, but I hoped I'd given him enough to keep him from demanding more.

"I see visions all the time. Not all come to pass."

How do I explain that I have bright dreams every night of a gorgeous young man–packed with muscle and fierce with drive–somehow related to the Blackthroat pack. Not a Blackthroat but near them.

Close to our enemy. The visions feel raw and intimate, not like other foretellings. They wake me in the middle of the night. Several times, it felt like the enemy wolf had also been awakened in dreamtime. Sometimes, he looked right at me.

Who is he? Why am I Seeing him? What does he have to do with me?

There's something inside me that longs to find him, but that's delusional. Especially if he's a Blackthroat.

He's the enemy. And I'm the Seeress. My power lies in my bloodline as a veilwalker, maintaining my virginity–and therefore my second sight–and being bound to the alpha of the Adalwulf pack.

Those tenets have been drilled into me since I was seven years old and selected to be Oma's acolyte. They said my magic was strongest. That I'd be able to hold the binding. And they wanted me to be trained early, so I knew nothing else but this destiny.

But they can't control my dreams.

Nor can they stop Fate. But I don't know what Fate wants for me. I don't know why she is sending me the images of this man. I have enough to deal with in the aftermath of Oma and Odin's deaths and Aiden's ascent to power.

Aiden assaults me with his cold blue gaze. "We will complete the Blood Bonding ritual during the upcoming lunar eclipse."

I reel, suddenly dizzy. The decree punches me in the solar plexus, and I have to struggle to breathe. Outwardly, I show nothing but acquiescence. I know better than to anger my alpha. Aiden's never struck me in the face the way Odin did, but I watched him kill his father in cold blood.

The Blood Bonding. Dammit. I had hoped Aiden would shun the old ways.

The ritual is the magical binding of alpha to seeress. Aiden resisted it until now because he knows the binding will siphon some of his life force and alpha power to me. He needed his strength after murdering his father and taking the helm of a pack that just suffered serious losses in the war with the Blackthroats.

Now, it seems, I've made it necessary.

I should have tried harder to receive a message for the pack, but the Grandmothers just weren't giving me anything I could say. Not without terrible repercussions.

But the lunar eclipse is less than a month from now.

My stomach churns.

Even though I have been groomed my entire life for this binding, the thought of completing it makes me sick.

But I have to. It is part of my role.

There's no other life for me.

"During the eclipse, you'll bind your magic, and your fate with mine. Then you will produce the guidance I require."

Still struggling to breathe around a constricted throat, I bow my head. "Yes, Alpha."

"You will give your visions to us."

"Yes, Alpha."

"If after the binding, you still fail to see beyond the veil, there's an alternative."

My head jerks up. An alternative? I thought there was only this one path paved for me. Without meaning to, I raise my gaze and meet Aiden's stare. His eyes flash silver, a sign that his wolf is ascendant.

There's a touch of an evil smile on his face when he utters. "You will be made into a sacrifice."

White-hot lightning strikes my body, burrowing a hole in my skull. My hands begin to twitch with the energy running through me. Still, I force myself to appear calm—not that Aiden can't smell my fear.

Still, I'm proud of how soft my voice is when I speak.

"So you're saying I must give you credible visions, or you'll kill me?"

Aiden pins me with his alpha stare, a cruel smile curving his lips. He enjoys my discomfort. Knowing he holds the balance of my life in his hands. He could tell me to drop to my knees right now to beg for it, and I would have no choice.

"No," he answers finally. "The Warden will breed you, so your children will become veilwalkers. But I don't want to wait for the next generation to find our true seeress, Aster."

I blink at him, looking at his throat to avoid the searing alpha gaze. My heart pounds faster than a rabbit's. Under my seeress's robe, my skin is cold and clammy.

"Don't disappoint me."

I shake my head. "I don't intend to, Alpha."

He lets that settle between us. I'm trembling, head bowed, hands clasped, legs shaking before him, and he simply makes me wait.

"Good. The Tiara of Ix-Chel is coming to the Gem and Mineral Museum in the city on Thursday. I will arrange a special viewing for you to see it up close."

It takes me a moment to refocus on the task he's giving me, my mind still spinning on the Blood Bonding.

"The Tiara of Ix-Chel?" I repeat to buy time.

"It's a headdress fashioned for the Mayan goddess of the moon, made with a giant moonstone. I want you to hold the headdress in your hands and evaluate it for its power. If you sense any, I will purchase it for the ritual."

I fold my arms in front of me, keeping my expression calm even though I'm freaking out. "Understood."

"We need all the power we can get. We live in perilous times. We're pressed from all sides by our enemies–" He means the Blackthroats. "And the humans are also becoming more of a threat." Aiden gazes off into the distance for a moment, while I try to figure out what he means. I never heard him acknowledge humans as equals, much less a threat.

What is he plotting?

Whatever it is, he doesn't see fit to share it with me, the seeress he treats like a servant.

"I need your visions, Aster. I need a true veilwalker who can guide us to victory, or we're all fucked. Understand?"

I don't, not at all, but I nod anyway. "I live to serve."

"You do." His voice is flat. He makes me wait for another interminable minute before he flicks his hand. "You're dismissed."

Chapter Two

N*oah*

I scrabble up the mountainside. Something tangles in my hind legs, catching me, pulling me back...

No. Fuck.

It's the sheets bunched, snagged between my legs. I sit up in bed with my heart pounding, sweat soaking my hair.

I need to shift and let my wolf run with a desperation that's driving me more and more mad. I have nowhere to run in Manhattan. No pack to hunt with. Brick Blackthroat may have hired me, but he hasn't invited me to join his pack. I don't think it's because I'm deaf–the entire executive team learned ASL to speak with me. Moon Co is an inclusive company. The Blackthroat pack seems progressive, perhaps a result of being led by a young, successful alpha.

I suspect my exclusion from the pack has more to do with etiquette. I gave offense to them by not presenting myself for inclusion the moment I moved to Manhattan. I was keeping my options open, hoping to get in with the Adalwulfs.

Go back to sleep, I command myself. My wolf won't get to shift and run this week. Probably not this month. I went home to Kentucky over Christmas, so at least I let him out then.

Before I slide back into the dream of hunting, I picture the waifish she-wolf with the long, moon-pale hair and skin as luminescent as starshine. I'd rather dream of her.

The Adalwulf princess.

The one I saw from a distance at Blackthroat's wedding. The one who came to me in a dream.

Find me before it's too late.

Trying to conjure her when I'm in hypnagogia is my favorite pastime.

I slip back into the place between sleep and waking. I'm on a hunt, chasing a deer. Then prowling around a stone mansion. Then I'm in a dark bedroom.

It worked! This is where I've seen her before. Where she seems to be a prisoner. I saw the way she stood behind Aiden Adalwulf, hands clasped, head bowed like a servant. Every time I remember it, I want to tear Aiden's throat out.

She sits up in her bed. She's exquisite. Slender and slight, her platinum blonde hair tumbles across her shoulders, which are bare, save for the tiny satin spaghetti straps holding up a cotton cami. Small breasts rise beneath the fabric. She looks a little too thin–like she's been starved into submission. The dark brown blanket on her bed is a basic rough wool, like a camping blanket, chosen for function over beauty.

Her wide blue eyes stare straight ahead, unfocused. I remember what Billy told me–she's the new Adalwulf Seeress. Perhaps she's having a vision.

Is it of me? Does she project these visions *to* me? Is that why it feels like I'm in two places at once? It feels like I'm right there, in her cold, harsh bedroom, but when I reach for her, my hands close on air.

Aster. I try out the name Billy had given me for her at the wedding. I don't know whether I actually speak it or say it in my head.

Either way, it pulls her out of her reverie. She jerks in surprise, her soft pink lips part, eyes suddenly focusing right on my face.

My heart pounds. Excitement is pumping through my veins.

Aster. That *is* her name.

You know me? she says, but her lips don't move. She projects the words into my head again.

I nod. My fingers move to sign, *I saw you–outside the Blackthroat wedding. You got out of a limo with Aiden Adalwulf.*

She doesn't look at my hands but seems to understand my words just the same.

Stay away from me. I don't hear her voice, but words lay themselves across my mind.

Stay away. She wants me to stay away. Does she know that I intend to hunt down their Moonborn?

The vision slips away. I'm out on a hillside staring at my paws.

No!

I will myself back to her bedroom by imagining it. I need to find out what she means to me. What she knows.

I find myself not in her bedroom but staring into the face of Aiden Adalwulf. He's on some kind of ridiculous throne. A metaphor? Or does this asshole truly put himself on a stone throne in his dark palace?

He looks down his nose at me with disdain. I watch his lips move as he speaks.

The Tiara of Ix-Chel is coming to the Gem and Mineral Museum in the City on Thursday. I will arrange a special viewing for you to see it up close.

I stare at him, puzzled, but then I realize he's not looking at me but at Aster.

He's saying something else–I miss it because I was looking her way, but her lips move to form the words, *Yes, Alpha.*

The dream or vision vanishes, and I'm in my tiny apartment. It's dawn. I throw the blankets off and surge to my feet with mad purpose.

The museum. Today is Thursday. The dream must have been guidance from the Moon Goddess. Fate is leading me to the Moonborn. A sense of satisfaction surges through me as I yank on my joggers and shirt for my morning run around Central Park. I can't shift, but at least I can run off the aggression. This morning, I'll probably sprint the entire six miles.

I'm going to find the Adalwulf seeress. She's the key. I know it.

I remind myself of her warning to me the last time I dreamed with her. *The war is coming. You must decide which side you're on.*

What if she's appearing in my dreams to seduce me to pledge fealty to her pack? She's an Adalwulf, after all. They are a dark, twisted, devious lot.

But isn't that what I wanted? My entire plan revolves around infiltrating the Adalwulf pack. That's why I came to the city and worked so hard on my degree and all the credentials that would make me a great candidate for Adalwulf Associates.

Except they didn't hire me, and now I work for their enemy, Brick Blackthroat. A twist of misgiving moves through me. I haven't been taken into the Blackthroat pack, but they're honorable. Brick is an admirable leader who has fought and overcome huge hurdles to hold his pack strong. Betraying them doesn't feel right.

But I didn't come to Manhattan to ingratiate myself with the Blackthroats.

I'm here to get in with the Adalwulfs. For revenge. For justice. And because they may still hold someone precious to me. Not Aster although something in me longs to protect her.

No. I've been working toward this purpose my entire life. I can't let a growing loyalty to Brick Blackthroat and his pack thwart my designs. They aren't my friends. They aren't my pack. They are just people I work for.

I step outside and hit the pavement running, trying to ignore the knot of misgiving that wars with the unquenchable need to meet the Adalwulf's new Seeress.

Chapter Three

ster

The bulletproof limo pulls up in front of the Gem and Mineral Museum. Aiden had a designer send a dress, shoes, and bag up to my tower for the trip, along with a long white rabbit fur coat. While Oma had insisted on our living in austerity to keep our gifts pure, Aiden sees me as a representative of the pack. Today, I represent him and his interests. I have to look good.

I braided my hair into a wreath around my head, and teardrop moonstones dangle from my earlobes. They were a gift from Catherine Adalwulf when I turned sixteen. She's the only person who ever remembered my birthday. I regret not being able to help her in the terrible position she was in. Her mate was a Blackthroat. She gave birth to Blackthroat pups and was hardly allowed to see them. And then Oma and Odin made her the instrument of her mate's death. Her own pups' father.

I can't imagine anything worse than that fate.

I haven't seen her since she defended her son's mate

"

from Odin's assassins. She's exiled now–a fate I'm sure she would've chosen for herself from the beginning.

Now that I'm Seeress, I hoped to steer the pack away from their feud with the Blackthroats. Away from the poison and hate and focus on tearing the Blackthroat pack down instead of building our pack up. Both sides have lost enough.

Of course, I haven't voiced that opinion. I wouldn't dare. But I plan to give them only the guidance that leads in that direction.

I plan to withhold any prophecies that support this war. It's all I can do to steer this pack towards a better path.

But I failed to earn their satisfaction with my visions, and now I'll be bound to the alpha.

I wonder if it will change me.

Did Oma become the hate-filled instrument of destruction through Odin's dark power, or did her black heart infect him?

I wrinkle my nose. The air in the limo is tainted, probably from Vera's aura. She accompanied me to the city, too, and was dropped off at her Manhattan apartment. We rode the whole way here with her staring at me, like she was watching me for the Warden. I ignored her. It was rude, but when I thought about being polite, my intuition whispered *Rat,* and I kept my mouth shut.

She's gone now, but the oily taste of her aura still lingers.

Blech.

I wait for the driver to open my door and offer me a hand before I step out onto the sidewalk. I wobble a bit in the heels–I'm usually in bare feet at the keep. My trips to Manhattan are infrequent. From the time they moved me from the Moonborn lair to the Adalwulf's Adirondack mansion to study with Oma, I've been to the city only a half-dozen times.

Today, I will get to go without Aiden or Oma breathing down my neck. Oh, I will certainly still be heavily guarded, but I'll be my own woman. I'm the pack Seeress. The men will have to respect me and my wishes.

I resist the urge to look around and gawk at all the noise and activity around us. Instead, I hold up my head, making my neck long and regal as I click up the marble steps to the glass doors, following Otto, my handler, in.

"Ms. Adalwulf is here for the private viewing of the Tiara of Ix-Chel," Otto tells the museum attendant.

"Ah, yes. I'll let the director know. If you could just pass through security here." She waves us toward the metal detectors.

Aiden's security team looks like any human security team, except they don't need to carry weapons. They *are* weapons. He chooses the largest and most ferocious young males the pack produces, and they all stand over six feet tall. They will shift and kill in an instant if Otto gives them the signal.

I send my purse through on the conveyor belt and walk through the metal detector, sandwiched between three of my six bodyguards. The remaining three follow me.

"Have a seat on the bench, right there," the young woman behind the counter tells us. "Director Houserman will be right with you."

I take a seat and look around. Several groups of young elementary school children move through the exhibits in twittering clumps. A bunch of high school students jostle and tease each other. Adult museum-goers meander through the exhibits, stopping to peer into the glass cases containing specimens of crystals and gemstones.

The energy of all the crystals and minerals in the building emits a frequency that makes my head feel like it's about to explode.

Pressure grows behind my eyes. I hope the energy doesn't bring on a vision.

A short, stout man wearing eyeglasses and dressed in a sweater vest and tie emerges from an office behind the desk. "Ms. Adalwulf?"

Otto steps forward like he's going to take charge of the conversation, but I ignore him, standing to offer my hand. "Yes." I am the Adalwulf Seeress, advisor to the alpha. I'm no longer just the acolyte they keep locked in a tower.

I sense Otto's surprise. For years, I've played ghost, trying to remain invisible. Now I'm pulling out alpha she-wolf energy. Somehow, the growing pain around my eye sockets cuts out the noise of second-guessing myself.

The director also ignores Otto.

Otto follows my lead. He won't slight me in front of the director—not when I've been sent here as the emissary of the Adalwulf family. Appearances are everything to Aiden, and diminishing his authority as bestowed through me in this situation would infuriate him.

Still, I do not doubt that the moment we're out of this situation, Otto will assume an alpha role over me again.

"It's a pleasure to meet you. I understand Mr. Adalwulf has arranged with the owner of the Tiara of Ix-Chel for you to have a private viewing while it's on loan here. I do hope if you decide to purchase it, you'll allow us to remain the custodian through this season, so it can be enjoyed by New York?"

Otto stiffens, about to take charge again. Oma taught me never to stammer an answer out when surprised by a question. I use her technique of turning the focus back on him and repeating his words. "You'd like the moonstone to remain here at the museum for the remainder of the season."

I sense Otto settle back, clasping his hands in front of him, bodyguard style. He's content to let me handle the business negotiations, at least for the moment.

The director colors a bit. Now he's the one stammering. "Well, yes, we only just received it this week, and we've been advertising its arrival for months. It would be a terrible shame to let down all the people of New York who were so excited to see the precious artifact that only recently resurfaced in the world."

I understand his desire to keep the tiara on display as an important historical piece. He doesn't understand that it probably also contains great power.

I keep my tone regal. "I see. Well, I'm sure the seller can compensate you for your sunk advertising costs. But we're getting ahead of ourselves. I'm not even sure yet whether we're interested. May I inspect it?"

"Yes, yes of course. Right this way." Dr. Houserman extends an arm to usher me into the large open atrium of the museum.

I follow, pretending the excruciating pain building behind my left eye isn't there. The pressure in my head is growing almost too fast for me to manage. Yellow and red horizontal lines squiggle in front of my vision as I walk, making every step in the Louboutin heels feel precarious.

"We'll take the private elevator." Dr. Houserman uses a keycard to open the doors to a small elevator marked "Employees Only." I step in first, followed by Otto, who holds the door for Dr. Houserman. It's so tiny, there isn't room for the bodyguards.

"What floor?" Otto asks in a brisk, military clip.

"Ninth." Dr. Houserman steps into the elevator and pushes the button.

Otto tips his head toward the stairs, and his men instantly pivot and charge up them.

The elevator doors close, insulating me a bit from the energy of all the crystals. I take a breath, my vision clearing.

Dr. Houserman gives us each a nervous glance. "They won't be allowed in the viewing room."

He's worried we're here to steal the tiara.

I have to play this down, or he won't let me in at all, and Aiden will have a fit. "Not a problem," I say smoothly. "The guards are out of an abundance of caution. We've had some death threats to the family recently, so my cousin's extremely protective of me."

"Your cousin?"

"Aiden."

"Oh, I thought he was your husband."

"No, no. I'm just the expert on gemstones."

"I see." His expression says he clearly does not see but is too polite to ask more. The elevator doors open. "After you, Ms. Adalwulf." He extends a hand again.

Three security guards wait for us at the entryway to the exhibit room. Dr. Houserman murmurs something to one of the security guards, and he nods, pulling a velvet cord across the entryway to cordon it off from other visitors.

My bodyguards arrive on our floor in a stampede, their footfalls ringing out against the marble steps. I hold up a hand to halt them. "Wait here."

They look past me to Otto who nods.

"You, as well," Dr. Houserman tells him. "Only one person may approach at a time."

Otto's jaw clenches, but he takes a position outside the room.

He takes me to a glass display case positioned in front of a giant window. I imagine on a sunnier day, the natural light would enhance the glow of the red moonstone.

I suck in my breath. The pressure in my head grows stronger as we approach. I hear the whispers of the Grandmothers murmuring to me.

The tiara is cast in gold, a delicate weaving of slender arcing lines. In the center, a red-hued moonstone dangles, meant to enhance the wearer's third eye. The moonstone's properties are strong. I don't even need to touch it to know. If this headdress was used in Mayan ceremonies, it would take on additional power through the belief of the people. What we honor as sacred becomes sacred.

The two security guards flank me.

Otto folds his arms over his chest from behind the velvet cord.

A muscle starts to tremble in my cheek. The intensity is getting to be too much for me. The jumbled noise of the Grandmothers is a cacophony in my ears.

"I can already see this is legitimate," I murmur. I need to get out of here before I have a seizure. The Sight is taking over, and I'm losing my grasp on control.

The seconds feel like hours as I watch Dr. Houserman unlock the case and open it.

I don't need to touch the tiara.

I don't even want to. The power is already too much for me to hold. My stomach lurches like it wants to empty. I sway on my feet.

I force myself to go through the motions. "May I?" My voice sounds far away. I reach for the tiara.

It scalds me. I bring my fingertip to touch the moonstone. Lightning strikes me right between the eyes.

My third eye explodes. Or at least that's how it feels.

I need to get out of here.

"I'm satisfied," I say, handing it back. "And if you'll excuse me, I'm..." I cover my mouth as my stomach heaves.

The director snatches the tiara back. I'm sure this seems like a heist with the way my fingers were shaking. He probably thinks I'm trying to create a distraction to steal the tiara or swap it with a fake.

I run for the door. "It's real," I say to Otto as I rush past him. He reaches for my elbow, but I slip out of his grasp, running blindly. "I need a bathroom," I say.

I can't see at all–patterns of light and colors collide in front of my eyes. Dimly, I hear the sound of an elevator nearby. Remembering that it helped dampen the gem frequencies, I dive in, bumping into people on the way.

My knees hit the floor, and blackness overtakes me.

* * *

Noah

Fate led her right to me.

I catch the luminescent blonde in my arms as she falls and sit on the floor of the elevator to drag her back against me, her ass onto my lap. The magnolia-peach scent of her skin enters my nostrils and charges up my wolf. My pants tighten at the crotch.

Everything happened so easily. I caught sight of Aster when she arrived at the museum under heavy guard. I followed them up the stairs and lurked around the elevator, waiting and watching. I don't know why my dreams showed me where Aster would be today, but I have to believe it's to move me on the path to find the Moonborn.

When I saw the Adalwulf female rush out, covering her mouth like she had to throw up, I slipped into the elevator just before she did and hit the close-door button before her retinue arrived. Dropping a tracker into her tiny purse was child's play.

But now Aster is having some kind of seizure. Her body shakes and trembles. Her eyes are open, but unseeing, the way they were at first in my dream this morning. She's completely vulnerable. Alone in an elevator with the enemy. I could kill the Adalwulf seeress right here, right now, with one easy snap of her neck. Weaken their pack by removing their ability to see into the future. It's tempting.

But I need to know why Fate led me to her.

"Aster." I say her name out loud, wrapping both my arms around her to hold her up.

Aster. This time I try it in my head.

Still no response. I suspect this is not a medical concern. Aster is a seeress. Perhaps she's having a vision.

According to my grandmother, the "moonborn" are created through the ritualistic interbreeding of witches with wolves during a powerful planetary influence like an eclipse. There's dark magic involved. The seeress is created through some kind of power bond with the alpha. It gives the Adalwulfs a distinct advantage but comes with a cost—some kind of warping or twisting.

Aster doesn't appear warped, but who knows what lies behind her luminescent exterior.

I rub her sternum to activate her calming reflex. *It's okay. I've got you,* I tell her telepathically. I have no idea if that works in real life or only when I meet her in dreams.

Her body starts to relax, just as the elevator dings. We're already on the first floor.

I hear the sound of pounding footfalls—her army racing down the stairs to meet her.

I scramble to my feet, lifting Aster with me. She lets out

a soft moan. One of her hands covers mine as she drags in a breath through her nose. My scent won't be on her because I covered it with a spray of men's cologne to keep her from scenting another wolf.

I prop her against the elevator wall and step out before her men round the bend.

Chapter Four

ster

A I haven't had such strong and debilitating visions since I was young. I step into the limo on shaky legs. The scent of men's cologne permeates my clothes, irritating my already frayed nerves.

A man in the elevator.

I can barely piece together what happened. Only snippets of memory bled through the excruciating visions.

"What was all that?" Otto asks when he settles in the opposite seat.

Another wave of pain shoots through my temples, making my stomach turn. I rub my forehead. "The stone held great power." My voice sounds thin. "It activated my Sight."

Otto makes a sound in his throat. He knows he's not high enough on the pay grade to ask me what I Saw, but I don't know if he believes me. He takes a water out of the mini-fridge and uncaps it to hand it to me.

I drink deeply, still trying to stabilize my nervous system. Chocolate would help. Meat would be better. It dampens the Sight, which is why Oma never let me have any, but Oma's dead, and my wolf is hungry.

I press the button to speak to the driver up front. "Find a hot dog vendor," I tell him. "I need food."

"Yes, Seeress," he says.

Otto studies me. "What happened in the elevator?"

I grit my teeth. I don't want to explain myself to this man, but he's a wolf, and he can smell the stranger's scent on me. "I lost consciousness for a moment, and a man helped me back to my feet."

It seems like a likely explanation, but that wasn't what happened.

I know that much.

The clamoring of the Grandmothers had grown so strong that I felt ill. I was running for a bathroom before I threw up, but I somehow ended up in the elevator instead.

And he was in there with me. Smelling like a human coated with harsh cologne.

He felt like the man from my visions, but I can't be sure. I might have been having a vision of the man and confused him with the stranger in the elevator.

I thought he said my name—not out loud but inside my head. Like we were speaking telepathically. But that doesn't make sense.

I bring my hand to my sternum and rub.

Did he touch between my breasts? For some reason, I feel he did. Not in sexual way but to calm me.

He *had* calmed me. I couldn't see anything, and my body was betraying me, but for some reason, I felt safe for those few moments in the elevator.

"What did he look like?" Otto presses.

I lean my head back against the limo's headrest. "I couldn't see."

"You didn't see him?" Otto's voice drips with doubt.

"I *couldn't* see him. The visions blinded me."

There were a thousand movies playing behind my eyes simultaneously. The input was far too great for me to sort through.

"You saw nothing? Nothing at all?"

I sensed the young man from my visions, but that might have just been another vision.

"Nothing. Was I alone when you found me?"

"Yes," Otto grumbles.

The limo pulls over, and the driver jumps out. I watch as he waves a big bill at a hot dog vendor to cut in line. A moment later, he opens my door and hands me a foot-long beef hot dog, smothered in neon green relish with yellow mustard squiggled on top.

Thank fate. I take the street food with shaking hands and devour the meat. It hits my stomach like a rock, but I don't care. I need that sinking stone in my center to weigh me down and ground me. Bring me back to Earth, so I can sort through what happened this afternoon.

When I finish, I wipe my mouth and fingers with a napkin, drink the rest of the water, and settle back in my seat.

Show me what it all means, I beg the Grandmothers.

Instead of hearing them, my mind fills with the memory of being in the elevator. I even smell the man's cologne–it must be clinging to my coat. Underneath the human-made perfume is his natural scent–warm amber, crisp pine. His scent, his presence, his essence feels familiar. It had to be the man from my dreams. The one associated with the Blackthroat pack.

And that means I was in grave danger. Alone and

vulnerable, in the grips of a vision with an enemy close enough to snuff out my life.

I should tell Otto right now. I probably should've sounded the alarm the moment I stepped out of that elevator.

What stopped me? Just confusion?

No, it's something else. Even now, I don't open my mouth to tell Otto what I suspect. Am I protecting the man?

Or shielding myself from Aiden's wrath if he found out I'd slipped my guards?

It doesn't feel wrong. What happened today doesn't feel wrong. Surely the Grandmothers would have warned me if I were in danger, and they didn't.

It doesn't feel wrong to keep my own counsel on this either. I haven't interpreted the visions yet. Until I do, they are mine to keep.

Oma would disapprove, but I don't care. Oma and Odin are dead.

I'm Seeress now.

When I learn what the man in my dreams means, I'll know what to do. Until then, he'll remain my secret.

Chapter Five

N*oah*

I pulled off that bit of espionage at the museum perfectly. So why am I so shaken by my encounter with the lovely and enigmatic Seeress?

Head down, I walk the city streets. I keep my steps measured, so I don't look suspicious, but my body is so wired with adrenaline it's all I can do not to break into a run.

What was that?

Fate sent me there. I do not doubt that. I'm a logical, even skeptical, person, but I can't deny that all these dreams of Aster led me to the museum and then to that moment in the elevator. It was destined.

The Adalwulf princess's delicate magnolia-peach scent still clings to my clothes. Warm and floral, at odds with her ice-princess exterior. There was something completely intoxicating about her. Like she's a magnet pulling me in. Part of me wanted to pick her up and carry her out with me.

Of course, I never would have made it out alive.

My hands shake just thinking about the feel of her ass

on my lap. My dick is still chubby. I shove my hands into my pockets, but my dick? Forget about it. There's nothing I can do but curse it and will my erection to go down. Thinking about baseball won't work; I don't watch human sports, so I have no idea how that game is played. My life revolves around my mission–infiltrating the Adalwulfs, so I can learn the truth about my birth. That's why I planted a bug on Aster–for the mission–not because I'm obsessed with the female who's haunted my dreams for months.

I'm not going to replay the moment she landed in my lap over and over again. I won't dwell on the way her white-blond hair looked so elegant, braided into a crown, but when it brushed my chin, it felt soft as corn-silk. It's probably long enough to hang down past her waist in a perfect curtain. If she were naked, it would brush the top of her ass...

And now my dick is hard again.

It's no use. I can't focus with the scent of peaches clinging to the stubble on my chin. All my thoughts lead to Aster right now.

The long walk does me good. By the time I clock back into work, I'm disgusted by the scents of the city–exhaust from the cars and buses, the concrete sidewalks covered in trash and gum flattened by a thousand dirty-soled shoes. The scent of magnolia and peaches is still there, but it's faded enough that I can focus.

As soon as I get to my desk, I get a message telling me to bring a report to the big boss' office. That's enough to kill my boner.

Brick Blackthroat is a beast in the business world, but humans have no idea how much of a beast he really is. I worked hard to qualify for a job here, and even though Adalwulf Associates was my first choice, my job at Moon

Co. has turned out to have untold benefits. Once again, it was like Fate was guiding me because I was able to befriend Madi, the human fated to be Brick's mate.

Fate, again. I might be a believer after all.

I make sure I wash my hands thoroughly and change my shirt and jacket before heading up to the big boss. Brick probably doesn't know what Aster Adalwulf smells like, but there's no sense smelling like an Adalwulf if I can help it.

When I arrive on the top floor, Brick's secretary sends me in. I tap on the door before I open it, even though I wouldn't hear if he told me to stay out.

"Here's the report, sir." I step up to Brick's desk and set the stack of unstapled papers on his desk. He's usually a "send it by email" guy, so I'm guessing he wants to go over it in person.

I watch his lips move. "Great." He doesn't look at the report–he looks at me.

I'm standing while he sits, but he holds the power in the room. His alpha nature is a large presence. Even his scent is dense and powerful–but there's a light citrus and spice essence that reminds me of his mate, Madi. Either she was just here, drinking her favorite vanilla latte, or her scent is now interwoven with her mate's.

Either way, it makes me want to smile. I don't, though, because Brick's mood seems serious.

"Do you ever let out your wolf, Noah?" He speaks the words at the same time he makes the ASL signs for *your wolf run?*, except he doesn't put the raised eyebrows we use to indicate a question. Still, the fact that my employer and his executive team attempted to learn ASL after I became an ancillary member shocked me.

No one but my grandmother learned to sign in my home pack. Our alpha wanted me to learn Total Communication, making me wear hearing aids as a child to teach me oral speech and lip-reading.

I arch a brow, surprised by this question. "I ran over Christmas." I both sign and speak out loud because he's still learning ASL. "When I was in Kentucky."

He gives me a cool look. His expression is inscrutable, but I can feel the power play. There's a challenge in his posture. The stare-down he's giving me. The alpha wolf has finally called me to the carpet over why I never petitioned to join his pack. Alphas don't like stranger wolves on their territory. It's in their nature to be suspicious of a lone wolf like me.

It's been two years since I started working here. I expected this conversation eighteen months ago. Now, it's been so long since I showed up in New York without requesting admission to his pack that I'd thought we'd both swept it under the rug.

Brick drops the game and shoots straight. "Why have you never requested to join my pack?" He doesn't attempt to sign the words.

I measure the air between us. My wolf doesn't sense an immediate threat. There's tension, but it's not deadly. Yet.

I have to answer him carefully.

"When I came to New York, I didn't know either pack."

Brick makes no acknowledgement; he simply watches me. His scent is one hundred percent his, cedar and leather and sandalwood, no *eau de Madi* to soften it.

"I think you know that I also applied at Adalwulf and Associates."

He nods.

"I thought it best to keep my options open, not knowing where I would land."

"Bullshit."

I can't hear Brick's words, but I can tell he threw an alpha command into them by the way they shove me square in the chest. If I were part of his pack, I would've fallen back a step.

Instead, the power wafts past me, like a punch that misses me by a few inches.

Interesting. I'm not one of his wolves, but I should still feel the pressure to submit to his Alpha commands. I felt the power, but it didn't touch me.

Is it like this for all lone wolves?

Of course, Brick is my boss. He could still fire me. And he's right. The reason I offered was bullshit. I'm not sure how or why he knows that, though. Or what he suspects.

I shrug, keeping my body movements languid to show I'm not distressed and try for something closer to the truth. "Honestly, I'm more of a lone wolf. I didn't want to get caught up in pack politics."

Brick's eyes narrow, like he knows I'm hiding something. His nose twitches–he's probably relying on his nose to clue him into my thoughts. "Why apply at the two wolf-owned companies if you weren't interested in pack politics?"

Well, that's an excellent question. One I definitely don't want to reveal the answer to.

"I was keeping my options open, I guess."

"You could have used the fact that you're a wolf to get this job. That would be the normal course of action. Show up, introduce yourself as a fellow shifter, and ask for a job. I would've given it to you. But you went through HR like a human." He shakes his head. "It doesn't make sense. Help me understand it."

Deaf Culture rejects the idea that we are disabled. Deafness is not viewed as a loss but is rather a gain. There's a whole community, culture, language, with an identity built in.

That said, I'm not human. I'm a wolf.

My mother had to sneak me out of my birth pack–the Moonborn sect of the Adalwulf Pack–to keep their alpha Odin from murdering me as soon as it was known I was "defective." My grandmother's pack in Kentucky wasn't so backward, but they still never welcomed me with open arms.

I don't want to do it, but it might be time to play the deaf card with Brick.

"Packs don't always accept my kind," I tell him.

It works. The aggression drops away from Brick's expression, and compassion seeps in. His scent shifts, growing less intense. He rises from his seat and walks around the desk to my side, no longer in punishing principal mode.

"You know we accept you." He attempts to sign again, perhaps realizing his lapse.

I nod. His pack is different–they've honored who and what I am from the beginning. That doesn't mean I want to join them, but I guess I do believe they would treat me as an equal if I were admitted.

"Yes. Thank you. I am grateful for all you have done."

He spreads his hands. "Yet you still haven't petitioned me to join."

I choose to bow my head. I don't lose anything by submitting now and placating the most dominant wolf I've ever met. "Forgive me, Alpha. I meant no offense to you or the pack."

"I take it as an insult."

I wince. I rack my brain for something to say that will allow me to remain free of the pack yet still keep this job.

My lack of a response further irritates my boss. He jerks his head toward the door. "Get out."

Fuck. Am I fired?

I don't move.

"I won't pressure anyone to join my pack. We don't coerce. If you don't want in, it's your loss. But if you ever go near the Adalwulf Pack, we're going to have a big problem."

I go still, staring at him. Do I come clean? Tell him I held the Adalwulf princess in my arms an hour ago? That I put a tracker in her bag and plan to find out where they keep the Moonborn?

No. I can't. My mission is more important than pleasing my boss. I'll have to risk his wrath.

"Understood, Alpha," I say.

"Apparently, I'm not your fucking alpha." The alpha command in his voice registers as another shove to my torso.

I tip my head to the side to show my throat. "Yes, sir."

"Get out."

This time, I obey. As I walk out, I sense danger closing in on me from more than one side.

I'll have to choose my path carefully, or I'll never have the chance to find my mom and free her from the cult that's kept her captive for so long.

* * *

I hole up in my cubicle, keep my head down like I'm getting to work. In between answering emails for my Moon Co job, I monitor the data the tracker in Aster's purse is picking up for me.

The tracker has an audio component, which I run through a speech-to-text translator, so I can speed-read the conversation.

> The Alpha wants to know if you think the
> tiara is worth purchasing.

> It's powerful. Maybe too powerful. The
> vision I had was strong.

I tag the second speaker as Aster and the first as her bodyguard.

I scan all the texts, but she hasn't admitted she met me. In fact, she's insisting that she doesn't know who I am.

> A stranger,

Is it possible she hasn't seen me in her dreams? They felt so real.

She's the enemy, I remind myself. She means nothing.

I know that's a lie. I can still smell her sweet floral scent, even though I washed it away before my meeting with Brick.

I need to focus. I can use the Seeress to get intel and infiltrate the Adalwulfs, but that's it. Beyond that, my interest in her needs to stop.

Bodyguard:

> So the moonstone will be an asset to the
> Blood Bonding.

Blood Bonding? What's that? I make a note to call Gran and ask her.

Aster:

> Maybe. There's a danger in using another
> culture's talismans to enhance our own
> rituals.

The speech-to-text doesn't give me any nuance, like

facial expression or tone of voice. I wish I had visuals, too, and not just so I can examine Aster's stunning ice-blue eyes and lovely face. I want to know how she feels about this Blood Bonding ritual. It sounds fucking painful, and knowing what Gran told me about the cult of the Moon-born, it's probably not a walk in the park.

Bodyguard:

A danger to whom?

Aster:

To everyone involved in the ritual.

Bodyguard:

I'll let the alpha know.

So that was the purpose of the museum visit. Seeing the tiara. Purchasing it for some sort of ritual.

Bodyguard:

Alpha Aiden has cleared the purchase. The sale will take place tomorrow at 6 pm. The museum is trying to negotiate, but the alpha will make sure the tiara is in our possession in time for the ritual.

I scramble. I have to get this tiara before Aiden does. Something tells me it's important.

And I know just the person who can help me.

I grab my phone and open a private app that connects me to a super secret forum.

I text my friend.

Hey

She's a witch who was also born into a creepy cult. Not the Moonborn but a family of underground dark magic users turned grifters.

Have you ever done a job at the Gem and Mineral Museum?

I don't wait long before she zings back.

Nope. But I cased it six months ago for shits and giggles. Why?

I grin. Once I tell her what I need, I know she'll want to help.

This is going to be fun.

Chapter Six

oah

Eleven a.m. the next morning, I wait by the bushes in a nearby park. I'm in wolf form, hiding so no one spots an unleashed dog that's bigger than a Great Pyrenees crossed with a Great Dane. My wolf is a bit smaller than most, so I can pass as a huge hound.

"There you are." Esme waves as she sidles up to me. She's in her usual outfit of black jeans and a cropped black leather jacket over a band t-shirt. Now I'm realizing she's always wearing the perfect outfit for an art or jewelry heist. Her long, dark hair is braided down her back, so it can be tucked away.

She crouches down, pretending to pet me, and slips a collar around my neck.

When I look up, she's holding a bright pink leash. *For the disguise*, she signs, tucking the leash under her arm. She and her family already used a series of hand signals for the heists and scams they run, so when we became friends, she asked me to teach her some ASL. *For the next forty-five minutes, you're Bubbles.*

Bubbles? I cock my ears, giving her a wolfish scowl.

She grins and keeps signing, *All part of the plan. My friend Ciara is going to walk you past the museum, and then you know what to do. I left your clothes in the second stall of the men's bathroom on the first floor. It has an 'out of order' sign on it.*

I woof to let her know I got it.

Awesome. See you tonight at the usual spot. You ready?

I rise to my feet. I put a little stiffness into my hips, so I'm moving like an older dog and let her lead me up the path. Because of her upbringing, she's used to shifters. She's fully human although I can scent a little extra about her. Underneath the scent of light roast coffee, there's an undertone of Old World incense that makes me want to sneeze but also something more that reminds me of the extra dimensions of Aster's scent. Maybe she has extra abilities, like Aster. That would explain why she's such a good thief.

A gorgeous brunette with brown skin a little darker than Esme's is waiting for us on the path. This must be Ciara. Esme greets her and hands her the leash. I read their lips as Esme explains that I'm Bubbles, and all Ciara needs to do is walk me through the park. "He's trained to do the rest."

Ciara cocks an eyebrow, looking skeptical, but nods. She's wearing a stylish camel-colored coat and cloying perfume that makes my nose twitch, but I get that she's dolled up to look expensive. She and I are going to be the distraction.

"Have fun." Esme backs up and pulls a cap over her head. She's going to get the jewel—she's done this before.

I never thought I'd have a jewel thief for a friend, but she's come in handy. I wonder if Ciara helps her with other jobs, too. This is my first time assisting with a heist, but I intend to pull my part off perfectly.

Esme heads off on her own. We wait until she disappears behind the art museum, and then Ciara and I stroll down the wide path through the park. I trot alongside Ciara, letting her camel coat brush against my fur. I let my tongue loll out like I'm a good boy.

When she stops on the path to check her purse, it's showtime.

I dart past the end of my leash, ripping it from Ciara's hand. She's wearing gloves, so it won't hurt, and this needs to look convincing. Ciara's supposed to wander around the park, pretending to look for me and then disappear.

Meanwhile, I race through the park and across the road, dodging cars, running like I'm chasing a squirrel. I reach the steps of the museum and tear up them, a wolf on a mission. There's a man in front of me about to enter the museum. I time things perfectly, so I charge through the door behind him and push him off balance enough to send him and his umbrella flying.

I take a moment to check on the guy I knocked over. He's red-faced but fine. Just to make sure, I leap onto him and start licking his face.

His mouth opens in a shout as he thrashes and tries to push me off. I'm too heavy.

It gives me a moment to case the space. There's a metal detector set up in front of me. There's no line, just three security guards who are whirling around, reacting to the chaos.

Two of them rush over to help pull me off the guy. I wait until they're almost on me, then whirl, bounding to the gate on the right side of the metal detector. It's meant to keep humans in, not dogs, so it's easy enough to leap over it.

And just like that, I'm in. I tear through the museum rooms, startling patrons and knocking over every able-bodied security guard I can find. They're armed with badges and flashlights, not guns, so it's perfectly safe. Just good clean fun.

Esme needs about fifteen minutes to get in, get the tiara, and get out. It's my job to keep all the attention focused on the front of the museum until then. I loop back towards the check-in counter and dive behind the cafe counter, grabbing a croissant as I go. I pause to wolf it down right in front of an entire class of sixth graders who are recording me on their phones. Then my entourage shows up–an assortment of security guards and heroic bystanders who are chasing me. I let them try to corral me, jumping up and down like it's a game.

Then I make another break for it. I dart behind a group with a crying child and yelling parent, then slip around a corner in a thankfully empty hall, running everyone ragged until I've lost them. I manage to reach the first-floor men's bathroom of the old 1920's building, where Esme told me she left my clothes.

Esme's scent is here, faint, on the artsy museum bag that she stashed in the out-of-order stall. I shift to human form, shaking off the tingles, so I can dress quickly. I exit the stall and force open the window, just wide enough for a big dog to leap out of. Then I exit the bathroom with the museum bag slung over my shoulder.

The whole museum smells like human sweat and stress. I keep my features neutral and walk up to a museum attendant obviously on the lookout for a giant dog to come tearing by.

"What's going on?" I sign while I speak.

The attendant shifts their focus to me, turning to face me fully when they realize that I'm deaf. "A dog got in here. It's big." They mime. "Have you seen it?"

I tell them no and take my leave, heading to the museum exit. Every human I pass is on high alert, either looking for a dog or talking excitedly about it and showing their friends footage on their phone. This event will be all over social media, but I bet the museum pulls strings to keep it hushed up in the official news media. Especially once they discover the tiara is missing.

I can't keep a smirk off my face as I stroll out the front door. It all went perfectly to plan.

I'll meet Esme tonight at our favorite coffee shop and get the tiara then. At that point, I'll have to figure out what to do with it. Esme might have some ideas.

One thing's for sure, the Adalwulfs will have to find another powerful gemstone to power their ceremony.

* * *

Aster

I'm seated by the fire in my suite's sitting room, trying to meditate, when I hear a roll of psychic thunder.

It's my only warning before the heavy wooden doors burst open, and Aiden storms in, with a wave of power that hits me like a tsunami.

"What did you do?" he growls. His alpha tone makes me want to bare my throat.

I tilt my chin slightly, averting my gaze, but keep my face impassive. Times like these, I remember how Oma used to let the alpha temper roll over her, never cowering. She didn't react. She was like a weathered stone standing upright and unmoved through a raging storm.

She also never answered a direct question. Instead, she asked her own.

"What has happened?" I ask, keeping my voice low and melodic. I project an aura of calm.

It helps that I was obviously meditating. I'm sitting on a cushion on the floor, breathing in the familiar scent of lavender and rosemary, the herbs I threw on the fire to break up the oppressive stuffiness of the room. The Adalwulf's city mansion is beautiful, full of art and antiques, but needs a good cleaning. I don't think the windows have been opened since the place was built in the Gilded Age.

With the herbs and velvet pouch of ancient bones in front of me, I look like a Seeress plying my craft, and feel less like an employee caught slacking off by their asshole boss.

"The Tiara of Ix-Chel. It's gone missing." Aiden paces the ancient Oriental rug, growling under his breath. He's dressed for work in one of his well-tailored gray suits.

"Missing?" I echo. It's a ploy to get more information, and it works.

"Houserman just called. Apparently someone broke in earlier today and took it, and he waited until now to break the news. I was on my way to purchase it." His lip curls, and I feel a moment of pity for Dr. Houserman, having to disappoint Aiden. No wonder he waited until the last possible minute.

"He suspects us."

"Us? Why would we steal it? We were going to purchase it."

"That's exactly what I told him." Aiden stomps around the room, sneering at gilt framed oil paintings and Tiffany lamps alike. "In fact, I would've taken possession of it immediately after you confirmed its power had I known the museum was going to completely bungle its security and allow it to be stolen." He marches around a Louis XIV era armchair to stand over me, glowering. "You didn't have any vision, any premonition that it would be taken?"

"No," I say clearly because it's not a lie. "When I have a vision that would help the pack, I share it." I'm still telling the truth. I just refuse to share any visions that lead us to war. Or put a spotlight on the man who held me in the elevator.

"Would you?" Aiden asks in a soft tone. *Danger*, my intuition blares. "Otto tells me you were reluctant to expose yourself to its power again. If I find out you had anything to do with this…"

A picture flashes through my mind. The man's face, the one I've been seeing, dreaming about. Could he be involved? My intuition says yes.

I lick my lips, and Aiden's eyes flash silver, as if his wolf has scented prey.

I need a diversion, and I need it fast. "Why would I? I seek power to guide the pack toward its purpose." I sweep a hand out toward the fire. "Ever since yesterday, I've been here, centering myself, preparing for the ritual." Beseeching the Grandmothers for a way to thwart it and avoiding Vera, who's staying in the room next door. "Do you think the director could've managed it? He didn't want the tiara to be taken from the museum. You can ask Otto."

Aiden stares at me. Testing me for weakness.

I inhale the soothing scent of lavender and wait for the storm to pass.

"Otto tells me you've been eating meat."

"I required strength after handling the tiara. It left me drained."

"The seeress shall not eat the flesh of any animal. So it

is written in the *Book of the Moonborn,* according to the Warden."

Yes, the *Book of the Moonborn,* the one that only the Warden is allowed to read. I'm sure it says a lot about how to starve the cult members as a way to keep them under the leadership's thumb. Liora, one of the Moonborn who helped raise me before I was sent to train with Oma, told me that every month there are long fasts she and the others are required to participate in, even if they're underage or nursing a pup.

I stop my lip from curling, but Aiden smirks, sensing my insubordination. "The Warden is keen to aid you in accessing your gift again. He will oversee your fast."

I know what's happening here. They want me weak. I'm already underfed. My wolf needs meat. I rise to my feet because I'm done taking this sitting down. "That won't be necessary."

"I think it is. And don't worry," he adds silkily, "I understand that all this opulence," he waves a hand at the over-decorated room, "Impedes your visions. You'll be returning to Adalwulf land immediately." He strides to the door where I can scent Otto and the others waiting outside, ready to drag me away. "There you will remain in isolation in the tower until you produce the intel we need."

"Exactly what intel do you need?" I ask. I'm feeling desperate, and he can probably smell it, but I'm getting better at asking questions, probing for information, taking the power back.

"Any intel that helps us destroy the Blackthroats."

I hesitate. This is the exact intel I don't want to give.

But what choice do I have?

Aiden opens the door and signals my handlers to enter.

"It's your choice, Aster. Give me what I want, or I'll give you to the Warden to breed a new generation, and he'll make sure your children will be trained to serve the pack properly."

Chapter Seven

ster

The tower is exactly what it sounds like: a big old phallic structure built of weathered stone. One of Oma's ancestors had it built, claiming they saw it in a vision. Maybe the same sort of vision that led Carl Jung to create Bollingen Tower although ours predates Jung's alchemical oasis by decades.

Unlike Jung's tower, this one is sweaty in the summer and freezing cold in the winter. There's no fire. No furniture. No creature comforts. Nothing that would distract me from my visions.

Six days ago, the Warden locked me in here with a bowl of water and no food, instructing me to cleanse my flesh. The water is replenished once a day. I use the medieval garderobe for a toilet. There's a guard at the door–I'm not allowed to leave at all.

The idea is to starve the flesh, so I retreat into my inner world. What my jailers don't know is that I have no problem seeing visions. I'm veilwalking constantly, and sapping my strength only means that it's harder for me to control them.

The visions wrack my body, leaving me sick and exhausted on the stone floor. They're growing stronger. I see visions of war, of Aiden becoming even more powerful as he brutalizes wolves and humans alike. I see sharp teeth and blood red eyes, a city on fire.

Most of all, I see the man I believe was the same one in the elevator, over and over again. I see his face and feel his presence, like a warm blanket wrapped around my freezing body. It's tempting to fall into him.

I feel like it's a test. I shouldn't want to be with the enemy. But I'm all alone, with day bleeding into night and no escape from the prison of my own mind, and his presence is a solace.

When someone knocks on the door, it takes me a long time to realize it's happening in real time.

The mists of my mind clear, and I open my mouth to croak, "Come in."

"Seeress." Liora's warm voice is a balm. I close my eyes, fighting back tears. Of all the wolves who helped raise me during my time in Moonhollow, Liora was the kindest. She's also a true believer, embracing the harsh rituals of the Moonborn. She once told me living simply makes her wolf happy. She revels in how connected she feels to nature, to the woods, to the earth.

She kneels beside me, offering me a steaming pot of liquid. My wolf leaps up, smelling the rich ambrosia of cooked meat. It's broth. The first thing I've been allowed to eat in almost a week. I cover Liora's hands with my own, and she helps me lift the stoneware to my lips. I'm grateful for the help because my hands are shaky. After days of visions, coming back to the real world is hard. The smooth surface of the clay pot feels too rough, too heavy. The guard outside the door clears his throat, and I shudder, my ears sensitive to the sound.

Liora seems to understand. Under my freezing fingers, her hands are warm and strong. She holds the pot for as long as I need, letting me drink the broth slowly. The taste is rich and meaty, almost overpowering. There's a tang of herbs, thyme and wild onion. It's the best thing I've ever tasted.

"Thank you." My voice sounds a bit less raspy. I'm still hungry and definitely dehydrated. Fasting is fine, as long as you're normally well-fed.

There are some bits of meat and bone at the bottom of the pot, and I want to devour them, but I hold off. I need to pace myself and be gentle with my stomach.

"Of course." She waits until I lean back and take a deep breath, then sets the pot in my lap. I rest my hands on either side of it, letting the warmth seep in.

Liora folds her hands in her lap. She's a beautiful woman with long sandy-blonde hair hanging past her waist. She's wearing a thick knitted sweater over a simple woolen dress. The Moonborn are forbidden to wear anything but natural, undyed fabrics. During the hot days of summer, many go without clothes entirely, embracing their "natural state" as a way of staying in touch with their wild side.

Right now, she looks so warm in her wool garments and fur-lined boots. I try not to shiver in response. I'm only wearing a thin white shift. I know she would've brought me a blanket or something extra to wear, but the Warden has forbidden it. Even if she dared defy him, I wouldn't accept anything that might get her in trouble. "I come seeking wisdom."

I straighten my spine. Of all the wolves in the Moonborn and pack, Liora is the only one I would freely give my visions to. Her gentle respect makes me feel like my gift is really a gift.

"Ask."

"During the next Blood Moon, the Warden intends to lead us in the Alpha Rites."

I nod. I'm keenly aware of the doomsday clock ticking down.

"He's chosen the females who are to be blessed and consecrated on the altar."

Blessed and consecrated. What a way to say "tied up with vines and gang-banged." Some of the girls will be willing, but they'll all be virgins, and the ritual doesn't leave much room for kindness or gentleness. In fact, it seems designed to make their first sexual experience as intense and traumatic as possible.

It's the Seeress' job to oversee the rites. According to Oma, that means I need to use my herbal tinctures to drug them. "It's a kindness," she would say. The herbs will help the females relax. It will also make them more obedient.

I think it's horrific. I don't want to drug a bunch of young females, so they'll submit to this atrocity. But if I don't, and the females rebel, they'll be punished and still raped. Not honored. Possibly killed.

If I had my way, I'd stop the ritual. But I have no idea how.

Liora hesitates, licking her lips as if she's deciding how she wants to phrase her request, as if she's reluctant to voice her true feelings. She's an obedient wolf, whether because she's a true believer or so beaten down she can't remember how to dissent. The irony is her gentleness makes me see how horrible the Moonborn's treatment of its acolytes really is. What sort of religion tortures its most faithful followers? A shitty one.

"Oriana is among the chosen."

Oh, no. Gooseflesh rises on my skin. Oriana is Liora's daughter. She's only sixteen.

I remember with a flash of intuition that Liora had been one of the chosen. She was young, too, probably the same age as Oriana now. During the lunar eclipse, she would've drunk the ritual wine and fallen into a drugged trance that made her pliant enough to be bound to the sacrificial table, but still aware of what was happening. She submitted then, but she wants to save her daughter now.

Maybe she's not fully broken.

"I asked the Warden if it would be better if she were fully grown. He says the decision is made. He doesn't want to take the chance that she'll become unclean."

Unclean. As if a mature female who's explored a little more of her sexuality and is more confident in making choices for herself is "unclean." The Warden doesn't want to wait for these young females to be old enough to know better, to fight back. My insides burn with rage.

Oma would say something about sacrificing for the good of the pack, but I won't spit that bullshit to my friend. I will not allow another generation to be victimized like this. I might not have much power, but what I have, I will use for good.

I take a chance and speak in a murmur, "Keep your head down. Don't speak of this again. As far as anyone's concerned, you are looking forward to the ritual."

Liora blinks her dark blue eyes. I'm asking her to practice deceit. It's not really in her nature. But she nods.

I inhale her scent–wintergreen mint and wild herbs with a touch of pine. Something about it is familiar.

I reach for Liora's hand. Mine is cold and bony, but she grips it like a lifeline. "I'm going to find a way for Oriana to be free of the ritual." *For all of us to be free.* I have no idea how I'm going to do that, but I feel the certainty in my chest as I make the promise. I can almost feel the approval the Grandmothers–but I shut that out as best I can because I don't want another vision to come on right now.

"Thank you, Seeress," Liora whispers. I squeeze her hand before I let her free. We sit in silence a moment before we become aware of the guard pacing outside the door. "I should go."

"Be blessed," I say, and, on impulse, I reach out and rest my hand on her forehead. A true blessing. Connection.

She closes her eyes and receives it before rising and making her silent way out the door.

Once again, I'm alone. I'm still weak–but she left the rest of the broth. I'll drink it and savor the scraps of meat, then call my wolf to chew the bones.

It's not much, but it will give me a bit more strength that I can use to figure out how to get us out of this mess.

* * *

Noah

I sit in my rental car, hidden on the side of the highway, behind a copse of trees. Twenty feet from where I parked marks the boundary line of the Adalwulf Pack land and Blackthroat property. When Madi was Brick's assistant, she helped him procure this land for the Blackthroats, swiping the sale out from under Aiden's feet.

If a member of either pack caught me here now, it could start another outright war. Or end my life. But that's the risk I have to take.

I maneuver the controls on one of the drones I bought to survey the Adalwulf compound, homing in on a stone tower where the bug I placed on Aster has remained for the past week. The bug is in her handbag, and she hasn't left the compound since she returned, so it makes sense the bag wouldn't move. But based on the conversation I recorded between Aster and Aiden, I suspect she's locked in that tower. The same one from my dreams.

It always looked like some kind of prison to me.

But the young woman in the museum didn't look like a prisoner. She looked every inch the high society bitch one would expect from one of the oldest and wealthiest families in New York. Like Catherine Adalwulf.

Then again, from the details Madi let slip, I think her mother-in-law was as much a victim of the family's terror as my mother is.

Maybe it's a misguided savior complex, but I have a fierce desire to liberate every female born to that pack. To dismantle the twisted underpinnings of the sick cult that breeds females and uses them like slaves in the name of religion.

Aster is one of those slaves.

No, I don't know that. But it's possible she could be flipped. She might be willing to tell me information about the location of Moonborn in exchange for the tiara. I left the tiara in a safehold in the city because having it close seemed to give me a headache.

My burner phone lights up, warning me of an incoming call from Moon Co. I left my actual work phone in my apartment but forwarded all messages and calls to the burner, so I wouldn't miss anything.

I keep the drone hovering and free a hand to check my messages. A shock runs through me when I see the transcribed voice message is from Brick.

Noah. Answer your phone.

I can't hear his tone, but I suspect he's pissed.

Why is the big boss himself calling me? I grab my phone, ready to message him back right away, but...I'm in the middle of a mission. I informed HR that I was taking a personal day. Wolves don't need sick days, so I can't use a doctor's visit as an excuse, but I didn't think I'd need to justify my absence.

Out of curiosity, I check my messages. There's one from Brick's assistant, informing me that Brick wants to meet ASAP.

Whatever's blowing up at work, I can't focus on it right now. But just as I'm about to turn off the burner phone, another message comes through from Brick himself.

Is this you?

Attached is a video clip. I play it and curse. It's a video of my gray and white wolf running through the museum lobby with a dopey, doggie grin on my face.

Shit shit shit shit. Esme monitored the news to see if it got out, but other than some social media posts by some of the sixth graders, it looks like the museum was trying to hush it up. Esme went ahead and commented on a few of the posts, claiming that "No way this happened, must be AI." But someone–probably Sully–discovered it. A shifter like him would recognize my wolf as another shifter right away. Sully isn't the head of security for nothing. He's paid to be paranoid.

It's also possible that Brick tagged me as a possible threat and is digging into my movements. One of Sully's spies would've noticed I was late to work the same day of the museum heist and put two and two together.

Another text comes through from Brick:

CALL ME

I can practically hear his alpha power vibrating through the phone. Forget firing me, I bet he's salivating to let his wolf out to rip me apart.

I'm busted, but there's nothing I can do about it now. I power off the burner phone and tuck it away. As soon as I obey Brick's summons, I'm getting fired and exiled from the city. And that's the best case. Worst case: Sully locks me up as a pack enemy and throws away the key.

But that's a problem for future me. I have a pack princess to spy on.

I dare to bring the drone closer to her tower, moving in from the top and slowly lowering at an angle. Is that window open? I inch the drone down a little further. Esme helped me source the best military grade drone–a dark drone that mimics the shape of a bird and the quiet sound of an insect. Still, getting it too close to the window could be a huge mistake.

I risk it, swooping in right against the cylindrical stone wall, then dipping below the top frame of the window.

I jerk in surprise, sending the drone on a wild wobble. Aster's face fills my phone screen.

She was standing at the open window.

Her hand snaps out, lightning fast, and she must catch the drone because the viewer blurs, then her lovely face comes in close. So close I can examine the exact color of her ice-blue eyes.

I drop the useless controller and simply stare.

She peers at the drone, then turns to look past it out the window.

The viewer blurs again and then clears, but it takes me a moment to figure out what I'm looking at: Aster's bare feet, kicking and jerking in a fit.

She must've dropped the drone and slumped back on a bed or chair.

I don't think. If I were thinking, I would know that what I'm contemplating is the worst idea I've ever had. I hop out of the car and sprint toward the entrance to the Adalwulf property. It's protected by an electric fence, which I clear in the best high jump of my life, thanking the Harvard track team for the lessons in catapulting my body in human form through space. As I sprint toward the compound, images flash in my mind.

Aster on the floor, clutching her head, her eyes rolling back.

Another image flashes in my mind: the location of the transmitter for an invisible infrared laser that must serve as long-range perimeter security.

Recognizing the nearby stone hut from my drone surveillance, I swerve and head for it without a plan. I don't know how to disable the alarm system, but I'm trusting in the visions.

When I arrive, I see the guard through the window. He spills his coffee down his front, curses, and gets up to walk to the kitchen. I take it as a sign and clap my hand over the laser transmitter to block it as I slip by.

Another image—some kind of underground tunnel—flashes in my mind at the same moment I trip over something and fall flat on my face. An iron ring protrudes from the earth. I wipe the dirt away to reveal the outline of a trapdoor.

The tunnel. I yank the metal trapdoor open and drop down into a dank tunnel.

Incredible. I've never experienced waking visions like this. Fate seems to be guiding me straight to Aster. No, to the Moonborn. To complete my mission.

Either that, or the wolf-witch is placing visions into my head to lure me into a trap.

Both possibilities seem equally likely. I know how corrupt the Moonborn are.

I take a moment to let my eyes adjust to the darkness. A sense of danger sparks all around me. I want to shift into my wolf form to run the length of the tunnel, but then there would be the awkward issue of not having clothes.

A dozen images flash in my brain, as if several movies are playing at 10X speed at the same time.

The image of Aster's jerking foot spurs me back into a run. I don't know why I care. I don't care—but it feels like my body won't let me remain still while she's in need.

I sprint into the darkness, trusting my senses will keep me from running straight into a wall.

I run for four minutes straight, and then I hit the end of the tunnel and an iron door. It has a ten-inch rusted hoop for a handle and an ancient-looking lock. I grab the hoop and tug.

The door doesn't budge. It's locked.

I detect a slight vibration in the door when I press my palm against it. There it is again-a thud against the door from the other side.

I duck back, pressing myself against the wall, so I can hide if it swings open. It doesn't move.

I press my palm against the door again to detect the vibration of any sounds from the other side. The inner part of the lock turns, but still the door doesn't open.

I feel the thud again and frown. A third thud.

Is she... trying to get out?

It's an insane risk, but something makes me grab the handle, put my foot against the wall, and heave with all my weight. The door swings back, and a slight blonde female stumbles out, doubles over, and throws up.

* * *

Aster

Oh fate, the visions. They came on again as soon as I caught that drone outside my window.

This time, I'm sure—it has something to do with the wolf I've been dreaming about. The young man on the periphery of the Blackthroat pack.

I saw him sitting in a car, looking at a phone screen that had my face looking back. After that I blacked out—the visions too fast and intense to interpret. When I woke up, I found myself here at a great iron door. Somehow, I know that I'm at the entrance to the secret tunnel that leads from the Adalwulf manor out to the guard hut at the edge of the property.

It's been in existence for over two hundred years. Oma once told me there was an escape tunnel dug in case the property was sacked by the Blackthroat pack. A way to get the pups and she-wolves out of danger.

I don't know how I even found it. How I even got out of my locked chambers. I remember Oma telling me of the tunnel's existence, but if she ever showed me this door, I have no memory.

But I trust the whispers of the Grandmothers, which tell me to go through it. I turn the ancient key in the lock counterclockwise and shove against the door.

It doesn't move.

I put all my weight into it, but I'm too weak from the vision spell. My stomach lurches—I'm going to throw up.

I try once more in desperation.

The door seems to swing open of its own accord. I stumble through it just as my stomach decides to empty its contents on the dirt floor of the tunnel. I double over, holding myself up with a hand against the dirt wall. The visions come even stronger now. I can't manage them. I can't see anything.

I throw up again, and it takes me a moment to realize someone is holding my hair back from my face.

Noah.

The name comes to me, and it sounds familiar, like I've spoken it before, yet I'm sure I haven't. Was it in a dream?

I reach blindly for him, and my hand hits a sturdy arm. Then I collapse to the floor.

No...

I'm not on the floor, but I *am* horizontal. I'm in a large wolf's arms being transported at a rapid pace.

I struggle to slow my breath and see through the visions as we race at breakneck speed through the tunnel.

The wolf smells like pine needles and amber wood–a scent I want to wrap myself in for all time.

"Stop." I finally manage to speak.

He doesn't stop.

In fact, he offers no indication that he heard me at all.

"Stop!" I shout this time.

"I know you're speaking, but I can't hear you," the wolf says in a flat tone.

Shock ripples through me

The pup with no ears.

The pup. With. No. Ears.

The memory of Oma and the Warden's murmured conversation ten years ago returns to me in a flood. I'd forgotten about it until now.

Could this be him?

And more–could he be the same man I've been dreaming about?

His energy feels the same as what I sensed in the elevator at the museum. I didn't see or hear him, but I feel certain this is the same man who held me on his lap while I had a fit. I'm almost certain that he's the man from my visions.

But if he's the wolf with no ears, that means *he's going to destroy the Adalwulf pack.*

My survival instinct kicks in, and I fight him, twisting to pry my body free, even though I still can't see anything. It's like fighting a stone wall. He's not hurting me, but I can't escape his grip.

I'm weak from fasting and the vision-sickness, and everything in me wants to sink into his warm, wild scent.

"Sorry, princess, but you're coming with me," he says.

"Coming where? Why?" I ask then remember he can't hear me nor can he see my lips move in the dark.

I hold my breath, reaching for guidance from the Grandmothers, but, like in the elevator, there's too much at once. I go into convulsions again, unable to process any of it.

I succumb to unconsciousness as I'm carried off by the enemy, but the visions crystalize into stillness. I'm in my bedroom dreaming, and I wake to see a young man is dreaming with me. He's in his bed but also somehow in the room with me. He sits up and looks at me.

"*Noah.*" I project the name without speaking. We're telepathically connected.

Noah! That *is* his name. I know his name. And now I'm

certain he's the same man from the elevator. The same man holding me now.

Somehow, I feel I've had this vision/dream before; I just didn't remember it.

I've been waiting to meet you for such a long time, I tell him, which I guess is true.

Who are you? he asks.

Disappointment jabs me in the chest. My dream self wanted him to know me. Thought that he would.

You don't know? I ask.

He shakes his head. *I want to.*

Chapter Eight

Noah

In for a penny, in for a pound.

I'm sure I just signed my death warrant. I had no intention of kidnapping the Adalwulf Seeress, but I suppose it's even better than stealing the tiara they want to use to enable her magic.

I'm not one to argue with Fate. I've never experienced the kind of clear guidance as I received today. While it may be that the wolf-witch sent the visions, it didn't seem to be a trap.

Perhaps she needed rescuing. She was at the top of what appeared to be a prison tower, and she's far too thin.

Either way, I'm certain destiny brought me to her.

If she were human, I would take her to a hospital to make sure she isn't dying, but since she's a wolf, I hold her in the rental car until she slips into unconsciousness, then take her to the nearby cabin I rented for the week.

She sleeps on the couch, her face peaceful, her breath slow. I crouch beside her, staring at her lovely visage.

She's like a china doll. Perfect, smooth skin—too pale to

be healthy. Long, dark lashes that fan in delicate feathers along her closed lids. She wears no makeup, and she's in the same thin white shift she was wearing in the dream I had with her.

The one where she warned me I would have to pick a side before the war came.

I assume she meant a war between packs.

But I don't know why she would think I'd be involved. That war has never been mine. I'm not a Blackthroat. I'm certainly not an Adalwulf, even if my mother is Moonborn. I have no allegiance to either pack.

I'd finally forced myself away from my fascinated study of her to cook dinner. She looks underfed, and after the fits she had, she'll need her strength back.

Logic dictates I should tie her up. She's my prisoner, after all. But nothing in me could make me do it. Nothing in me wants to do anything but brush the backs of my fingers along her cheek to see if it's really as soft and smooth as it appears. So I do. Just once, just to see.

And it is.

But instead of focusing on her beauty, I should be formulating a plan. I have Brick Blackthroat breathing down my neck over the tiara heist.

I just stole the Adalwulf's biggest prize. If the Adalwulfs decide the Blackthroats are behind her kidnapping, I could've triggered a war. And more than that, I have a slender, lovely but powerful she-wolf sleeping on my couch and no plan for how I'm going to keep her from running away.

* * *

Aster

The scent of steak wakes me. If the smell didn't pull me

from unconsciousness, the sound of my stomach growling would have. I feel fuzzy but comfortable. A fire crackles nearby, sending sweet, sweet heat to warm me through. I'm so relaxed and cozy, I'm definitely not in the tower.

But where am I?

I crack my eyes. I'm lying on a couch of faded blue fabric. Someone covered me with a soft, gray blanket. I'm so comfortable, I don't want to move, but I make myself sit up a bit and look around.

I'm in a fire-lit room that looks like a cabin of some sort, with walls of knotty pine. There's a small window framed by blue curtains to my right and a braided blue and brown rug on the floor, pitted with a few sooty black stains.

Behind me is a tiny kitchen area with wood cabinets and a small round table between two chairs. Everything is made of the same knotty pine–as if whoever built the cabin used the leftovers to decorate.

The door is across the room. Even as I spot it, a man comes to stand beside me. It's him, the wolf who carried me through the tunnel.

The wolf who held me in the elevator.

The wolf from my dreams. *Noah.*

"Welcome back, Aster."

He knows my name, too.

The firelight gilds his hair, picking out the golden streaks in the blond. He smells familiar, like warm amber and pine. My nose tells me I'm alone with him.

"Where am I? What time is it?" It's dark outside.

"A little before eight. You passed out after your seizure and stayed asleep the whole way here. I let you sleep. I think you needed it." There's the shadow of a smile hovering around his mouth.

I swallow. He kidnapped me. I shouldn't feel so relaxed.

"I need to go to the bathroom." I do, but I also want a moment alone to buy some time. I want to see how long a leash I have.

"It's there." Noah nods to a door near the kitchen. "Through the bedroom."

My insides knot at the mention of a bedroom. Who is this wolf? What does he want with me?

Automatically, I glance at the front door, the closest exit. It's a mistake because Noah catches it.

"Don't try to run." His expression turns serious. "I'll catch you." His eyes glitter with a golden light.

He's a wolf shifter–alpha stock, judging by his size, and even if I were at my best, he's bigger and stronger than me. Dangerous.

An enemy.

My stomach chooses that moment to growl. My mouth is watering, reminding me that I'm smelling steak. I glance at the cast-iron pan on the small stove.

Noah's grim look softens when he catches my glance, and I see the glimmer of a smile. "Stick around, and I'll feed you."

I ease myself up off the couch. It's a good sign that I'm still dressed in my shift–if barefoot–and allowed to move around freely. I'm not chained in a dungeon. I'm not being brutalized.

Yet.

My wolf wants me to hide how weak I am, but I can't keep my legs from wobbling as I take my first steps towards the bathroom. A wave of dizziness sends my head spinning, and I lose my balance and have to grope for the couch to hold me up—

Noah's warmth hits my back and side as he catches my elbow, supporting me with a hand at my back and my arm.

His touch sets off a fresh burst of colors in my Sight, and I gasp.

I twist so he can see my lips. "I've got it," I choke, but I definitely don't.

"It's okay, Seeress. We all need a little help sometimes."

Seeress. Just hearing my title makes me stand a little straighter. I control the visions, banishing them for the moment. I nod with queenly grace and let him escort me to the small room.

Once inside, I grip the edge of the sink and give myself a pep talk. My eyes look sunken. I scoop water into my hands and drink it, then give up and drink straight from the faucet. Damn Aiden and the Warden for weakening me like this.

Damn, if this strange wolf isn't treating me better than I've been treated by my pack, except for Liora.

Noah is waiting for me when I open the door. He offers his arm as if it's the 1800s, and I need an escort to help me cross the street.

Respect. It feels nice. And maybe he's just softening me up before he turns on me and starts an interrogation, but for now, I'll play along.

This time when I touch his arm, I brace against the visions, but they don't start. Instead, I feel the low thrum of a pulse between my legs.

What is this? Sexual attraction?

It can't be. I sublimated all sexual desires to augment my Sight. That's why the Seeress must remain a virgin. We lose our powers if we have sex.

I look up at the alpha wolf as we walk. He's achingly handsome—more handsome in real life than the man in my dreams. His square jaw is lightly dusted with stubble. His sandy hair falls across his forehead in a way that softens the troubled storm behind his blue eyes.

"Noah." Thunder rumbles outside, like nature is punctuating this moment.

He nods.

"You're a Blackthroat."

He shakes his head and pulls out a chair for me.

Okay. We're playing Twenty Questions.

I sink into it and look at the place setting on the simple wooden table. Filled water glasses. Two placemats. Two plates. Cloth napkins with forks and steak knives resting on them. It seems like a consideration that a kidnapper wouldn't take. I mean, he's presenting me with a weapon.

But he told me not to run, so I'm definitely a prisoner. Rain descends in a sudden burst, pelting the roof and windows.

I glance at one of the windows, and he follows my gaze then flicks his brows.

"Are you kidnapping me?"

He doesn't answer, and for a moment, I think he's stonewalling until I realize his back is turned to me as he picks up the skillet. I wait for him to fork a large steak and drop it in the center of my plate and try again. "Am I your prisoner?"

Golden light rolls over his irises again, and I feel the prickle of danger. "For now." He forks a steak onto his plate and serves us each a portion of broccoli drizzled with fresh lemon and salted butter, judging by the scent.

For now.

What in the hell does that mean?

He slides into the chair opposite me. "What do you want with me? Are you selling me to the Blackthroats?"

A frown creases between his brows. "No." He taps his index and middle finger down on his thumb around his fork in what must be the sign for no. The syllable is decisive, and his distaste with my question is clear. He cuts into his steak.

I don't smell a lie. I cut into mine and take a bite. I'm ravenous. I gulp down two more bites, hardly chewing before I notice Noah glowering at me.

"You were starving."

Is it me, or does he seem angry about this?

I swallow down a hunk of meat and draw myself up straighter. I don't want him thinking I'm weak. Especially not if I'm his prisoner. "Fasting aids in the Sight."

He studies me without comment. I don't think he buys it. He reaches across and cuts a corner of my meat into small squares, as if I were a child. "Smaller bites. I don't want you choking."

I glare at the smaller bites and then decide I'm too hungry to quibble. I stab one and swallow it down. "What do you want with me?" I repeat.

He shrugs. "It's not you I want. But fate delivered you to me, and I know better than to argue with fate."

Fate delivered me to him? A shock of surprise ripples through me as my mind quickly catalogs the events.

Grandmothers, is it true?

Maybe he's right. Maybe fate was at work in sending me straight into his arms. I still don't know how I got out of my locked and guarded cell, nor how I found my way to the tunnel entry. The visions were coming too fast for me to interpret, and then suddenly I was out, and Noah was there waiting for me.

Noah continues to stare at me as he eats, as if he's listening intently, not with his ears but with his other senses. His aura is powerful, a serene but intense blue that radiates from him. I can almost taste his alpha magic.

"You've been in my dreams," he says.

I choke on my steak. He lunges forward like he's somehow going to save me from asphyxiating. When I hold up my hand, he slowly sinks back into his chair, gaze still intent on my face.

I pound on my sternum with my fist and swallow, then pick up my glass and guzzle down half the water. "You saw my dreams?" I rasp out, my eyes still watering from choking.

That golden sheen rolls over his irises again. It sends a shiver down my spine. He's so beautiful it makes my chest ache.

"You saw *my* dreams." He points at me, then uses a flat hand on his chest. I enjoy seeing him talk with his hands. Something in me yearns to see him sign. The way his hands move is beautiful.

A hint of a smile plays around his lips, and I realize he might be teasing me. The sight of it sends butterflies fluttering through me. He has beautiful dark blue eyes. Kind eyes.

He feels familiar, even though we're total strangers. I know he was the man who helped me in the elevator. I keep imagining it, wishing I'd been able to see him or had been more aware to understand what was happening.

The smile vanishes as quickly as it came.

"When? Which dreams?" I demand.

"Most of them I don't remember, but I know I've been dreaming about you. There was one in your bedroom. You sat up in bed and were looking at me. It was like we were in two places at once."

I gasp. That's the same vision I remember. "What did I tell you?" I ask, testing him.

Something in his face closes as if he doesn't want to have this conversation. Does that mean he didn't have the same vision? Or doesn't remember it?

"You said I would have to choose sides for a war coming." His expression is dark.

Ice sluices through my veins, and I shiver.

He remembers. And he understands the warning.

Has he already chosen a side? He said he wasn't with the Blackthroats, but I know that's not true.

Warning bells sound in my head. They should've been sounding this whole time, but I was weak from fasting in the visions. Now I'm finally waking up to the disaster of my situation.

Noah kidnapped me and is holding me prisoner. He intends to use me against my pack, I'm sure.

This wolf is the enemy.

* * *

Noah

I narrow my eyes at my lovely captive. "I don't care about your war."

Her pale brows lift toward her hairline. "No?"

"No." I sign the word as I speak it.

"What *do* you care about?"

I watch her lips move. They look plump and soft. Kissable. My wolf is riled up being in the same room with her. She's the most beautiful creature I've ever seen.

But I shouldn't be thinking about that. Especially not when she's at my mercy. It would be wrong to make any kind of move on her. Besides, I couldn't trust her motivations if she reciprocated. She could be doing it to get free.

And I still haven't ruled out the possibility that she lured me to her to win this war she warned me of.

So I ignore the question and her delicious peach

blossom scent, putting a bite of steak in my mouth and chewing.

She does the same. It satisfies my wolf to feed her. Her arms and legs are too thin. She was so weak, she was barely able to walk to the bathroom, and the way she tore into the meat made it seem like she'd been starved.

I'm sure the fits she has during her visions sap her strength, and she also mentioned fasting to improve the visions, but something makes me think there's more to it. My impression from our shared visions was always that she was a prisoner of some kind.

Which should make me feel all the worse for keeping her my prisoner now.

But I have no choice. As I told her, fate delivered her to me. She must be the answer to finding the Moonborn.

Aster finishes the steak and moves onto the broccoli. After she cleans her plate, she wipes the butter from her lips with her cloth napkin. My cock stirs at the thought of licking it off for her. My wolf wants me to keep feeding her, but I don't want her to get sick. She devoured her food too fast.

Now I wish I'd purchased extras from the grocery store before I checked into the cabin. Wine would be nice right now. Or something sweet.

"Are you still hungry?" I sign and speak the words, and she pays attention to my fingers, like she's committing the signs to memory.

I watch her lips move, still wanting to kiss them. "I'm okay. Thank you. That was delicious."

I touch the tips of my fingertips together, contemplating the situation. I don't know what in the hell I'm going to do with her. I can't very well let her go now because the moment I do, the war between packs begins. Or perhaps it already has–I don't know. I still haven't returned Brick's messages.

"I have a question," I say.

She stills, her face arranging into an inscrutable mask.

Fuck. I don't want her so guarded.

"How old are you, Seeress?"

She relaxes a bit. "Twenty-two."

"What were you doing up in that tower?"

Wariness returns. "Receiving visions."

"And you were fasting to receive them?"

Aster pushes back from the table and stands, drawing herself up tall. Tall for her is up to my shoulders, and she's so thin I could break her in half with one hand.

I also stand, picking up our plates and silverware. "Were you a prisoner there?" I try again.

Something in the way her eyes jerk to my face tells me I'm right, but she immediately covers it, throwing her shoulders back and lifting her chin. "Of course not. I'm Seeress to the most powerful pack in New York. There is no female wolf who ranks higher than I."

I don't smell the acrid scent of a lie, but I'm still certain that she's hiding something. She worded her answer very carefully. She didn't come right out and say she wasn't a prisoner in that tower. And if the Adalwulfs treat their Seeress so poorly, how do they treat the rest of the females in the pack? Do they imprison and starve them to the point of weakness?

My Nan hinted that before my birth, my mother was brutalized in some kind of ritual. Maybe I'm reading too much into Aster's situation, but my gut says no.

The thought of my mother being treated like Aster makes my wolf hot and itchy for revenge, but I hide my violence. I'm adept at hiding all emotions and urges. Being deaf gives me the advantage of being underestimated. Written off. I learned to become the observer who stayed out of pack dynamics and plotted his revenge on the Moonborn in a long game.

Aster props her hip against the table. She's still not steady on her feet but doesn't want to show me her weakness. I want to question her more, but my wolf won't allow it.

"You're tired, Seeress. Take the bed. I'll clean up."

She glances toward the door. I shake my head. She wouldn't make it two steps before I caught her.

Of course, my wolf wants her to run. He wants to chase. He wants the dance of the full moon runs, where the males chase and catch the females, forcing them into sexual surrender.

Once more, she squares her shoulders, picking up her empty glass and carrying it past me to the kitchen sink. Her hip brushes mine as she passes, and I get a hit of her scent–fresh summer peaches. I reach for the faucet to turn it on for her, dying to keep her close, to breathe that sweet scent until I drown in it. I'm crowding her into the corner against the cabinets, but she doesn't seem afraid. No, the flutter of her eyelashes as she darts a quick glance at my face tells me she knows I'm not trying to intimidate her.

I can't help it. I have to touch her. I turn off the water after she's filled her glass and rest my hand on her lower back. "Come. You can wear something of mine to sleep in."

And I'm happy to undress you if you need my help.

Another darted glance at my face, and she acquiesces, allowing me to escort her to the bedroom where I pull out a flannel shirt and a pair of too-big sweatpants from my duffel bag.

"Thank you." She reaches for the clothes with pale, slender fingers.

I've never wished I could hear a voice. School administrators tortured me when I was a child with devices to help me hear–that was how I learned how to talk, but I have long-since abandoned them. But right now, I'd give my left nut to know the tone of her voice. Whether it's light and breathy or low and sultry. Maybe it's an unpleasant shrill sound, but somehow, I doubt it.

"Good night, Seeress."

She inclines her head, making it harder for me to read her lips. "Good night, Noah."

Something about seeing those pouty lips form my name does something to the room. The floor tilts. My heart pounds. My balls grow heavy.

I have participated in full moon runs with my pack back in Kentucky. I've shared a bed with she-wolves for the night. I explored my sexual needs with a handful of human females during college. But I have never once let a female distract me from my mission of freeing my mother and taking down the Moonborn.

Right now, though, I'm tempted.

Aster Adalwulf is the most fascinating female I've ever met, and if she wasn't the prize possession of my sworn enemies, I might allow myself to explore my wolf's apparent interest more.

But I'm in no position to do that.

I will have to keep my hands off this beautiful she-wolf before she tempts me into making a mistake.

Chapter Nine

After

The dreams begin almost the moment I lay my head on the pillow. Visions that come in splintering speed, too fast to interpret. Not that I want to analyze and predict right now. I just want to sleep. My body is bone-tired. My nerves are beyond frayed. The steak will help me recover by tomorrow morning, but right now, it's just making me sleepy.

Noah insisted I leave the bedroom door open. Maybe he thinks I'll climb out the window and run.

I probably should be planning my escape. The rain and darkness would help cover my scent and footprints, and it would be hard to track me. But right now, I'm too depleted to even contemplate it.

After I crawled in bed, I listened to Noah wash the dishes and clean up then heard him standing in the doorway, like he was watching me. The visions quieted while he stood there, but my body heated as thoughts of what I would do if he came in and pulled down the covers bombarded my brain.

My body seemed to think I *wanted* that to happen, which is new.

I've noticed attractive males before, but it was always from an intellectual point of view. I admired tall men. Men with perfect physiques. Men with symmetrical facial features. Noah's handsomeness hits every time I glance his way. My knees go weak. A flutter starts in my belly. I have the strangest urge to giggle–and I almost never laugh.

So would I fight him if he tried to climb in bed with me?

Yes. I'd have to. Protecting my Sight is far more important than indulging my body's sudden whimsical interest in a male. But I know it's a moot point. Noah is a gentleman. He's not going to force himself on me tonight.

I surrender to the visions and let them carry me into sleep.

Oma startles me awake. I'm in the prison tower. Her wrinkled face is right in front of mine.

"What are you doing, child? You can't be with a man!" She points a gnarled, bony finger at me.

"I'm not *with* a man! I'm his *prisoner*." It's not like me to talk back to Oma. This dream self sounds shrill and defensive.

She slaps my face. "Don't lie to me. You walked out of the tower!" Her voice is a screech. "You're going to ruin everything I worked three generations to achieve. Get back to your confinement. *Now!*" She puts her fingertips on my temples and sends searing pain into my head.

I scream as the visions return, so fast they turn into a blinding white light that makes my head explode with too much coded information.

I need to throw up. I pray I'll pass out.

My body feels like it's falling through the air–like Oma

threw me out the tower window, and I'm tumbling to my death, except I don't hit the ground.

Someone catches me.

Noah.

His amber and cedarwood scent curls into my nostrils. His warmth seeps into my body against my back. One of his strong warm hands cups my nape, the other curves around me to press against my sternum. He's rocking me.

I've got you. His words enter my head the way my clairaudience does.

The blinding white light begins to fade. I hear the murmurings of the Grandmothers, but it's as if someone turns the volume down until their chatter disappears.

Is this a vision?

No. I feel Noah's breath feather across my shoulder. He climbed in the bed with me after all–not to force himself on me but to hold me.

To comfort me.

When I was young–before I was sent to the Adalwulf manse to train under Oma–I was cared for by the mothers, the group of Moonborn female wolves who live in the simplicity and oneness of nature at Moonhollow. In my earliest years, I was loved. I was cuddled and held and guided, even as I was taught the importance of my future role as an acolyte to Oma.

But the moments of comfort since I left Moonhollow have been few. Perhaps it's just from my exhaustion from everything I've been through since the day I went to New York, but I suddenly feel so safe.

I feel so safe, and it releases a dam of emotion I didn't know I carried. A sob rockets from my throat. My stomach twists up, and tears stream from my eyes onto the pillow.

Noah shifts his fingers from my nape to my temple, where he lightly strokes me with his thumb.

Don't cry, starlight. His projected words reach me. *I won't hurt you.*

"I know." I answer out loud then remember he can't read my lips when he's behind me. I try again but speak the words in my head to him.

His body jerks in surprise.

He heard me. This isn't a vision. Or is it? A waking one?

Noah tugs me toward him, rolling me onto my back and peering down at me with concern. He brushes my hair back from my face. "What did they do to you?"

A lump forms in my throat, and fresh tears spill uncontrollably from the corners of my eyes. "Please." I shake my head. "Don't."

I don't want him to uncover how vulnerable I am. Don't want him to know or understand my pain. *I* don't even want to explore this sudden ocean of grief welling out of me. I can't trust that he won't use it against me and my pack.

My body starts to tremble, a violent shaking like I'm going into shock.

Noah's eyes glow gold, alarm scrawling across his features, but then his lips crash down on mine. His fingers curl behind my neck, angling my mouth toward him.

I gasp against the kiss, more shocked than I've ever been. My hips buck with need, the ache between my legs amplifying to a steady beating pulse. The sobs vanish, every nerve ending electrified by this male's kiss.

My first kiss.

He pulls away like he's surprised. Like he didn't know that he was going to kiss me before it happened. But then he plunges in again, kissing me hard, lips slanting across mine as he blankets me with his body.

I rub against his thigh pressed between my legs. My breasts tingle, nipples tightening to tight buds against the flannel shirt he lent me.

His tongue sweeps into my mouth.

I'm kissing him back now, hungry. Greedy.

Wait...*no.* Oh, Fate. *What am I doing?*

I press both hands against his chest and push away. "No! I can't."

Noah shakes his head as if to clear it. As if he doesn't know what just happened. "I'm sorry. I didn't mean to–"

But then I tug him back down, needing to feel the intense pleasure of our joined lips again.

There's power to the connection. Every second his lips stroke across mine heals me more.

His free hand strokes across my shoulder then cradles my breast. I've never been touched there before. He pinches my nipple beneath the flannel, and I feel the answering tug between my legs.

"Wait. No. Wait...please." I push at his chest.

A shudder runs through Noah's body, as if it pains him to stop kissing me, but he sits back and wipes his mouth with the back of his hand. His eyes still glow gold.

My pulse races. I want to kiss him again, but I know it wouldn't stop there. I had chastity culture drilled into me from the time I was a toddler. I know you can't excite a male wolf and then stop him from claiming you. Not without getting badly injured.

"I can't, Noah."

I can't have sex with this gorgeous male.

I'm not even interested. I don't know why I enjoyed that kiss so much.

"It's okay." Noah moves off me and rolls me back to my

side, settling behind me in spoon position, the way he was before. "It won't happen again."

He wraps a strong arm around my waist and pulls me back against him. For a moment, I wait, breath held, body singing at his closeness. My heart pounds at his audacity. Is he going to stay in this bed with me? All night?

There's no way I'll be able to sleep with him here.

Except he starts softly stroking my hair with his free hand, and it feels so good, I forget about my objections. His breath steadies into a slow, deep rhythm, guiding me into relaxation. The rain outside has slowed to a gentle lull.

I keep my eyes open for a few moments, afraid the visions will come back, but when they drift close, there's nothing but darkness. Nothing but darkness and the feather touch of Noah's fingertips stroking my hair. Somehow, by some unknown miracle, I fall into a deep and dreamless sleep.

* * *

Noah

Aster's peach magnolia scent rolls over me like a heady drug. I didn't mean to kiss her. I meant to soothe her. To ask why she was crying and say the right words to make it right. Not that words are my specialty.

The idea that she might be crying because I am holding her here as my prisoner gutted me. But then she projected words right into my head and said she knew I wouldn't hurt her.

I shouldn't be so shocked. We're obviously telepathically connected. That was how we've been dreaming the same dream. She's a powerful Seeress. Somehow, she's created a connection into my mind.

She was crying because of something else. Maybe the thing that made her meet me in that tunnel. I wanted to make it better, and then suddenly, I was kissing her.

Not tenderly. Not gently. Not with consent.

I kissed her like a male crazed with passion. Like a wolf who's met his mate.

The idea occurred to me before—that I've been seeing her in my dreams because she's mine.

She belongs to me.

I have to admit that holding her as she sleeps feels like a fucking privilege. I'm telling myself I'm doing it to keep her from escaping. I'm doing it to soothe away her nightmares or the fits she has when she gets her visions. But those are lies.

Holding her, touching her, breathing in her scent feels like home.

Maybe fate didn't bring Aster to me to help find my mother. Maybe fate wanted me to rescue her from whatever nightmare she's living out in that prison tower. Or maybe the moon goddess was connecting two mates.

Fuck. Even though the idea brings a kind of chaotic excitement to my cells, I don't want to examine this possibility.

Mating the Adalwulf Seeress–their most protected asset–isn't a possibility for me. I've spent my whole life working on this long game to infiltrate them and find where they keep their Moonborn. To try to talk sense into my mother, and if I can't, to bring down the entire violent cult that indoctrinated her with their warped ideology.

They bred my mother like a slave. They tried to kill me at birth.

They need to be extinguished.

So yes, I will use Aster to get what I want, but complicating this plan with romance? With mating?

Not a possibility.

Chapter Ten

A*ster*

I ease awake from a dreamless sleep with a deep sense of peace in my body. The scent of a delicious male with amber and pine notes fills my nostrils.

For one moment, it feels right. Like I'm somewhere familiar. Like I've woken this way a thousand times, and every time was sweetness.

Then I remember where I am.

I gasp and try to sit up, only to discover Noah's still in the bed with me, his heavy arm wrapped around my waist.

He jerks at my sudden movement and then slowly releases me. Something hard brushes against my ass. My body is untouched, but I've witnessed the Alpha Rites. I know what this means.

Noah's aroused.

I quickly roll off the bed, squaring off to him. The soft flannel shirt sleeves of the shirt I borrowed from him flap open, hanging far past my hands.

He sits up, and I get a full view of his naked and muscled torso. When he lifts a hand to rub his mussed hair,

I see the tattoos that trace his forearms, which give him a rugged, alpha look. I want to examine them up close. To see what he chose to ink on his body. I suspect it's something intentional. He doesn't strike me as someone who did it on a whim. Or for looks. Tattooing a shifter is a painful process involving adding salt to the ink mixture to keep our natural healing from absorbing it.

His nostrils flare like he's taking in my scent. He throws off the covers and swings his legs off the side of the bed. "You said you weren't scared of me."

My gaze darts to the tent in his sweatpants. How big is he? What would it be like to...

Ack! Why am I thinking this way? I'm not interested in this male. I'm not.

He glances down and adjusts himself. "You're scared of my dick." He samples the air again and grows thoughtful. "No, you're scared of your body's reaction to me."

Heat flushes up my neck. Damn him. He must smell both my fear and arousal. I hold the flannel closed at the neck, as if to keep him from seeing my throat. As if that, alone, would be too much of an invitation.

"I'm sorry I kissed you." He holds his palms up. "That's not what I want from you." He turns and stalks out of the bedroom, almost like he's a little pissed.

At me? Or at himself?

"What *do* you want from me?" I call toward his back, forgetting he can't hear me.

I chase him into the kitchen and tap his shoulder. "What do you want from me?"

"We'll get to that." He pulls open the refrigerator door and pulls out a carton of eggs and a slab of bacon. "After I feed you."

He wants to feed me. That shouldn't make my heart flap its wings like a trapped bird in a cage.

It's the word choice. Not *after we eat*. Or *after breakfast*. *After I feed you.*

That sounds like something a male wolf says to his mate.

Grandmothers, is that what this is? Goosebumps race up my arms, and I start to tremble with the revelation.

Is Noah my mate? Is that why I've been dreaming of him? But that can't be–he's also the wolf with no ears. The wolf who will destroy the pack.

Fate wouldn't put me in that kind of position. Fate wouldn't pair me with the enemy.

Or would she?

"There's enough hot water in the tank for one of us to take a shower." Noah pulls the cast-iron skillet out of the dish rack and drops a chunk of butter into it.

Shower. Fate, yes. That's what I need right now. And to escape this male's presence, so I can get myself back together.

"I can make it quick," I offer.

"Nah, take your time. You need it more than me."

I cock a hip. "Are you saying that I smell?" Dearest Grandmothers–am I flirting?

His gaze alights on my hand at my waist and that golden sheen rolls over his irises. "Only a little." He sniffs and scrunches up his nose, pretending he smelled something bad.

We're flirting. Tingles of excitement fizz all around me. I laugh, and a strange look comes over his face. Something akin to...longing.

"You're smiling," he says.

My smile falters.

His own lips quirk although his smile looks a little sad. Wistful, almost. "I haven't seen you smile before, Seeress."

I shrug. "I didn't have anything to smile about." I turn and go into the bathroom, turning on the water and stepping in as soon as it's warm.

Fates, the hot water feels good. The shower is surprisingly roomy for a three-room log cabin. The only soap is a bottle of hand soap from the sink, but it smells like honeysuckle and lemon, and it feels luxurious to use it to wash my hair and whole body. My wolf is preening. She wants to look good for our sexy captor.

He's not sexy, he's holding us hostage, I scold her, even though I had no problem flirting with him in the kitchen. Nor cuddling up with him in the bed. I slept better than I have in years, maybe ever. It was like my wolf knew I had a protector who would keep me safe, so I was able to let go and rest.

That would make sense if he were my mate.

He feeds me better than anyone from my own pack, that's for sure. Even the clothes he gave me to wear were so soft and warm—and smelled like him.

But what if it's a ruse to break me down? I don't have experience with being courted by men. I've been protected from males my entire life. I need to be cautious. I can't fall for it. Even if we're sharing visions...

Oma is screeching at me from the grave, but...I don't know if her advice is in my best interest.

I don't know what to think.

I wish I could stay here in the hot water all day, but I remember Noah said there was limited hot water. I really should save some for him. I turn off the shower, feeling better. Feeling clean.

The scent of bacon and eggs filters through the closed

bathroom door, and despite my huge meal last night, my stomach rumbles.

He wants to feed me.

I'll let him, for now. That way I'll have the strength to make my escape.

* * *

Noah

Aster is still in the shower when I finish making us a bacon, cheese, and mushroom omelette. I turn off the stove and cover the food to keep it warm while I review all the messages Brick sent me.

He and Sully have been blowing up my work phone. I can't avoid them any longer. I need to keep an eye on Aster, but I also need privacy to contact Brick.

I stick my head in the bedroom, and the bathroom door is closed. If I make this quick, I'll be done before Aster's finished enjoying all the hot water.

I exit the cabin and pace to the edge of the woods, far enough that she won't be able to hear me. I scrub a hand over my face to wipe away my thoughts of her. I need to get my game face on for this conversation.

My burner phone acts as a clone of my regular work phone, so I can see all the messages and calls from Moon Co and Brick specifically. Between Brick, Sully, and his assistant, I have over ten messages ranging from texts and missed calls to emails.

This is going to be a hard conversation. He's going to be pissed. I'm probably going to be fired.

I shoot a text to Brick's assistant, saying I'm available for a video conference. I get a reply immediately, along with a link to the virtual conference room. My stomach flip-flops for a moment, but I center myself. *He can't hurt us,* I tell my wolf, even though I'm feeling disappointed.

I've lived below my means to save up most everything I've earned, so I can survive without the job until my mission is complete. Still, I worked hard to earn Brick's approval and trust. I actually like my job. More than that, he's a good alpha, and I don't want to hurt him or his pack.

I make sure my back is to the forest, so my background will be pines and newly budding beech trees. If Brick looks closely, he'll see trees and bushes that might as well be in Kentucky as upstate New York.

I hope.

I click the link, and Brick's face fills the screen. His eyes are bright amber. Shit, he's two seconds away from going full wolf.

"Where the fuck are you?" Brick says, speaking slowly and clearly while wagging his finger in the sign *Where?*

"In Kentucky," I say. My instincts tell me to turn and show Brick a glimpse of the log cabin. "I had a family emergency. Is everything okay?"

"You know it's not. I've been trying to reach you for the past fifteen hours."

"Sorry." I duck my head, playing submissive. "My connection out here isn't good," I wave at the woods and rustic-looking cabin, "and I just realized I had my phone off. I told HR I'd be working remotely."

A shadow falls over Brick's face, and I bet it's Sully in the background, listening in on the call. Brick fixes me with an alpha stare. "If you planned on working, why did you leave your work phone in your apartment?"

Shit, this is bad. I bet they shook down my apartment, searching for me. Ready to drag me in front of Brick.

Leaving my work phone was a good call because I bet Sully has tech on it that allows him to trace its location.

He probably has tech to trace any call, though, so I need to keep this phone call short. If he and Brick find out I'm in upstate New York, I'm a dead wolf. They'll think I'm an Adalwulf spy and make an example of me.

"I forwarded all calls and emails to my personal cell but didn't check them until now. My grandma needed me."

"That's the excuse you're going with?" His expression tells me he's practically breathing fire. With his bright eyes, he looks like a dragon. "Your grandma was sick?"

I say nothing. I could fool a human boss, but Brick isn't buying it.

"I sent you footage taken at the Mineral and Gem Museum uptown. Was that your wolf?"

I feign surprise. "No, sir." I'm lucky I'm not getting grilled in person. If I were, Brick would smell that I'm lying.

Even now his eyes glimmer. He doesn't believe me. Why would he? I'm acting cagey as hell. "You have until the end of this week to present yourself to me in my office. Understand?"

Today's Wednesday. He's giving me three days. Fuck. That's not enough time. Not with the Adalwulf princess as my captive. I need to interrogate her about the Moonborn's location and then figure out what to do next.

But I dutifully nod. "Yes, sir."

I know what he's doing. When I'm in front of him, in person, he's going to make me shift in front of him, and once I do, they'll know I was the wolf in the video at the museum. Then again, I might be able to resist. I felt his alpha command in the office, and it hit me, but I'm much stronger than I was the last time an alpha used it on me. It seemed to bounce off my chest.

Maybe I could resist. I could tell him I'm a defective wolf who can't shift, and that's the real reason I never asked to run with his pack.

But if he does make me shift, I'm truly fucked.

"I'm disappointed in you, Noah," Brick says. "I thought you had potential. I gave you an executive position. But you're hiding something. I need to decide whether you're team Moon Co material. Get your ass back to New York and prove to me you're a team player. Otherwise..." He lets the threat hang in the air.

"I understand, sir." I nod quickly. I have to end this call before Sully traces my position.

Brick's eyes narrow. "You befriended my mate. She trusts you. If I find out you're lying to me, to us, then I'll take that as proof that you're a threat. And if you're a threat to me and mine, there's nowhere on Earth–"

I end the call. I have to. My palms are slick, and my wolf is geared up to fight.

That...did not go well. I don't know if I'll be able to explain away my actions at the museum in a way that satisfies Brick. Which means I might not ever be able to go back to New York.

I knew this day would come–I planned on it. The Ivy League degree and Wall Street job were only a means to infiltrate the impenetrable Adalwulfs and get to the Moonborn. Still, disappointment makes my gut clench. I like Madi, and I respect Brick. It sucks to have lost their trust.

Even though I was never officially part of the pack, my wolf loved being around other wolves who were willing to accept me as a friend. I guess I'm less of a lone wolf than I thought.

I've lost the only chance at having a shifter community.

But I have bigger things to worry about.

* * *

Aster

I hear the front door open and close and quickly towel off.

Did he leave me here alone? This could be my chance.

I pull on my panties, yank the flannel around my shoulders and quickly button it.

I come out of the bedroom and find he's nowhere to be seen. The cabin is empty. A quick check of the windows shows him outside by the tree line. He has his back to the cabin and seems to be talking on the phone, having a video conference.

I duck so no one can see me. My heart's pounding fast. Noah left me alone.

I definitely should run.

I don't take the time to finish dressing or finding my shoes. I don't know where I am—but he can't have brought me far from the Adalwulf land. The woods look the same, so we're probably still in upstate New York or close to it.

If I stay, there's no telling what he'll do to me. I'm the Seeress. Aiden and the Warden will have wolves out looking for me.

When they find us, they'll kill Noah and throw me back in the tower. My wolf whines at the thought, but I'm not worried about myself. I'm worried about Noah. I can't bear the thought of harm coming to him, even if he is my captor.

Noah's flannel shirt sleeves hang over my hands, and I ball the soft fabric up into a fist. My mouth waters from the scent of breakfast, but it feels like a trap. If I stay, I get to eat and have another conversation with this gentle alpha. But he's my enemy. I can't trust him, can I?

My tension grows as I walk to the door. My wolf doesn't

want me to leave. She likes Noah. The idea that he's my mate, and my magic drew him to me makes me hesitate for a second... but no. I have to remember that he's associated with the Blackthroats. He was the wolf Oma saw who could destroy the Adalwulfs. I need to separate myself from him. Besides, I can't mate. I am Seeress. I would lose my magic if I let myself succumb to my physical desires with this male.

I would check in with my visions, but they'll just torture me. The steak Noah fed me gave me the strength to run.

I crack the door open and try to hear who Noah's talking to.

"I understand, sir," Noah says, and I realize what the conversation is about. Noah's checking in with his superior. An alpha growl rumbles from the phone speaker–I can't hear what the other wolf is saying, but a flash of insight tells me who it is.

Brick Blackthroat. Alpha of the enemy pack.

Noah's probably confirming my capture and getting orders on what to do next. He didn't feed and clothe me out of kindness. He has an agenda. And if I don't give him what he wants, he'll probably drag me to the Blackthroats, and that's when the real torture and interrogation will begin.

The wind catches the door, and it swings open with a creak. I jump at the sound, but Noah still has his back to the cabin, and he can't hear me.

This is my chance. I don't think, I don't hesitate. I just run.

Chapter Eleven

oah

I race after Aster, following the trail of broken branches and her small, hurried footprints in the mud.

I don't need to hear her. Wolves track by scent, and Aster's is a sweet perfume laid out before me like a highway a mile wide. If I had to, I'd follow it forever.

Catch her! My wolf urges me. He's enjoying the chase. He thinks this is wolf courtship, where she runs, and I chase.

Where there's a juicy reward when I catch her.

I speed up, following the flash of white-blonde hair disappearing between the aspens. I catch up to her in no time.

She's weak. It's not a fair match.

I slow down, one part of me enjoying the fuck out of the flash of her long, bare legs under my flannel, the other part pissed that she might be cold. Or that she was so desperate, she thought she had to run without putting on shoes.

I could let her run and tire herself out, but then she stumbles and slips in the mud, and my protective instincts take over. I launch through the air to grab her, carrying us both off balance enough that we go crashing down into the mud.

I make sure I break her fall then roll to pin her beneath me. She thrashes, fighting me, even though it's futile.

I pin her wrists to the soft earth beside her head. I don't want to hurt her, but I am pissed that she ran. I thought we had a connection. We do have a connection–the visions.

Did I do something to spook her?

You held her prisoner, my wolf reminds me.

Well, yes. There's that. But still. We had a vibe.

"Stop," I command, and feel her body freeze in response to my dominance. I must've thrown alpha command into my voice.

I didn't know I could do that.

We're covered in mud, and I can smell iron, which means she's bleeding. The scent makes my wolf howl.

I stare down at her–my lovely captive. Her blue eyes are wide and round. Mud coats one side of her cheek. I want to kiss her again.

Desperately.

She's panting, her chest rising and falling quickly. Her hair–still wet from the shower–is now covered with wet leaves and dirt.

Kiss her, my wolf urges.

I can't. She doesn't want that. Plus, I promised I wouldn't do it again.

Fuck. Her nipples peak the flannel of my shirt like she's turned on.

Claim her.

Definitely not.

Except my hands don't obey my mind. I grasp the edges of the flannel shirt and yank it open, sending the buttons flying in all directions.

Aster gasps.

I lower my head and suck one of her pert nipples like my life depends on it. Her body softens, knees drawing up to cradle my hips. I release her wrist to frame her breast with my fingers, squeezing lightly as I suck. Her free hand doesn't push me away. She clings to my shoulder with it at first, then burrows her fingers into the hair at the back of my head, as if urging me on.

My cock is rock hard. I want to devour her. She smells like nirvana. Tastes like divinity. Her soft, yielding body beneath mine sings like a choir of fucking angels.

I suction my lips to her nipple and tug until it releases from my lips with a pop.

Fuck. I want more.

My ability to stop left me at some point during the chase. My wolf thinks she's mine now.

If she gives me any indication she doesn't want this, I'll stop, I promise myself. I may have to strangle my wolf, but I'll do it.

I'm not the kind of male who forces himself on a female.

I'm not like the Adalwulf alphas.

I switch to the other breast, using more finesse this time as I lick a slow circle around her nipple, then flick it with my tongue before I suck it.

I feel the vibration of a sound from her, so I lift my head to gaze at her lips, but her eyes are closed, lips parted.

It must've been a moan.

My wolf loves that. He wants to make her moan all day.

But not out here in the mud.

I sit back, pulling the wrist I still have manacled to lift her easily over my shoulder, then I straighten. Her bare legs draped across my chest are almost too much for me. The scent of her arousal makes me hungry to taste that sweet honey.

I give her upturned ass a sharp slap then rub away the sting.

Her scent drugs me, lowering my inhibitions. Making me do crazy things I wouldn't normally do with a female.

She's gone still in my arms, but I can feel the tension in her body.

Her feet are scratched from running barefoot over the sharp rocks. She's a wolf–she'll heal fast, but I hate seeing her hurt.

"That was a mistake, Seeress. I told you not to run."

I don't sense the vibration of any sound against my back indicating an answer.

Back in the cabin, I take her straight into the bathroom to wash off the mud. When I set her on her feet on the rug, she wobbles on her long, coltish legs. The flannel shirt flaps open, buttons gone. She tries to pull it closed, but I'm too quick for her, yanking it down her arms, so it falls at her feet.

Claim her.

Mate.

This gorgeous she-wolf is completely naked with me in a small room, and I don't know if I can hold myself back.

* * *

Aster

Running was a mistake. I should've known I couldn't escape him. It only irritated the man and excited his wolf.

Now his glittering gold gaze promises punishment.

Or a rough claiming–it's hard to tell which.

I can't tell whether I'm scared or thrilled.

Noah's eyes glow with his wildness. His cock tents his jeans. I'm trapped in this small room with him–naked and weak and no match against his strength.

What is he going to do to me?

He grips my shoulders and turns me to face the sink countertop. I meet his golden gaze in the mirror. Mine looks startled. His, feral.

He presses between my shoulder blades, folding me forward until I brace my forearms on the cool marble.

Prowling closer, he positions himself beside my hip and strokes his large palm down my back to arrive at my ass. He squeezes me roughly then lifts his hand away and brings it down with a clap.

I get lightheaded. Dazed. Wet where I've never been wet before. It doesn't hurt. Not at all. But my wolf is riled up.

Especially when he immediately rubs away the sting, massaging, and squeezing my ass before he delivers the next spank. I'm panting, breathing in short little gasps, awash in sensations. The steady thrum between my legs grows louder. I want him there.

No. No, I don't. That would be crazy. Surrendering to this burning desire would mean I lose everything–my entire identity. My life's training and dedication to become the honored Seeress.

It's not possible. There's no way.

Yet, still, I don't move to stop him. I'm not sure I could if

I tried, though he seems more in control than he was out in the mud. And even then, he didn't claim me.

Noah peppers my ass with spanks–light ones interspersed with caresses. It sends all the blood rushing between my legs, and the scent of my arousal fills the room like a hedonistic perfume.

I imagine him kicking my legs wider, gripping my hips, and taking me roughly from behind.

My body revels in the idea. My mind rebels.

Noah clasps the back of my neck and uses it to lift me from my position and rotate my body to face him. His lips crash against mine with bruising intensity.

I open for the kiss, apparently as eager as he is. His tongue sweeps into my mouth. He sucks at my lips.

It's...transcendent. The most honest interaction I've had with anyone in my life. It's like all my defenses and self-protective measures have crumbled, laying my true essence bare. I'm raw and open and impossibly sensitive to every nuance of this man's touch.

Still kissing me, Noah tugs me toward the shower, where he turns on the water then picks me up by the waist and lifts me inside under the spray.

I rinse the mud out of my hair and from my face and legs, acutely aware that Noah is stripping out of his clothes. In a moment, he will be naked. I will see everything.

I've seen naked men before–witnessing the Alpha Rites. I found them almost repulsive. Frightening. But right now... I can't look away. Noah's body is built of solid, chiseled muscle. He slides his jeans and boxers off, and I get a view of his powerful thighs and ass. And...oh my.

Oh...wow. His cock flies at full mast for me, thick and hard. My body instantly readies for him, the slick between my legs hot on my inner thighs.

Oh fate. I need to stop this.

The moment he steps into the shower, I dance out of it. Surprisingly, he lets me go. I grab a towel and wrap it around myself, facing the shower, watching the spectacular show of Noah rinsing off the mud under the spray of water. The ache of need between my legs extends upward, into my womb. My heart thuds against my breastbone.

I need to talk to him. To explain before anything happens.

"I can't have sex." I raise my voice to speak over the spray of water before I realize it doesn't matter.

Noah turns the water off and faces me, his attention on my lips. I hand him a towel, which he thankfully wraps around his waist.

"I can't have sex," I repeat. "Or I lose my ability to see."

He cocks his head, not understanding.

"My visions." I point to my eyes. "I have to be a virgin."

Noah considers me, standing there in his full male glory, droplets of water running down his cut muscles. I want to lick them off his body. I want to throw myself at him and beg him to finish what he started.

"You have to be a virgin," he repeats.

I nod. A trembling has begun in the backs of my knees, born of temptation. Of fear that he'll be angry or force himself on me. Borne of navigating this foreign landscape with a man I barely know.

Except he feels so familiar.

Mate, my wolf whispers.

"I can't be your mate," I blurt, panic setting in. The trembling in my knees grows stronger. I can barely stand.

Noah's eyes, which had been flickering gold, blaze into a full fiery glow. His canines lengthen.

My pussy contracts, breath heaving with the instant

recognition. He's ready to mark me. The mention of the word mate brought on his instinct to claim me. To sink his teeth into my flesh and forever leave his scent embedded in my skin to show I'm his.

If I'd had any doubt before whether he was my mate, it evaporates now.

I back away, reaching out to clutch the bathroom counter to steady myself.

"You can't have sex." Noah ignores the mate part, even though he must know the truth now, too. "No orgasms or no penetration?"

I blink. Swallow. Goosebumps travel down my arms although I'm not sure what the Grandmothers are trying to tell me.

"No...penetration, I guess."

In a flash, Noah moves, lunging for me.

I try to turn and twist away, but he catches me by the waist and lifts me from the floor. I kick, but all he does is sit me on the marble counter. My towel jostles loose, and I clutch the ends together.

Noah's eyes still blaze. His teeth are long, dripping with the serum to mark me.

"Don't mark me," I whisper.

"I won't mark you. I just want to taste you." He holds my gaze. "Spread your knees, starlight."

I realize he's waiting for consent. He could pry my knees open himself, same as he lifted me. His physical mastery over me is unquestionable.

He lifts his hands—slowly—as if showing me he's not a threat, and gently tugs open my towel.

The soft whimper that comes from my lips isn't resistance. It's more like surrender. Noah cradles my neck between his palms, then lightly strokes down, across my shoulders, to cup my breasts. He brushes the pads of his thumbs across my nipples.

My entire body is trembling now. The sensations are so intense I can barely contain them.

Noah starts to push me gently backward. I catch my weight on my hands, and when he keeps the pressure up, lower to my elbows. He looks down pointedly, to my knees, then lifts his gaze back to my face.

Another whimper escapes.

I slide my knees apart. He wants to taste me. I'm not even sure what that means.

Noah traces down my body, licking, kissing, and sucking his way from my breasts down my fluttering belly and around the soft silk of my mound. He trails kisses up my inner thigh before his tongue reaches my sopping core.

He starts with just a flick of the tip of his tongue.

My body violently jerks in response, the sensation making me cry out.

His tongue delves between my folds, tracing a tiny circle at the apex.

I let out a sobbing breath.

This I haven't seen before. The Alpha Rites don't involve female pleasure. The female devotees are bound on their backs to the stone dais with vines. The chosen alpha males move among them, rutting inside each one until every female holds the seed of every male. It takes hours, and sometimes the males use the female's mouths to ready themselves between she-wolves.

What I witnessed made me happy to forego sex.

But this? Fate, this is like picking up the chessboard of my life and dumping all the pieces. This pleasure is so intense, I'm going to combust into a burst of flames. No, rose petals. Because there's no violence to this—only the most beautiful velvet-soft pleasure.

"More," I find myself saying, even though he can't hear me. I burrow the fingers of one hand into his hair and urge him on.

He lifts his face and smiles at me, his lips coated in my juices.

"More," I say again.

"I heard you." He's still smiling. He taps his temple. "In my head. Your words projected into my head." Wonder and celebration shine in his eyes, and I'm hit with the significance of his words.

I project my thoughts into his head without even trying.

That must be how he found me in the tower's tunnel.

Mate, my wolf insists.

But I can't focus on that problem because Noah returns his tongue between my legs. He's more aggressive this time, laving me with his perfect tongue then using his thumbs to part my labia. He suctions his lips around my clit and pulls at the same time he strokes his thumb over my slick entrance.

"Please," I beg. "Please, please, please." I grip his head, my fingers winding into his hair and tugging. I need more.

I need it all.

No—not all, not...oh, fate. Oh fate.

I scream, my hips bucking against Noah's mouth as he continues to suck hard on my clit. "Yes! Yes, please! Yes, yes, yes!" My internal muscles squeeze and pulse in a glorious release.

Oh fate, it feels so good. I've never experienced this kind of ecstasy.

Didn't know it existed.

When the tremors finally quiet, I tug Noah's head up

and throw myself at him, winding my arms around his neck and my legs around his waist. Clinging to him with a desperation I don't understand.

Noah lifts me off the counter, his forearm propped under my butt, his other arm banded around my waist.

I've got you, Starshine, he projects the words into my mind.

I burst into tears.

Chapter Twelve

Noah

Oh fuck.

The scent of Aster's tears drains all sexual aggression from me. My wolf was glorying over making her come, but now he whines, needing me to fix whatever went wrong. At least I have the privilege of holding her through it.

I'm sorry. She speaks telepathically. The apology only worries me more.

"Sorry for what?" I ask out loud, except I can't see her lips with her face pressed into my neck like this.

She lifts her head and looks at me. "I don't know why I'm crying." I think that's what she says. It's hard to tell when her lips twist with emotion.

Lip reading is imperfect at best. Most say it's only 30 percent accurate, but I usually get the general idea. I have the benefit of a keen sense of smell to read people's emotions which helps me decode a little more.

She wipes her tears. "Thank you." She attempts to sign

thank you, but instead signs *fuck you,* flicking her fingers under her chin which is adorable.

Her smile is sheepish. "That was incredible."

Pride kicks through me. "Yeah?" I smile.

"Yeah."

I carry her into the bedroom and set her on her feet while I fish out one of my henleys for her to wear. I tug it over her head, and she threads her arms through the sleeves and lifts her wet hair out of the neckline to cascade down her back.

I cradle her face and steal another kiss. We've blown past my broken promise not to do it again.

We've blown past any doubt that she's mine.

The question is—now what am I going to do?

She can't mate me. Not without giving up her magic.

Besides, the Adalwulfs would never let me take her. She's their prized possession. The asset that gives them a leg up over the Blackthroats. And I'm not joining the Adalwulfs.

So I can't mate her. Not without giving up my life's mission of bringing down the Moonborn and freeing my mother from her mental slavery.

Fuck.

I don't see a way out of this mess, and it seems I'm getting in deeper with every minute I spend with Aster.

I break the kiss, troubled.

Aster searches my face, and whatever she sees there makes her turn away. She pulls on the sweatpants I lent her last night without underwear, since those got dirty in our roll in the mud. Is it weird that all I can think about is the fact that her bare skin is coating my clothes with her scent? Yeah. Probably weird.

"Come. I'll re-heat breakfast." I take her hand and lead

her to the kitchen. She's probably starving. She still seems weak.

A few minutes later, we both sit down to the plated omelets and mugs of hot chocolate. She digs in right away–hungry, as I expected.

We devour our food in silence until Aster sighs and pushes her plate away.

"Full?" I ask, showing her the ASL sign for *full stomach*, lifting my flat palm from my stomach to my chin while puffing out my cheeks. Aster laughs and copies it. I teach her the signs for *Hungry, Stop, Ready,* and *Sleepy*.

"Why did you fly a drone to the tower?" She mimes a drone swooping around.

I frown. I don't know how much to tell her. Just because she's my mate doesn't mean she can be trusted.

"Were you looking for me?" She points at her chest.

I shake my head. "No."

"Why were you in the tunnels?"

I hesitate. I should be the one interrogating her, but I'm too drunk on satisfying her sexually to want to push her right now. This information is about her, so it seems fair to share. "I knew you were having a seizure because the drone fell. I ran for the tower, and you showed me the way in."

Aster looks at me with wide eyes. "But then you took me prisoner."

I shrug. "I didn't know you were my mate." There, it's out in the open. We need to acknowledge this thing. "At the time, it seemed like fate delivered you to me for a different purpose."

Her gaze sharpens. "What purpose?" she asks, ignoring the part about being my mate.

I turn the questions around on her. "Where do you keep the Moonborn?"

She chokes on her hot cocoa.

I sip mine, studying her.

"What do you know about the Moonborn?" she asks.

I lean forward. "I know they brainwash females into serving as sex slaves."

Aster recoils. "Not true." But I see doubt creep over her expression.

"I know they snap the necks of pups born without hearing."

She goes still, her entire body coming alert. "You know you were Moonborn."

I nod.

A frown mars her forehead. "The prophecy–" Her hand flies to her temple, and her face crumples with pain. She starts to jerk and shake.

I lunge from my chair, not able to catch her in time, but throwing my hand between her head at the floor as it hit.

Fuck.

I scoop her jerking body up and carry her to the couch, where I sit, cradling her in my arms.

It's all right, Seeress. I've got you. I project the words to her. *You're safe.*

Her eyes roll back in her head. Her feet tangle and thrash around mine.

Come back to me, starlight. I pour energy into her. It's not something I've done before, but it must be what an alpha wolf does with his pack members when he lends his strength for their healing or to help them when they first learn to shift.

Somehow, I'm sure she's absorbing it. In fact, it feels like she pulls it from me until her fit gradually eases, and she slips into a quiet slumber.

Damn.

Her visions take so much out of her. My wolf wants to rip someone apart. To give her something–some kind of tonic or medicine or talisman–to take this burden away from her.

I push away the lewd thought that I have exactly the thing that would take this from her–my dick.

I kiss the top of her head, unwilling to lay her down or remove her from my arms. As she naps off the after-effects, I mull over what she said. *There was a prophecy about you.*

What was the prophecy? And was the seizure a reaction to the prophecy or just that she was thrown back into her vision world?

As I stroke her silky hair, grim thoughts march through my head.

The prophecy is probably that I am the wolf who will destroy the Moonborn. But what if, in doing so, I destroy my mate? What if I take from her something she loves?

Fuck.

She's not even my mate. As long as she, too, remains brainwashed by the Warden and the Adalwulfs, she won't give herself to me.

What's more, any harm I do to them could harm her.

And that, my wolf may not allow.

* * *

Aster

Visions of hundreds of years of the Grandmother's wisdom and millions of their memories spear my mind, moving in fast forward, too jumbled to read.

Then, they crystalize into a single moment. A memory.

. . .

"Are you spying on me?" Oma glares at a younger Warden as she leaves the yurt of one of Odin's females. His face paint is even more dramatic than how he wears it now.

He falls into step beside her. "Is she pregnant?"

"No."

"Odin needs an heir," the Warden warns. "If he doesn't produce one soon, Catherine's Blackthroat pup will have a claim to the throne."

Oma stops walking and turns to face the Warden. "The problem is not with the Moonborn females. Odin's seed is sparse. He's incapable of siring a child."

The Warden's eyes flare. He runs a hand over his bald head, his scent full of dismay. "Who have you told about this?"

"Do you think I'm an idiot?" Oma hisses. "No one."

"Not even Odin?"

"He knows. But no, we do not speak of it."

The Warden stares off into the trees for a moment, then he snaps his attention back to Oma. "Use the Alpha Rites to choose a Blood Heir. We'll use all the Moonborn females of a suitable age and genetic makeup. They'll all be bred by Odin and the males you hand select. Ask the Grandmothers to select the next alpha from those conceived. The first-born pup will be the chosen Blood Heir."

"That kind of magic requires a great sacrifice to the Grandmothers."

"Then give them what they need! If you can't make this happen, the Blackthroats will take over our pack, and we will lose everything."

Oma looks like she ate something sour, but she inclines her head. "Very well."

The Warden turns and walks away, his robes flapping about his legs, his hands clasped behind his back.

. . .

The vision fades.

I'm engulfed in the deepest sense of warmth and safety. Amber and pine and delicious male fill my nostrils. I draw a deep breath and try to force my eyes to open.

I remember sitting at the kitchen table across from Noah, and then there was blinding pain as a vision filled my head. It was the same one Oma described so many years ago.

Noah, wearing the Adalwulf mantle, standing on the broken stone dais, destroying everything. Fate, this is bad.

I start to tremble again with the significance of it.

Strong arms tighten around me.

Noah.

My eyes finally remember how to open, and I twist to look up at him.

I'm in his arms again, nested on top of his body on the couch. He quiets the visions. Soothes my frayed nerves. I stifle a groan. My stomach is queasy, but I draw in a deep breath to calm it.

Noah kisses my forehead, and something warm and syrupy pools in my chest.

I blink up at him. He's the enemy. The male who could destroy my pack. And I'm snuggled in his arms, melting over forehead kisses.

I scramble back out of his arms and onto my wobbly legs. How long was I asleep? He must've held me the entire time!

It's crazy how much I want to crawl right back onto him, to drape my body over his and soak up that feeling of safety he gives me.

But he's not safe. I'd be a fool to believe he was.

He climbs off the couch, his brows down with concern as he watches me square off to him.

"You're here to take the Moonborn down, aren't you?" I demand.

He looks at me for a long moment then nods.

"Because they wanted you dead?"

"No." He shakes his head. "For my mother."

His mother. Of course, he has a mother. I don't know why I'm so slow to put this all together. What had Oma and the Warden said about him all those years ago?

He was born of the Blood Heir Alpha Rites. *The true first-born.*

The pup Odin Adalwulf should have claimed as his own. Instead, Oma swapped the pup with Aiden because Noah was born deaf.

Noah is the true alpha of the Adalwulf pack. Chosen by the Grandmothers to lead.

A sensation like lightning shoots through me, and my knees buckle. Noah arrives at my side in a blur, catching my elbow to steady me. Should I tell him? If he knew, would he stop his assault on the pack and the Moonborn?

But no. There will be war regardless. He'd have to kill Aiden and win over the pack to lead. I don't want him harmed.

He's still holding me. Once again, he's my support, a solid frame I can lean on. We fit together perfectly.

I can't lose him.

I lick my lips and force myself to speak. "Wh-who is your mother?"

Noah hands me a laminated photo from his back pocket. It's worn, like he carries it with him at all times. It's a photo of a teenage girl with brown hair and kind eyes.

She looks familiar.

Then I realize she looks like Oriana, Liora's daughter. Same gap between the teeth and dark blue eyes.

But this photograph is old. It's not Oriana.

It's Liora.

I gasp. "Liora is your mother."

Noah nods. "You know her."

"Yes. I-I *love* her. She was one of my mothers until I was sent to serve as acolyte to the Seeress."

"Not your biological mother," Noah clarifies, and I can read the alarm in his eyes.

"No," I assure him with a relieved laugh. "We're not related." I point between the two of us.

His shoulders relax. "Good. I need to see her."

I nod. "Of course you do," I whisper, blinking back tears. The Liora in the photograph has a sweet, peaceful smile. The Liora I know is capable of smiling, but all I can remember is the pain in her voice and the shadows in her eyes as she pleaded with me to save Oriana.

I don't need the Sight to see that Fate brought Noah on this mission right now because Liora needs him. She came to me for help. She saved her son from Oma and the Warden's machinations, and now she's trying to save her daughter. I'm not strong enough to wield any influence over the Warden and Aiden.

But Noah is. He's the true Adalwulf heir. An alpha wolf. More powerful, even, than Aiden.

Ignoring the realization that I'm betraying my pack, my family, and everything I've worked to become, I square my shoulders. "I'll take you to Moon Hollow."

Chapter Thirteen

A I can't stop the knot in my stomach from tightening when we step onto Adalwulf pack lands. Noah didn't want me to come, and we argued over whether I'd be safe, but I assured him I would be, and there was no way for me to explain how to get there without taking him myself.

We stopped at a mountain convenience store on the way to buy me some clothes. All they had were touristy souvenir gear, so I'm looking campy in a pair of sweatpants, a sweatshirt with a wolf howling at the moon, and a pair of soft leather moccasins.

I smell the familiar scents. Pack should feel like safety, like home. The only time I felt that was when Liora was raising me. She was a true caretaker, and her gentle strength is the only kindness I've known.

I owe her.

Beside me, Noah is silent. His expression is closed off in hawk-like focus. We argued fiercely about whether I was allowed to come with him on this mission. He thought he could infiltrate Moon Hollow without my help. In the end, I pointed out that even if he could get to Liora, her first reaction would be fear of a strange male. I could help bridge an introduction and make their meeting easier.

He didn't like it, but he agreed. I can tell he's got a lot of complicated feelings about meeting his mother for the first time. I can't imagine what he's going through, knowing his mother gave him up to save him, but chose to stay with the pack that wants him dead.

Noah sends up two scouting drones. By watching the screens for them and my intuition, we're able to bypass the guards without too many close calls. Once or twice, we catch a whiff of a patrol and crouch down to wait, but no one discovers us.

It helped that I chose our point of entry. We hiked up Moon Rise, a giant bluff overlooking pack land–the guards are lazy and rarely patrol up this way. Moon Hollow lies in the valley at the foot of Moon Rise. We're deep in the forest, surrounded by ancient trees. I sense the spirits of this land watching us as we sneak down the hill and head to a secluded spot Liora loves. It's her favorite spot to rest and meditate, and my intuition tells me that she'll make an appearance there.

If any guards come upon us, we'll have to run. But this part of pack lands is so remote, I'm hoping we don't run into anyone. Or if we do, Noah's drones or my visions will warn us.

The danger is our scent. Mine isn't so much an issue as Noah's. The place we're headed is coated in my scent, but one whiff of a strange wolf like Noah, and the residents of Moon Hollow will alert the guards.

I did what I could to mask both our scents. Back at the cabin, I gathered lots of wintergreen leaves and crushed them to release their minty-fresh scent. We stuffed them in our pockets just before we stepped on Adalwulf land. The plant is known as Eastern teaberry and is plentiful in the forests here, especially in the groves ringing around Moon Hollow.

Oma used the fertile soil around the Hollow as an extensive garden and ordered the devout to tend it. I extended the garden up the wooded slopes. There are secret spots where I've planted sweet woodruff and American ginseng, and that's where we're headed now. Liora is the only one I trusted to tend to the herbs when I'm not able to, and she usually makes the rounds around this time of day.

We make it to the base of the cliff, and for a moment, the sense of the land swirls around me, making me dizzy. There are benevolent spirits here but also darkness. A death place.

Noah starts to lead us on a well-worn path, and it jerks me from my stupor.

No. I tap my index and middle finger to my thumb to sign. *Stop.* Noah taught me a few ASL signs, so we could quickly communicate, but I don't know how to sign, "That way leads to The Celestial Cradle, the sacred clearing where the Alpha Rites will take place under the Blood Moon." My pained expression and tense posture probably say it all.

He nods and lands the drones in trees where they can recharge with solar, then pockets the controller he's using to pilot the drones, so he can take my hand. His fingers flex around mine, and warmth rushes up my arm. Just his touch is grounding and healing. I lean into him for a second, smelling amber and pine sap under the sharp scent of the wintergreen leaves. Then I lead him off the worn path and head towards Liora's favorite gardening spot, a place where she likes to sit and meditate after her gardening chores.

With Noah at my side, my tension swirls away. I know these lands like the back of my hand. And fate is guiding us. The Grandmothers require this trip; I can feel it.

For once, my actions and my visions are aligned.

Today is warmer than it has been. In the shady patches there's still snow on the ground, but it feels like spring is around the corner. Purple crocuses and native violets peek out from under the oak leaves, the first flowers that promise more to come. Here and there are bundles of thin green leaves. The daffodils haven't bloomed yet, but they will soon.

We come to the little grove Liora and I love. There's a flat rock here that's perfect for sitting and listening to the birds singing in the beech trees above a thick carpet of sweet woodruff. A stream runs past us, sweet clean water that takes on the grassy vanilla flavor of the woodland herb.

The sun is starting to set. Liora should come on her evening walk soon. I lead Noah to the rock and climb on it. His brow furrows, but he settles beside me. I turn my face, so he can clearly see my lips, and whisper, "Liora usually takes an evening walk. We'll wait for her here."

He nods.

The rock chills my butt and legs at first, but I close my eyes and start to meditate. Beside me, Noah's aura is a turbulent storm. There's still plenty of the cool blue and soothing gray, but more darkness, with lightning flashes of red. He's in turmoil.

I rest a hand on his arm, lending him a little of my calm.

Noah lifts his head and sniffs a few moments before I detect the sound of soft footfalls and sense a wave of grief coming towards us.

Liora.

I still haven't caught her scent. Noah's sense of smell must be incredible.

He's gone rigid beside me. I nod at him. He doesn't get up, so I stay by his side. Liora approaches us with her arms full of herbs and her head down, like she's lost in her thoughts. She's alone, as I'd hoped.

"Liora," I say softly, to get her attention.

Her head jerks up, and she stifles a gasp, her gaze riveting to Noah.

He still doesn't move. There's no expression on his face–he's gone completely wooden.

"Liora...this is Noah."

Her arms fall to her side, and she drops the herbs. The leaves flutter in a cascade to her feet. "Noah," she whispers. She touches her chest and then brings her index and thumb in front of her forehead and makes a cradling motion with her arms with her eyebrows raised. Maybe it's the sign for "my baby"?

I don't know how or when she learned ASL. Fate, it breaks my heart. She must've hoped she'd meet him again one day and prepared for that possibility.

Noah is stone-faced, staring down at the petite woman who looks so like him. They have the same dark blue eyes and sun-streaked sandy hair.

Liora's lip trembles, and her eyes grow glassy, like she's holding back tears. Noah still hasn't moved. "Why are you here?"

I open my mouth to explain, but before I can, Noah signs as he says, "I want to know why you abandoned me."

* * *

Noah

I've waited so long for this moment. To meet the mother who sent me away.

And now I'm here, and my whole body is awash with hot and cold sensations.

Nan always told me Liora was a sweet, loving person. She insisted that her daughter, who came from a powerful alpha bloodline and could've been a pack luna, was sucked into a cult that degraded her, brainwashed by them. She told me my mother loved me. I used to look at her photograph and imagine her tucking me in at night and singing me to sleep. But I don't understand–if she loved me, why would she give me up?

Liora winces. I can't think of her as my mother, not yet.

"My son," she signs fluidly as she speaks, "I did not abandon you. I would never abandon you." She emphasizes *never.* "I had to give you up to save your life."

Why didn't you come with me? If this place is so terrible, why did you stay? I sign. I shouldn't be asking these questions. I need to stick to the plan and convince her to leave, so Aster and I can get her out before we're all discovered and killed.

Instead, I'm rehashing the past. But I can't help it. I have to know.

I was afraid, Liora signs. *I was young and powerless, and I knew if I disappeared with you, the pack would hunt us both down. This way, I could sell the lie that I'd lost you. Because I did lose you. And I grieved.* There are tears shining in her eyes now.

I harden my heart, even though I want to go to her. I feel too conflicted. There are too many emotions bubbling up in my body.

I sense Aster stepping close to my side. All the times I

imagined reuniting with my long-lost mother, I never imagined I'd have my mate by my side, but I'm glad she's here. Her sweet scent steadies me, lends me strength.

Now's your chance. I came to get you out.

No, she signs, and even though Nan warned me she wouldn't come, I feel it like a blow to the chest. A second abandonment. But then she adds, *I want to. But I can't. Oriana.* She fingerspells a name I don't know, tears her gaze away from me, and looks to Aster. Speaking and signing, she says to Aster, "The Warden has her. She's locked in the tower now. They all are."

"All the females for the ritual?" Aster asks.

"Yes. When you were found missing, the Warden gathered them up and locked them away. We're all on lockdown. I shouldn't even be here, but I had to, I had to..." she breaks off, her whole body trembling.

Aster leaves my side and goes to her, pulling her into a hug.

"You shouldn't be here," Liora says, her eyes still on my face. "It's not safe. It's too late for me."

I can't read Aster's lips with her back to me, but Liora answers, "I'm not leaving without your sister."

Her sister? I sign.

Liora releases Aster and faces me. *Your sister.* She nods her head, her eyes intent on mine. *Oriana. Your little sister is in trouble.* Her eyes fill with tears.

I have a sister?

Goosebumps race across my arms. My breath leaves me in a whoosh. I. Have. A sister.

All the particles in the Universe seem to break apart, leaving chaos as my mind is forced to re-arrange around this new information.

Aster didn't tell me! Maybe she thought I already knew,

but Nan hasn't been able to contact her daughter since the day she met her in a New York City subway station to take custody of me as a newborn pup. Liora never sent letters, never made contact again.

It never occurred to me that she might have had other pups. That she has her own family here. The news makes me want to retreat into myself. To go even more wooden than I was before.

While I possess alpha traits, I don't consider myself a leader. My whole life I've self-isolated. I had Nan, but I stayed apart from her pack, and I avoided joining one out East. I decided early on to make it in the human world with my intelligence and the hell with the shifter world. They didn't involve my plans, other than to take down the Moonborn and free my mother from her servitude.

But right now, some protective alpha instinct comes screaming to the surface. If I have a younger sister, she's under my domain. In my pack. My previous pack of one.

Two, my wolf rumbles.

He's counting Aster. Our mate. Except Aster isn't part of my pack. She's another problem I haven't worked out yet.

I frown. *What trouble?* I sign.

Liora's chest sags, like a cinderblock just lowered on it. "She was selected to be bred by the alphas."

I stare at her, sickened.

Then we'll take her, too, I sign.

I see a flash of hope flare in Liora's eyes before she looks over her shoulder.

I tense, not sure if she heard something.

"She's locked up and under guard." The tears shine in her eyes again. "I don't want her to go through the Alpha Rites." She fingerspells the words Alpha Rites, so I know it's the proper name of a ritual. She shakes her head. "They're terrible, and she's too young." She looks at me with that sliver of hope again. "I can't leave without Oriana." She's pleading with her eyes. She wants me to help.

To save my sister from some cult ritual.

I shove my hand in my pocket and pull out two tiny trackers, like the one I slipped into Aster's handbag at the museum. "Can you get one of these to her?" I sign. "They're trackers, so I can find her when I come back. Find both of you."

Fuck, I want to free all the females in Moon Hollow who've been brainwashed into serving males instead of being protected by them.

Liora takes the tracker, looking over her shoulder again. "I need to get back before they come looking for me. When will you come back?"

"When is the ritual?"

I catch the scent of a male on the breeze and jerk my head up, scanning the direction she came from. Liora's eyes fly wide, and Aster tenses.

On the lunar eclipse. Liora's fingers fly as she starts to back away. *Run!* She hurriedly scoops up the herbs she dropped and darts back down the path as Aster grabs my hand, and we race through the woods in the opposite direction.

My heartbeat thuds in my ears as we flee down a worn path, the one I started to follow earlier before Aster stopped me. The stress returns to her scent, and I understand why when we reach a stone thronged clearing, and I smell the fear staining the area. The whole place stinks like death, pain, violence, and old blood. The ground is worn from many feet, as if throngs of pack members stood and participated in the ceremonies conducted on the massive obsidian stone lying in the center of the granite pillars. The air is heavy, almost too dense to breathe. There's a buzzing in my head, a pressure like claws scratching on the inside of my skull.

Aster's face is pale and pinched. If I'm picking up uncomfortable vibes, she must be suffering. I pull her along faster, and she follows my lead without hesitation, picking up speed even as we race uphill towards the bluff. It's a relief to disappear into the woods and leave the clearing behind.

The hike back is long and grueling, with sweat trickling down my back. I can only imagine how hard it must be for Aster. My muscles and lungs scream for a break. As soon as I can, I stoop and lift her into my arms, ignoring her mouth moving in protest as I run. She's light as a daisy, and it's a pleasure and privilege to carry my mate to safety.

Finally, we emerge on the road where I hid the rental car.

"What was that place?" I ask Aster after we climb in the car.

Her scent is sour, her voice sad. "That's the Celestial Cradle. The Hollow within the Hollow, where the rituals take place. They tie the young females to the altar and force them to breed with the chosen males."

"The Alpha Rite?" I feel sick, imagining my mother going through that.

"Yes. That's where you were conceived in the Blood Heir Alpha Rite and where I'm to be forever bound to Aiden Adalwulf."

Chapter Fourteen

Aster

Noah's eyes flash gold. He normally feels safe to me, but a sense of violence blasts from him, reminding me he's a dangerous alpha. He's more of an alpha than Aiden, and I know what Aiden is capable of.

I freeze. We haven't really discussed what we are to each other. Noah said I was his mate, but I didn't acknowledge it even though I know it must be true. I haven't unpacked what that means. We certainly haven't agreed on what we're going to do about it.

Now, I suddenly realize I may not have a choice in the matter. Noah may not let me go.

"That's not going to happen," he snarls. Again, I feel the blast of violent power, but when I jerk back, he cups my face, showing me a tenderness I never experienced from an alpha male.

I'm still shaken from the hike. I wish I could sag back in my seat and sleep forever.

But I can't. The scent of Liora's fear clings to me, along with the older, heavier energy from the ritual site. The visions clawed at me, blinding me, but I held onto Noah and refused to let them in. They weren't visions so much as memories of the terrible past, all the psychic shock of the females and males sacrificed to the greater good. Ritual rape and murder.

I want to puke.

Touching me seems to subdue his violence. His eyes change back to blue, and he recovers that steadiness that makes me feel safe. He has incredible self-control for an alpha.

"He wants to claim you?"

I shake my head. "Not claim. I must remain a virgin to keep my power. It's a ritual to bind me as the Seeress, to him as the alpha of the pack. I will share in his alpha power, and it will enable me to receive visions for the highest good of the pack. Seeress is a sacred position." I repeat to him the words that have been drilled into my head by Oma.

"You want this?" Noah is careful, like he's holding back all the ferocity of his power to hear my answer.

What if I said *yes*? Would he let me go?

That's when I'm sure: I will have a choice. Noah may have kidnapped me, but he respects my will. He's not a tyrant like Aiden and Odin.

Do I want to be bound to Aiden? The need to retch wells again. "No," I admit, wondering if the Grandmothers will strike me down for the blasphemy.

I want to be Seeress, but I don't want to serve Aiden. I don't want to go back. That's when I realize that I already made my choice. I made my choice the moment I snuck Noah into sacred Moonborn land.

I'd made the choice without a second of deliberation. Mate first. Over all else.

"Then I won't let him touch you. None of them. I'll kill them before I let that happen."

I believe him, but I feel so weak right now.

"The Alpha Rites are only a week away. Aiden and the Warden will do everything to make sure both rites happen, no matter the cost."

"I won't let them have you. And we'll get Liora and Oriana out. Both of them. Got it?"

"Got it," I say and make the fist nodding sign *yes*. And I do sag back and rest while Noah turns on the car and gets us the hell away from Adalwulf land.

Noah is silent on the ride back to the cabin. I'm sure he has a lot to process about seeing his mom. Learning his sister is scheduled to be bred.

When we arrive, I get out, but Noah walks around and sweeps me up to carry me inside. "You're weary," he says.

I tuck my face into his neck. I've grown stronger these past few days, but the trip took everything out of me.

He carries me into the bedroom and lays me gently in the center of the bed, pulling off my moccasins, then kicks his shoes off and stretches out on his back beside me. I roll into him, resting my hand on his chest. He covers it with his.

"Was it hard to see your mother?" I ask then realize he didn't hear me. I push up on my elbow to show him my face and repeat the question.

That wooden expression takes over his face again, and I sense his chaotic thoughts. Feel his struggle to contain them.

I send love through my palm on his chest, trying to soothe him the way only a mate can. "Do you hate her for giving you away?"

I see a flash of grief before he hides it again. He scrubs a hand over his face.

"You didn't tell me I had a sister."

"Oh! I'm sorry! I thought you knew. I should have."

"Is she deaf?"

"No."

"How does Liora know ASL?"

My eyes fill with tears. "She must've studied it on her own in hopes of meeting you."

Noah's eyes redden, and grief creases his face.

"She must have suffered being apart from you."

Noah's pain washes across me. I lay my cheek on his chest until I feel it pass.

"It must be hard to not know her."

"I understand it. She wanted to save me. I just don't understand why she stayed. Why would she stay?" His forehead screws up with fresh pain.

I hesitate.

Noah sees I'm holding something back and immediately jumps on it. "What? For power?"

I blink, surprised. "No. Not at all. Liora holds very limited power. She's honored for being the most devout. But..." How do I explain? It's the same thing that makes me reluctant to give up my role as Seeress although, if I'm honest, there may be some enjoyment of power mixed in there for me.

"The draw of the Moonborn is the magic. Not the Alpha Rites magic–that's been twisted and corrupted. But the communing with the earth. Living in harmony with nature. Feeling her gifts and returning our reverence. Running naked with the moon and feeling the Moon Goddess' answering pulse of power. And for me, it's hearing the Grandmothers."

Noah cocks his head. "Grandmothers?"

"Two hundred years ago, when the Adalwulfs first came to the New World to settle it, they bonded with a coven of witches. The wolves provided physical protection, allowing them to self-govern and avoid the Puritans who wished to burn them. The witches offered their command of nature and their gift of Sight. They made sacred vows that forever bound the pack to the witches. The rite that binds me to Aiden was developed by them. It's a way of bolstering the witches' power and benefitting the pack. I am a descendant of both witch and wolf. The Grandmothers are my foremothers. They provide me with constant guidance."

"The Grandmothers led me to the tunnel to find you," Noah says, and goosebumps race across my arms.

"They must have." I nod. "And they led *me* to the tunnel to find *you.*"

But why? Because they wanted me to find my fated mate? It doesn't make sense. I would forever lose my connection to them if I let him claim me.

Or do they want me to help Noah take his rightful throne? Do they want me to be bound to *him* as Alpha of the Adalwulfs–not Aiden?

It's true that my visions and the chatter from the Grandmothers was blindingly loud the first few times I came in contact with Noah.

Even the visions in the museum might have been set off by his presence rather than the moonstone tiara.

The tiara!

"Did you steal the moonstone tiara from the museum?"

Noah gives me the fist-nodding sign for yes.

"Why?"

My heart pounds. Did the Grandmothers guide him to secure it for his own alpha bonding ritual to me?

The idea doesn't frighten me the way being bound to Aiden does, but for some reason, I don't like it.

He shrugs. "I figured if it was important to Aiden, I should keep it from him."

Relief trickles in. It was only revenge motivated for him.

But why should I be relieved that he's not aiming for the throne? If I truly cared about and served my pack, I would do everything in my power to help him win it.

But these last twenty-four hours have been the best of my life. I feel free here. Safe. Excited by the male I'm with. I don't know if I want to go back to the pack.

Not yet anyway.

He studies me. "Is it important to you?"

No. I make the sign, wanting to learn and practice to speak with my hands like he does. "Aiden wanted it to enhance the Alpha Bonding ritual."

Noah's eyes flash gold again. "Then I'm glad I kept it from him." In a sudden motion, he rolls our bodies to flip me on my back, pinning me beneath him. "You will *never* be bound to that wolf."

* * *

Noah

I've wanted to end the Adalwulf reign for all my life, but it was from a place of cold, calculated revenge. Now, I want to tear Aiden Adalwulf apart with my claws. I want to rip his head from his shoulders and smash it—

I force the rage back down into the tight box in my chest and put a lock and chain on it. I scared Aster earlier by showing my wolf's possessiveness over her.

I stare down at my luminescent mate, my swollen cock pressing against the zipper of my jeans in the notch between her parted legs.

The need to claim her is excruciating.

But we haven't even talked about a future. I don't know if she'll accept my claim on her. She wants to keep her virginity to maintain her power.

That may kill my wolf, but if that's her decision, I'd accept it. But that doesn't mean I will ever let another male near her.

Fuck, I don't know what it would mean. I can't imagine ever letting her go.

No.

Hell no.

I won't let her go.

It's impossible.

If she won't let me claim her, I will still dedicate my life–however short that may prove to be before moon madness overtakes me–to protecting my beautiful mate.

She will never be locked in another tower.

She will never be starved again.

Never fall to the floor blinded by her visions without my arms around her.

She's mine, whether she wants me or not.

"You're mine, starshine," I tell her. "If you want to keep your powers, I will respect that, but no other male will ever touch you." I know my wolf shows in my eyes, but Aster doesn't seem afraid. She reaches for my face and pulls my mouth down to hers, kissing me boldly.

My cock surges painfully against my zipper. Her sweet tongue tentatively tastes my lips then parts them. I let her lead for a moment, but my wolf can't take it. Can't wait any longer to taste her.

I kiss her hard, devouring her mouth, scraping teeth across her lips. I pull back to see her eyes. "I love you."

Her long lashes fly wide, then her eyes fill with tears. "What?"

"You heard me." I want her naked so badly, it hurts. "You're my mate. You are all that is precious to me. I would walk away from this revenge plan right now if it meant you came with me," I tell her, realizing it's true.

Her eyes glitter with unshed tears.

"My beautiful starshine. Come with me." I cup her face. "We'll get Liora and Oriana out and run away."

Now I suddenly understand how my mom could give up her own freedom to ensure mine. She felt this kind of love.

Aster doesn't answer, though. A tear escapes one of her eyes, running down toward her ear.

Fuck.

I asked too soon. She's not ready to leave her pack, her life, her elevated role with the evil pack that's all she's ever known. And she just took the time to explain to me what she loves about it. I can't ask her to give up her magic. Who she is. Everything she's known.

"Nevermind," I tell her. "Don't answer. It's too soon. I'm sorry."

To distract her, to soothe her, or maybe just to appease my wolf, I apply my mouth to her neck, kissing and sucking as I slide a hand up her sweatshirt to cup her supple breast. I push the shirt up to her armpits and apply my tongue to one nipple, tracing a spiral around her areola, starting on the outside and working my way in toward the beaded peak. I flick her stiffened nipple with my tongue.

A full-body shiver runs through her body, and my wolf gets smug.

Aster yanks her shirt off over her head and works on unbuttoning my flannel as I apply my tongue to her other breast. Her hips roll beneath mine, rubbing over my hardened dick, making me pant like I'm running a race–and wolves rarely get out of breath.

She tugs at my shirt, yanking it off my arms before I kiss my way down the soft plane of her belly, then swirl the tip of my tongue in her belly button while my hand strokes down her hip to squeeze her ass.

I want to claim her. My canines have lengthened. My dick throbs. What if I could mark her without taking her virginity? Maybe that would stave off moon madness. My wolf would know she was mine, but she would get to keep her powers.

Fuck.

I should have paid more attention to the birds and bees talks our alpha subjected us to in high school.

Must. Taste. My wolf is growing frantic from the scent of her arousal leaking between her legs.

Yes, I can taste her. I can still pleasure our mate whether she lets me claim her or not.

I yank her sweatpants down and pull one of her knees up and open to spread her sex, resting her leg over my shoulders. Her belly flutters in and out on shuddering breaths. I lick into her with a firm, hard stroke.

She gasps, arching her bare breasts up to the ceiling. Her leg clamps down on my shoulders, inner thigh trembling.

That's right, starshine. You're so beautiful when you scream for me.

And I do intend to make her scream. I will spend the whole night with my head between her legs if she wants me there. I slide the tip of my tongue around her entrance, making a hardened point with it to penetrate her. I take my time, fucking her with the tip of my tongue until she starts tugging at my hair with an urgency that can only mean she's getting close.

My wolf is getting feral, though. He wants me to bite her thigh. To mark her now before I've even made her come.

So maybe marking *is* possible without penetration. But of course, I won't do it. Not without her consent.

I have to get my wolf back under control.

I drag deep breaths in through my nostrils to put him on a leash as I work on making my mate come. I lave her swollen clit with my tongue, giving it the attention it deserves. As it swells longer, I'm able to affix my lips over the tiny nubbin and suck.

I feel the vibration of Aster's scream as her pelvic floor muscles gather up, pulsing and squeezing while her knee squeezes against my shoulder. The scream goes on and on as her body jerks on the bed, powerful pulses ripping through her body, her arousal leaking down my chin.

I wait until she finishes, then kiss her mons, down one side of her labia and up the other, over her swollen entrance, along her inner thighs. I shower kisses between her legs with the reverence of a man at worship.

My cock is harder than granite, but I ignore the pain.

"Expect more of that," I tell her when I lift my face, licking her juices from my lips. "All fucking night."

"I love you," she blurts, like she's been waiting for me to lift my head and read her perfect pillowy lips. "How do you sign it? Like this?" She gives me the arms crossed at the chest sign for love.

I smile. "Yes, that's the way." I return the sign, pointing slowly at myself, crossing my arms and pointing at her. "Also like this." I hold up my thumb, index finger and pinky in the ASL sign *ILY, for I love you.* "Or this." I point at myself, push my closed fist away from my chin, then point at her. "That one is more for casual. Like I love chocolate. This one is for lovers." I go back to the first sign of arms crossed over the chest in the sign for hug.

She repeats it back to me. "I love you, Noah. I just…"

No. I sign. "Don't." I don't want to hear if she's telling me she can't be mine. "Just wait. I pushed. I don't want you to decide anything yet."

Aster spells *O-K* with her fingers, her eyes soft. I devour her with another ravenous kiss, but when my descending canines nearly puncture her lip, I pull back.

Fuck. I need to take care of this hard-on before I do something I'll regret. I back off the bed and hold up a finger to let her know I'll be back in a minute.

In the bathroom, I close the door and pull my cock out. I'm so hot for my mate this will only take a minute.

I face the tub allowing myself to remember the way Aster looked under the spray of water.

Mine.

The possessive word lays itself across my mind at the same time Aster reaches around and grips my cock. A shudder of pleasure runs through my body.

My wolf celebrates the fuck out of her claim on me. On my dick.

I move my hand, so it covers her smaller softer palm fisting the base of my root. My fingers close over the tops of hers, and I savor the feeling of her touch, her scent, as I slowly guide her fist up toward the tip, working the blood into the head.

She wraps one slender arm around my waist, pressing her naked body against my back. I turn to the side, so I can watch her in the mirror.

Mine.

I feel her assertion with more force this time. She is as

possessive as I am. Or her wolf is. She may not be fully on board yet, but her body knows we belong together. Her wolf is making an alpha female claim on me.

I'm dying to be inside her. To fuck her long and hard. To drive into her and watch her face contort with pleasure when I make her come. To experience the privilege of sliding in and out of her tight channel as I coat my dick with the nectar she's making just for me.

Aster slides her free hand down past my waist to caress my balls.

Oh fuck. Oh fate.

That's all it takes. My balls pump and cum shoots down the length of my cock, spurting in ribbons into the tub.

Next time it will be into Aster's mouth. Or over her tits. My thoughts turn disrespectful as I catalogue all the things I want to do to my gorgeous mate now that I know she's a willing participant.

We can survive me never coming inside her if that's what she wants. There are plenty of other ways to please each other. Especially if I can mark her.

I grab a washcloth and clean up, keeping one arm around my mate to keep her close.

Thank you, I sign.

She shakes her head at me, frowning.

Mine. She lays the word down fiercely in my mind.

I smile. *Yes,* I sign. *I'm yours.*

I love that she's finding non-verbal ways to communicate with me. Finding a way into my world instead of asking me to push into the hearing world. She spent the afternoon asking me different signs and practicing her alphabet for fingerspelling. Which must mean she's sticking around, right?

Fuck, I hope so.

I pick her up to straddle my waist. After carrying her to the living room, I set her on the couch and make a fire to warm the night chill from the place.

Hungry? I sign.

She remembers the sign from yesterday, and her face lights up. She signs *yes*, with a smile that nearly brings me to my knees.

This is what my mate looks like when she's sated. This is what it's like to care for her needs.

I can't think of any greater privilege.

Chapter Fifteen

ster

The next morning, I wake relaxed. I slept with my head on Noah's shoulder, nestled against his large, muscled body. He fed me pork chops, mashed potatoes, and green beans last night, then used his clever tongue between my legs before I fell asleep in his arms.

He must already be up. I smell the scent of bacon and pancakes from the kitchen. I jump in the shower and dress in one of Noah's shirts again. I like having his fresh fir tree scent engulf me–it relaxes me.

I find Noah monitoring his phone screen as he works the knobs of a controller. I look over his shoulder to see an aerial view of the Celestial Cradle. I rest my hand on his shoulder, and he startles, twisting to look at me with a quick grin.

"Sorry, I didn't mean to sneak up on you."

He pulls me onto his lap, and I twine my arms around his neck. "I'm just making a plan for getting back in." He takes the drone higher and lifts it up above the treetops, then sweeps it over the entire compound.

"So this is the tower where Oriana is being kept?" He points at a tower and raises his brows.

I nod.

"Do you know how I can get in?"

My stomach tightens. "It will be heavily guarded. We'd need some kind of distraction."

Noah shakes his head. "No *we*. I go alone. I don't want you in danger." He lands the drone in a tree to give me his full attention.

"No. I know the land, the buildings, and the people. You need me."

A stubborn look comes over his face. "I won't put you in danger again."

I bare my teeth, gathering the power of the Grandmothers to me as I show him my wolf and my magic. "I *will* go with you."

Fascination coats his stare as the corners of his lips twitch. He seems to drink me in, long enough that my fierceness starts to fade, and I blush.

"You're so beautiful it hurts," he says.

"I'm going with you."

He frowns. "I don't like it."

I kiss his temple. "I know you don't." I try to think of how we might pull this off. The best thing would be if they believed Oriana and Liora escaped on their own. That way nothing would be traced back to Noah or the Blackthroats.

"Noah, what is your relationship with the Blackthroats? You said you aren't one of them, but my visions showed me you near them."

"I work for Moon Co."

That tracks. "Brick Blackthroat's company."

"Yes."

"But you didn't join their pack?"

"Right. I'm a lone wolf. I came to New York to take down the Moonborn, and I didn't want to involve them in that."

"And they were okay with you not pledging your loyalty?"

He flicks his eyebrows. "No. Not really. Brick took offense. And I'm in deep shit with them right now over the tiara heist. I'm supposed to present myself by tonight, or I assume I will lose my job or maybe worse."

I stare at Noah, shocked by the stress he's been silently carrying. "Are you going to go?"

He frowns. "No. It was nice while it lasted, but it's over now. I found the Moonborn." His expression softens, and he reaches for my cheek. "I found you."

"You're not sorry? You didn't like your job?"

He hesitates, and I know he does. I'm hit with a flash of Noah at a wedding, and he seems happy.

"Are they your friends?"

His expression closes off again, and he shrugs. "I thought we might be friends. They learned ASL."

I blink in surprise. "That sounds like they care about you. I didn't think the Blackthroats cared about anyone but the Blackthroats."

I feel Noah's sudden stab of pain as if it's my own.

"No, they are good people. Brick comes off as a hard-ass, and he can be, but he was always more than fair with me. His mate is–*was*–" Noah winces, "a friend of mine."

"Catherine Adalwulf was barely allowed a relationship with her children by their father."

"Brick's mother." Noah nods. "I heard something about that. The war between packs has caused unnecessary suffering. But Brick isn't like that."

He pulls out his phone and scrolls before showing me the screen.

It's a picture. I take the phone to study it better. It's a group photo taken in some sort of conference room where everyone is dressed in business attire. Noah's off to the side, but still included in the group. Even though it's obviously a work function, everyone looks relaxed and happy.

"Is this the Blackthroat pack?"

"These are the top wolves–Moon Co's Executive Team." Noah points to one young woman, a slim brunette with shoulder-length hair who's looking up at a much bigger, bearded man. She's not the most beautiful woman I've ever seen, but there's something about her face. It's almost as if she's spotlit from above. I feel lighter just seeing her smile.

"That's Madi, my friend," Noah says. "She's Brick's mate. A human."

Yes–the human. I remember our visions of a human who would be the Blackthroat's downfall. Odin and Aiden were excited to have our enemies weakened.

Judging from this picture, it looks like the human is not only part of the pack but a central part. And the Blackthroats aren't weaker, even though everyone in my pack would say Brick mated with a "lesser" species.

The Sight grips me, darkness swirling around me.

"Aster?"

My fingers spasm, and I hear a thud as Noah's phone hits the carpet before I'm lost to the world.

A vision's coming on. A big one.

Noah pulls me close, steadying me so I don't hit the floor. *Don't fight it. Let it come,* he murmurs in my mind.

His strength pours into me, and I feel so secure between his arms. I let my head lean against his shoulder. He steadies me when I quake with the power flowing through me.

The images flit through my mind so fast I nearly don't catch them. There's Madi, sitting at a restaurant table with a stately older woman who looks a lot like Madi, except she has gray hair. They're both sharing a meal, and everything looks normal except... there. In the corner lurks a narrow-faced woman with long brown hair, watching Madi with malice in her gaze.

Vera.

Her smoke-gray aura swirls over the humans, a green-black taint tinging the edges. The dense miasma covers Madi, blocking her from view.

Something horrible is happening. When the smoke clears, Madi is slumped over the table, and the older woman is screaming.

I gasp and come back to the room. I'm on the couch lying in the circle of Noah's arms. He must have moved me here when the vision started.

"Easy." Noah rocks me a little, soothing me as if I just had a nightmare. Which, I guess I did. "I've got you."

His gentle tone helps my muscles relax a bit more, but I'm still aching with the force of the vision. My back is clammy with cold sweat. I rub my eyes, and let Noah help me sit up and drink some water.

He watches me with worried eyes but doesn't pry. If Oma were here, she'd be impatient to hear what I Saw. Not Noah. He's worried about me.

I sigh and lean into him, indulging in the moment. Noah's got me. He'll keep me safe.

But then I remember what I saw and lick my lips. "It's Madi. Something terrible is going to happen."

Noah's forehead creases, but he simply rubs my back,

soothing me. The rest of my muscles unclench, so I tell him the whole vision in a rush. For once, I don't have to hold anything back.

Noah won't let anything hurt me.

I describe Madi and the older woman and how Vera was lurking in the background.

He frowns and leaves my side to grab his phone. "Was this her?" He shows me another picture that looks like it was taken at the same event. Madi stands next to an elegant woman with short gray hair.

"Yes." I didn't see the woman's features clearly but got a sense of who she was.

"That's Eleanor Harrington, Madi's grandmother. Madi didn't have a relationship with her until recently, but now they're close. Eleanor chose Madi as her successor to take over the family business."

"So they'd eat together regularly." Which means I don't know if the vision I saw was from the past, present, or future.

"Something terrible is going to happen. I don't know how exactly, but Vera plans to harm Madi."

Noah's forehead knots. I can smell the worry in his scent. Madi is his friend.

I lick my lips. I can't believe what I'm about to say next. "We have to warn her."

Chapter Sixteen

N*oah*

"This is a bad idea," I say just to make sure someone says it. Aster sits next to me in the passenger seat of my car, her mouth set in a stubborn line. It's late afternoon, and we've driven to the Berkshires.

"You're sure about this?"

"Yes," she says, but shakes her head. Her body is contradicting her words, a sure sign she isn't sure, but she opens the door and gets out. I follow quickly, feeling the need to protect her.

We're parked right on the edge of Blackthroat land. We're not sneaking in. No, we're going to walk right in and wait for their guards to sound the alert and capture us.

It won't take long.

I've already sent an email to Brick saying that I'm practically on his front doorstep. "You wanted me to present myself by the end of the week? Well, here I am." I may have sounded a bit more cocky than I needed to, but my wolf required a show of strength. Brick might be the alpha of the biggest and most successful pack in the States, but I'm an alpha, too, and I have a mate to protect.

Beside me, Aster shivers. All her life she's been told the Blackthroats are evil, and now, here she is, about to walk on their land and claim sanctuary.

It's like handing your enemy an atomic bomb and asking him not to use it on your pack. Except you're the bomb.

I can't imagine what this is like for her. I want to toss her over my shoulder, bundle her back in the car, and drive until New York is a distant memory. Fuck these packs and their twisted hierarchies. Fuck destiny. I just want to be with her.

Maybe when this is all over, and I've gotten my mother and half-sister out.

"It's all right. I won't let them hurt you." I wait for her to sign *ok* and take her hand, lending her my warmth and strength. After a moment, we both start walking. We leave the car hidden in the woods and enter the forest, tromping silently over the leaves.

The air seems to shimmer when we step on pack lands. I can smell the sentry markings. At one point, I think I see a furry head disappearing into a grove of mountain laurel, but the markings around the boundary are too strong for me to catch the wolf's scent.

Maybe I was imagining it.

At the foot of a towering pine, a cluster of purple and yellow crocuses are in bloom. Aster stops a moment to take in the sight. I take it as a good sign.

The next moment, we're surrounded by wolves.

They were so fucking fast, I never even scented them. Aster must not have heard them either.

There's at least five of them, four in plain sight and one a dark shadow in the trees.

I wonder how long they've been watching us.

I start to raise my hands in a show of surrender, and the wolf closest to me bares long white fangs.

Sully steps out of the shadows. *Noah*, he signs. "We've been expecting you. But who is this?"

"I'm Aster Adalwulf. The Adalwulf Seeress. I claim sanctuary."

Instantly, the rest of the wolves bristle. A hand movement from Sully I don't catch, and behind him, a wolf I didn't even notice before dashes off, probably to send a message.

Shit, we're in it now.

They march us through the woods on foot. Sully leads the way, and his enforcers close ranks around us but make sure they don't get too close. I keep my arm around Aster. She's a bit glassy-eyed, and her steps are unsteady. Maybe she's fighting a vision.

This whole thing sucks. I like Sully. And I have no doubt he'd slit both my throat and Aster's if we make a wrong move. Any trust the Blackthroats had in me is gone. If I'm lucky, they won't think I'm a traitor. I'm counting on them to be smart enough to hear us out.

Finally, the Blackthroat Mansion appears. It's one of those Gilded Age mansions with multiple wings and a large circular driveway in front of the house. We leave the forest just as a helicopter is setting down on a helipad on the manicured lawn some distance from the house.

Two figures exit the helicopter. One is tall and broad-shouldered, hovering over the smaller figure. Brick and Madi. They're quickly surrounded by the phalanx of enforcers waiting to escort them from the helipad to the house, but a minute later, Brick comes striding straight towards me.

I don't need to catch his scent to see he's spitting mad. *What have you done?* he signs with clumsy but forceful fingers. This time he remembers to raise his brows to ask the question. My nose twitches at the searing scent of his rage. His eyes glow amber.

I put my arm around Aster.

"This is the Adalwulf Seeress," I say, hopefully loud enough that every wolf can hear. "She's claiming sanctuary."

Brick looks like he's about to blow steam from his nostrils like a dragon.

But then his head jerks to the right, as if someone's called for him.

He half-turns, so I can only catch half of what he's saying, but the first word is "Madi." His hands fly out to signal her to stop. He doesn't want her to get close.

Madi marches right up the hill to stand beside Brick, ignoring the guards crowding her.

What's going on? she signs, looking at me. I bet Brick didn't tell her anything about the situation. He knows Madi and I are friends.

I was hoping she'd be here, to get Brick to listen and smooth the way. For someone new to pack politics, she's great at diplomacy and dealing with wolves.

We're here because you're in danger, I sign back. My statement is like a bomb threat, sending all the wolves around us into high alert. The guards around us close in.

Brick steps in front of Madi, his mouth open wide like he's shouting. "Are you threatening my mate?"

Beside me, Aster winces but she raises her hands. *No,* she signs and puts a hand out like she's going to protect me. My wolf points out that she's barely one hundred and fifteen pounds soaking wet, but she's trying to protect me. My mate is fearless.

The wolves around us are restless, ready for violence. *We're here to help you*, I appeal to Madi. *Someone's infiltrated your ranks. Someone close to your grandmother. She plans to poison you.* My friend's face goes pale, and her shoulders curl inward, her right hand going to her belly. She lets Brick maneuver her back a step, so he's between us and his fragile human mate. He's snarling something I can't catch.

He's too upset to listen, and now Madi is in shock.

At that moment, the sun breaks from behind the clouds. A sunbeam seems to spotlight Aster, shining on her white-blonde hair and face. She looks like she's glowing, otherworldly. I can't take my eyes off her.

The wolves around us go still.

"She wants to kill the heir," Aster says, her lips moving slowly and clearly enough for me to follow. Her eyes have gone white. She's in the grip of a vision, speaking straight to Madi. "Your pup is in danger."

Aster faints into my arms.

* * *

Aster

"How are you feeling?" Noah asks, as if we're at a party, and I just had a dizzy spell, instead of blurting out a vision in front of my pack's sworn enemies.

I still feel a little shaky but calm. "I'm good." I drink more of the bottled water our captors, or hosts, offered us.

After all the terrible things I heard about the Blackthroats, I'm amazed we're not in a dungeon. We're in a room with no windows, but it's pretty luxurious. The gleaming heart pine wood built-in bookshelves lining the walls makes the room into a mini library.

Noah drums his fingers on the table. When they searched us, they took Noah's phone.

A big wolf with dark hair opens the door. He's dominant and scary, his aura impenetrable black.

"Sully," Noah greets him. "I can explain–"

Sully cuts him off with a sign. He doesn't bother to speak.

"It's not a trick or a trap. I'm sure you don't believe us, but it's not."

"Save it for the alpha."

"May I see him?"

"This is your summons." He glances at me and jerks his head toward the door. "Both of you."

Noah helps me up from the chair, then puts a hand protectively on my lower back as he ushers me out. My heart pounds in my chest, but I hold my head up high, trying to pull on the mantle of respected Seeress rather than she-wolf caught on enemy pack land.

Sully escorts us to an office where Brick sits behind a giant wooden desk. Madi is on his lap. She tries to get up when we come in, but he tugs her back down, stroking her thigh with his hand.

He's in protective mate mode. His female is pregnant– of course, any threat to her would turn him ferocious.

The walls are lined with the male wolves from the photo Noah showed me. Brick's inner circle. They are all standing at attention, ready to attack. I can barely take in their auras–there's too much power in this room all at once. It's hard to breathe.

I force myself to keep my shoulders back and stand up straight, but the pressure comes from all sides.

But I am the Seeress. I was trained to stand in the presence of Alphas and guide them. My pack might have tried to crush me, control me, but I'm still here, standing on my own two feet. And I'd rather stand strong and be slain by the Blackthroats, my pack's sworn enemy, than cower before them.

In the room full of intense Alpha energy, Madi's aura is sweet and light, but grounding. Like a good cup of cinnamon tea after a long walk through a storm. It helps to remember Noah considers her a friend.

Madi signs something to Noah. I catch what I think is a thank you—an open hand from the chin.

Noah nods gravely. He's also in protective mate mode, keeping me tucked against his side, on edge as he faces off with the most powerful wolf in the state.

But then again, according to the Blood Heir Alpha Rites, Noah is also a powerful male. Perhaps powerful enough to take on Brick, not that I want to see that happen.

Madi points at me and spells *O-K* with her eyebrows raised.

Noah's fingers fly too fast for me to decipher what he's saying, but my intuition tells me he's explaining the fits I get when I have powerful visions.

"I wasn't honest with you, sir," Noah begins.

Blackthroat frowns. "No shit." His aura pulses with power—reds and oranges burning like hot coals and rising into a fierce, fiery amber.

Madi rests her hand on the back of his neck and kneads the muscles there. Just her touch softens the anger in his aura a little.

"My grandmother isn't sick."

"I'm stunned." Brick's flat expression and voice drip sarcasm.

"I was born into the Adalwulf pack."

This startles Blackthroat, not that he shows much emotion. But he does blink as he absorbs the information. His aura pulses bright, and his lips flatten into a thin, dangerous line.

"Have you heard of the Moonborn?"

Brick narrows his eyes. "The witchy cult where Odin bred his fanatics?"

"Yes. My mother is one of them. But Odin would've killed me because I am deaf, so she told everyone I died and gave me to her mother to raise."

Some of Brick's irritation seems to drain away as he listens.

"I came to Wall Street to work for Adalwulf Associates to infiltrate their pack. When they wouldn't hire me, I tried to come at it from another angle."

"Working for me."

"Yes."

"What is your endgame?"

Noah looks down at me. Then stares at the desk for a moment, like he's thinking. "It's changed."

"Because of her." Blackthroat lifts his chin toward me.

"Aster is my mate."

"I knew it." This comment comes from one of the males against the wall.

Noah doesn't see him because he's focused on Brick, but when I look over, he follows my gaze.

The man signs and speaks to him. "I remember when you saw her outside Brick and Madi's wedding."

I look up at Noah. "You saw me?"

He nods, that hint of a smile playing around the edges of his mouth as he stares down like he's drinking me in. "I recognized you from my dreams."

Blackthroat clears his throat, so I lift my chin in his direction to shift Noah's focus. My mate looks back at his boss. "I planned to destroy them. Now I just want to get my mother and sister out."

Brick runs a hand over his beard, considering us. "The tiara heist was you?"

"Yes, sir. Just to fuck with them. Aiden wanted the tiara for a Moonborn ritual, so I took it. I ran into Aster there and put a tracker in her purse to locate her. I found her imprisoned in a tower. Starved." His arm tightens around me.

I flinch. My pride detests that he's outing Aiden's treatment of me, but his indignation also makes my nose burn. Seeing it through his eyes brings home just how mistreated and abused I was. I spent my life excusing the mistreatment as necessary for me to achieve the role as Seeress, but none of that seems to matter anymore.

I don't care so much about being Seeress. Or about the Adalwulf pack. Not the way I care about the male standing beside me.

The human, Madi, looks at me with a form of shocked sympathy. Brick also turns his penetrating gaze on me as he says to Noah, "So not only were you reckless, showing your wolf to humans, you also kidnapped the most powerful member of the Adalwulf pack and dumped her on my doorstep."

"He didn't kidnap me," I say. My voice is a bit raspy, but it comes out strong. "He rescued me."

Brick's eyes narrow, and I feel the full weight of an Alpha stare. The pressure is so intense, I can't draw a full breath. "I'm supposed to believe that?"

"We came here to warn your mate. I mean you no harm."

"This vision. What did you see?"

I describe the lunch-time scene. Madi with an older woman, with Vera hovering nearby.

When I describe Vera's narrow face and beady eyes, Madi sits up straight. Brick automatically turns and puts all his focus on his mate.

"Could she mean..." Madi taps on her phone and shows Brick something. Sully crowds close to see it and then leaves the room, signaling several other wolves to come with him.

"Is this who you saw?" Brick shows me Madi's screen. There's a picture of Madi and an older lady–the one from my vision. Beside the older lady is Vera.

"Yes. That's Vera. And that's the older woman I saw."

"Eleanor," Madi murmurs. "My grandmother. This is her new assistant."

"Vera's an Adalwulf. Her orders must have been to get close to you by any means possible. That's how she was going to poison you."

Madi sits back in her seat, looking pale.

"Until you conveniently showed up." Brick's eyes glitter amber, a sign that his wolf wants out. He's not shaken like Madi, and he's definitely not convinced. And he's an Alpha, so when he's under threat, his instincts make him attack. "What else did you think you'd gain by warning us?"

"Nothing else," I say. I fight the urge to crumble under that Alpha stare. I feel so tired, drained. "Noah cares for Madi–as a friend," I add quickly. "I...couldn't let an inno-cent child die."

"You think I should believe you, an Adalwulf?"

"Your mother is an Adalwulf," I say without thinking. I'm channeling–I completely forgot about Catherine, but the Grandmothers prompted me to bring her up. Brick blinks, and his gaze flickers away.

Noah puts his arm around me, and I lean into him,

grateful for his strength. It's the only thing keeping me from slumping over in my seat. I draw energy from him and use it to sit up straight again.

"I intend no harm to you or any member of your pack, Alpha," I say as formally as I can. "I swear it on the Grandmothers."

Thunder booms in the distance, making Madi startle in her seat. All around us, the wolves growl, their eyes lighting.

The glowing lamps flicker and go out. It's daytime, so it's not so dark, but no one says anything. After a second the lights come back on as if nothing happened.

Even Brick looks stunned. He's half out of his chair, blocking Madi with his body as if protecting her from a threat. What does he think–I'm going to leap across the table and savage her? She tugs him back down.

"Well," says a wolf with a polished British accent, "that's good enough for me."

The wolves around him shake themselves. One of them checks the window and returns, muttering, "Doesn't look like rain."

I send a silent thank you to the Grandmothers for giving the Blackthroats such a clear sign. Brick seems to buy it although, now, he and everyone in the room are unsettled.

Noah rubs my back. I close my eyes for a moment and accept his kiss on my forehead. There's cold sweat all over my body, but I feel less exhausted.

"What is your endgame, Aster?" Brick asks.

I hesitate. For some reason, the question makes tears spring to my eyes.

This is the moment.

I knew it would come, and I've been delaying its arrival. We both have.

But I have to decide which side I'm on. I have to declare

an allegiance. Choose between the two packs. Actually, for me, the actual choice is between keeping my powers–my gift of Sight–or submitting to my mate's claim on me.

Noah wraps both arms around me, as if to shield me from the pain of this moment. This decision.

"She's helping me free my family," he says.

"That's not what I asked."

A buzzing grows in my head. The Grandmothers are talking–all of them at once. I rub my forehead. The room starts to spin. My teeth chatter. Pain stabs at both my temples at once.

Noah pulls my face into his chest. *Forget them, starshine. It's just you and me here. You're safe.* His words lay across my mind.

"She hasn't made her choice yet," Noah's spoken words cut through the noise.

I scrabble against the nausea and the distortion in my vision, trying to find my way back. "Yes, I have," I hear myself say. My voice sounds clear and confident, even though my body's overwhelmed with convulsions. "I'm leaving with Noah."

Chapter Seventeen

I gather Aster up against my body, crushing her with the force of my emotion.

Fuck, I've kept my desire on lock from the moment I first touched her. I kept my wolf on a leash. I wanted to ravish her.

To stake my claim.

Mark her skin.

Make her every promise in the world to win her submission to our fate.

But I couldn't push her. I didn't want to scare her off.

I knew she could be as brainwashed as my mother about her pack and their cultish ways, and I needed to give her time to arrive at a decision on her own. Without me influencing it.

And she chose me.

Knowing that she's mine–that Aster chose me over pack and power and all the magic she possesses–makes me want to drop to my knees and praise the Moon Goddess. I want to get her alone, strip her naked, and worship her body all night to show my gratitude.

I swing Aster up into my arms and appeal to Brick. "We only came because Aster had the vision that Madi was in danger. I'm not asking to keep my job. I'm not asking for your help, or your permission to free my family. I just need you to let us go, so I can get them out before my sister is raped by every alpha in their pack in one of their sick rituals."

Madi blanches.

Everyone looks over at Sully, but his lips aren't moving. I look back to Madi, who bares her teeth, and hinges clawed hands together in the sign for *growl*.

Brick's expression remains inscrutable as he studies me. "How do you plan to get them out?"

"I'm still working on that plan. I have a tracker on each of them."

Aster's body trembles in my arms. Her breath is coming in shallow gasps. I need to get her out of here. I want to get her alone. I twist toward the door and back. "May we leave?"

"Give them a room in the East Wing," he says to Sully. To me, he says, "Attend to your mate. We'll talk more about this plan of yours tomorrow."

I follow Sully to the room without taking my eyes off my beautiful mate. I can feel her heart pounding with her decision. Like she's scared and excited at the same time.

I know what this means to her. She's giving up her role as Seeress. Giving up the magic that she loves. Giving up her visions.

I know they are her source of power, but part of me rejoices that she won't suffer through them anymore. I hated seeing her so vulnerable, weakened by the debilitating side effects of them.

I love you.

Aster's words project into my head. She's speaking to me telepathically. My beautiful, magical mate.

I try to project it back. I don't know if she can hear me, but I know she must feel the ecstatic sense of soaring in my body. The avalanche of love pouring out of my heart and into hers.

Sully says something that makes Aster smile.

"What?" I ask.

He turns to face me and signs as he repeats it. "I said get a room, you two." We arrive in front of a door, which he pushes open. "Here's a good one. I'll instruct the guards to give you some space tonight."

Aster blushes.

"Here." Sully hands me my phone. I thank him, pocketing it with relief. I'll be able to access the trackers, but not the drones.

"Noah," Sully hesitates, all glimmers of amusement disappearing. "You did the right thing, coming here. The Alpha Rites are an abomination. They should be stopped at any cost." A visceral blast of cold comes from him, and from the menace in his glowing eyes, I can see why Brick chose him as pack enforcer.

Aster gasps, eyes widening, like she's Seeing something about Sully.

Thank you, I sign.

He nods gravely to both of us and walks away.

I gently set Aster down and close the door. We're in a large, stately bedroom with an en-suite bathroom. A dark mahogany four-poster bed stands in the center, covered in what looks like a fluffy feather blanket wrapped in a plum silk duvet. Matching plum pillows in all shapes and sizes adorn the head of the bed.

"What was that about?" I ask.

Aster shivers. "I think…Sully knew a wolf named Moira. She was an acolyte killed by the Warden while trying to escape the rites years ago."

Goosebumps race across my skin. "Fate guided us to him for this reason." I turn to Aster and cradle her face between my hands.

"Yes."

"Just like fate guided me to you, starshine."

She smiles up at me, her face luminescent.

"But I was a fool. I thought she brought you to me for my mission. I didn't know" –my throat closes as I speak– "I never dreamed…she would gift me the most exquisite jewel on the continent." I brush her hair back from her face. "My mate."

I still can't believe she chose me. I am punching way above my weight.

Aster's eyes flash silver, and she leaps, crashing into me. She straddles my waist, attacking my mouth with hers.

I stumble back as our tongues twine until my ass hits the bed, and I lie down, letting her climb over me and rip open my shirt.

"I want you," she says. The scent of her arousal permeates the room.

It's too much. My wolf goes wild. The need to claim her, to mark her, overwhelms me. I flip her over on the bed, a growl ripping up my throat. With a swipe of my arm, I clear the bed of all the decorative pillows, then tug her shirt off over her head.

I somehow remember to yank the covers down, so we don't stain the silk bedspread between feral kisses.

Mine, her wolf growls in my head as she unbuttons my shirt.

Yes, I'm yours, Aster Adalwulf. Until the day I die.

I kiss the fuck out of her as my hips roll over hers, the hard bulge of my straining cock grinding in the notch between her legs. She reaches between us to undo my jeans as I lower my head to suck one of her nipples.

Freeing my erection, she fists my cock, and a sound rockets from my throat.

She pushes at my shoulders. "Roll over." Her eyes are pure silver.

I comply, and she crawls over me, pulling my jeans and boxers off. She wraps her fist around my cock and tugs, further engorging the head with blood. Pre-cum drips from the slit.

Aster holds my gaze as she lowers her head and flicks her tongue over the head, tasting my essence.

I groan. "Fuck, Aster. You're killing me."

She takes my murder to the next level by opening her mouth and fully engulfing the head of my cock.

I shudder with pleasure, my fingers reaching for her hair. My canines have already descended, sharp and ready to puncture her skin. She's playing a dangerous game. She's going to get me so excited I won't be able to hold back. And it's her first time. I need to be gentle.

I should come now, so I can take that pressure off and take my time claiming her. Yeah. That's a good plan.

I lie back and receive her gift. Her hot, wet mouth slides over my cock at the same time she cups my balls. I show her how to use her fist in conjunction with her mouth, stroking along my length as she moves her head down and up to make it feel like she's taking all of me.

I surrender to the sensations. Allow the exquisite pleasure to wash over me until I reach a peak.

My fingers tighten in her hair, and I use them to pull her off then flip her over onto her back and give my cock a few jerks. With a shout, I come all over the flat plane of her belly.

She runs her fingers through my essence and brings them to her mouth.

I yank off her sweatpants. "Do you want me to use a condom?" I somehow remember to ask.

"No."

I'm surprised by her immediate answer, but then she already made her choice. I suppose a she-wolf who has lived in harmony with nature, guided by Fate would embrace the possibility of conception with her mate. Even on their first time.

With her full permission to coat her with my seed, I use my cum to lube up her entrance, painting her plump folds, rubbing it all over her clit. She arches, rolling her pretty pussy into my hand. I screw one finger into her, prying her open, readying her for my dick.

I fucking love seeing her pussy painted with my cum. Claimed with my essence.

O. K.? I sign.

More, she signs back.

Fuck, yeah.

I screw in a second finger and curve them up to stroke her inner wall. Some of the tissue under my fingertips tightens, and I know I've found her G-spot. I stroke it, loving the way it makes her writhe and kick in pleasure. Then I pump my fingers in and out, hitting the spot every time I plunge in.

She screams something. I can't see her lips because her head is tilted back, but I feel the reverberation in her body. Her inner thighs squeeze around my wrist, her ass clenches up tight, and then she squirts in a glorious display of female ejaculation.

A growl reverberates in my throat, and I pull my fingers out, hardly waiting for her to finish her orgasm.

Judging by the wild silver of her eyes, she needs me inside her as much as I need to be there. I rub the head of my cock through her juices, and she reaches for my hips, lifting her knees up to tip her sopping pussy up for my ravishment.

My teeth dig into my lip as I force myself to slow down instead of impaling her in one violent thrust. Blood drips into my mouth. I gently press against her entrance, but her nails score my hips as she pulls me over her, taking me all at once.

"Aster," I choke. "Fuck, yes."

Her eyes are round, her mouth open as if in surprise. I freeze, buried deep inside her to give her a chance to get accustomed to my size.

"O.K.?" I mouth.

She nods and starts slowly moving beneath me, rubbing her clit along the base of my cock. My body shakes with the effort, but I still don't move. I want her to lead this. To show me what she's ready for.

She finds a rhythm, rocking her hips and sliding beneath me, and I see the exact moment she surrenders to the pleasure. She moans and her breath deepens.

I draw back and sink in deeper, and she rocks to meet

me. My upper lip curls as I drive a little harder, my hips snapping to bury myself deeper with each thrust.

Aster thrashes beneath me, her head sliding over the luxury sheet, her eyes rolling back in her head with pleasure.

I give it to her hard–harder than I mean to, but I'm losing control. My wolf is in charge now, and he needs to claim Aster with a ferocity I've never felt before. I catch her nape to keep her head from hitting the wall each time I shove into her. I grip the fronts of her thighs, lifting her pelvis off the bed, so I can slam in hard. My loins slap against her ass with a satisfying smack, reminding me how much I want to spank her gorgeous ass again.

We dance together this way for an eternity. Or maybe just a few minutes. I lose track of time completely, my brain fully embedded in my balls.

Aster's lips are moving. It takes me a moment to focus on what she's saying. "Mark me."

Mark. Her.

"*Mine.*" I don't even know if the syllable is intelligible with the growl rising in my throat. My wolf goes insane. I drive into her so hard the bed bounces. My jaw hinges open and snap down on the place where her neck meets her shoulder. The moment I sink my teeth into her, I come like a freight train.

Even though I just orgasmed from the blowjob, an endless stream of cum pours out of me into my convulsing mate. Aster jerks and spasms beneath me, her ass squeezed up tight as her internal muscles clamp around my dick, milking it for every last drop of my essence.

I force my jaws to soften and ease my teeth out of her skin, licking the wounds to help them close and heal.

Rocking my pelvis over hers, I shower kisses along her hairline, down her jaw, across her throat.

"Mine," I repeat.

Aster smiles up at me, luminescent in her post-orgasmic glow. She touches the place I bit her, then touches my cheek. "I'm yours."

* * *

Aster

Noah gazes down at me like I'm the most beautiful female in the world. "I'm so fucking lucky," he says.

I bask in the glow of his regard. Every cell in my body seems to sing with joy at his claiming.

Mate, my wolf keeps whispering. *Mate.*

There's a satisfaction that runs bone deep.

My wolf will keep speaking to me, even if the Grandmothers will now be silent. I reach for them, testing our connection, but feel nothing. Not even their disappointment with me over this choice. It's just...quiet.

Which I guess is a relief.

My entire life I had this internalized sense of judgement. Maybe human kids have the idea of Santa Claus always watching. Or the Boogie Man. But I had the Grandmothers. Oma was always lecturing about not shaming myself with them. That they'd know if I broke a rule, and they'd tell her, so I could be properly punished.

Now they're no longer in my head. No longer watching over my shoulder.

I'm...free.

I'm free!

I throw my arms around Noah, nearly strangling him in

a wild hug. All the pressure to perform, to be a conduit for the pack's visions, to survive in a toxic environment is gone.

It's just me and Noah.

And soon, we'll have Oriana and Liora. We'll be a pack of four until Noah and I have pups of our own. We love each other. We'll find our way.

I push away the nagging anxieties about whether we can safely get Liora and Oriana out without my Sight to guide us.

Or if Noah will lose his job. What Brick Blackthroat will do with us. Or worse, what the Adalwulfs will do if they ever find me. Kill me, most likely. If they find out I've lost the Sight, then I'm not only worth nothing to them, but I've taken their greatest asset from them. Such a loss would be punishable by death.

But with Noah, it feels like I can face the most insurmountable problems and come out on top. Look at the miracles that have already happened—I'm out of that prison tower! I won't be magically bound to Aiden Adalwulf.

He eases out of me, and I release his neck. "One minute." Noah holds up a finger as he slides off the bed then returns a moment later with a warm washcloth. He cleans between my legs then lays more kisses along my skin, traveling from my mons up to my throat.

I love you. He shows me the "ILY" sign, but this time his middle and index fingers are crossed.

I shape my fingers into the same sign.

"It means, I really love you," he explains. "The R is for really."

"I really love you," I whisper as I wave my IRLY hand in front of his face.

He grins and holds up his finger again, this time going to

the bedroom door and cracking it, even though he's naked. He bends down and picks up a tray from the floor outside.

There's a tray with a red rose in a vase, a bottle of Moet champagne on ice with two flutes, and a charcuterie board with cheeses, meats, and fresh bread.

I gasp. "What's that?"

He shows me a note. *"Congratulations, Noah. You punched above your weight."* It's signed by Billy and the whole pack.

"'Punched above your weight.' What does that mean?"

"It means I mated someone far, far above me." He leans in and kisses me.

"That's not true," I protest.

"Oh, starlight, it is." He looks smug.

"Which one is Billy?"

"The wolf who noticed me mooning over you when I first saw you. He's my direct boss and an asshole. And we all tease him because he definitely mated someone better than him. And he knows it."

I can't help my smile. Noah seems to know these wolves so well, and they also seem to have accepted him even though he's not pack. It warms my heart. "Do you think we're still prisoners?"

Noah sets the tray down on the bedside table and pours the champagne. "Probably. But I think Brick might be willing to help us." Or *Sully,* he adds in ASL.

I take the slender stem of one of the filled glasses from him, and we clink them together. "To us," I say.

His eyes grow serious. "To you."

"No. To *us.* There's an us now. We're a team. You're not a lone wolf anymore. Not ever again."

Noah's eyes grow moist, and he leans his forehead

against mine for a moment then kisses my lips. "We should tell my nan. Do you want to meet her?"

My heart squeezes in my chest. "Of course."

Noah sets our champagne glasses down, and we pull on our shirts before he videocalls his grandmother with the phone propped up on the tray of food in front of the ice bucket.

A woman who looks like an older version of Liora except with dark hair cut into a shaggy layered bob answers. For a moment, their hands fly, and no one speaks out loud, so I'm lost, but then the she-wolf says, "Aster, it's so wonderful to meet you." Her eyes are damp with tears.

"Aster, this is Nan," Noah says.

"Hi, Nan." I wave and smile.

"Look at your beautiful mark. My darling! I can't wait to hug you in person." She signs something to Noah, who chuckles.

"Yes, she's a wolf. She's an Adalwulf, actually." Noah signs and speaks out loud, so I can follow.

Nan's smile fades and concern creeps between her brows.

"She helped me find Liora."

Nan goes perfectly still, her body on rigid alert. "And?"

"And I have a little sister."

Nan's face turns pale. Her lips start to tremble. "Will she leave? Can you get her out?"

Noah nods. "We're going to figure out how to get them both out. Liora wants out now, too. For Oriana–her daughter."

"But they're not with you now?" I can see the alarm on Nan's face. She knows enough about the Moonborn to know it's not easy for anyone to leave.

Noah shakes his head. "No, but I will go back for them. I have a plan."

Nan frowns but nods then turns her attention back to me. "Aster, my child. I'm so happy you and Noah found each other. Please be careful."

I nod. "We will."

"Take care of each other," she says.

"We will." Noah gives her the "ILY" sign, and they hang up.

"*Do* you have a plan?" I ask. Because I'd like to hear it, so I know what we're going to do.

He pops a square of cheese in my mouth. "No. Not yet. But I'm working on it."

Chapter Eighteen

ster

A I'm awakened by a soft glowing light. At first, I think it's a vision or a dream, but then I come fully awake and remember–I no longer have the Sight. I feel relief followed by a sense of loss. It's worth it, though. I'd trade anything to be with Noah.

Beside me, Noah is looking at something on his phone. That's the source of the light that woke me. The bedroom curtains are still drawn, and there's a little light slipping in, but not much. It's probably just after dawn.

"Hey." I touch his arm gently and wait for him to turn to me before asking. "What are you doing?"

"Did I wake you?"

"It's okay." I snuggle closer to him.

He shows me his phone screen. On a black field, there are two glowing green spots signaling where Noah's trackers are.

I go to ask a question, and Noah puts a finger to my lips. *Eyes and ears,* he signs, pointing around the room.

I widen my eyes. If I'm understanding correctly, Noah thinks the Blackthroats are surveilling us.

"Really?" I mouth. I remember Sully telling us the guards would keep their distance, but maybe that promise ended at dawn.

He points to one of the green lights on the screen. *O* he signs. For Oriana.

L, I sign and point to the other green light. He nods.

I sigh, settling closer. This is why he's awake so early. He's watching his mother and half-sister, trying to figure out how to free them. The mark on my shoulder throbs, and my heart swells with tenderness for my caring, courageous mate.

The green light that represents Liora is on the move.

"Gardens," I mouth to him. Looks like she's up early to do her chores. "I wish we could see her."

"I have audio." He switches over to a text file and hands it over to me. "The tracker listens, but it's one way. I can't communicate with her, and I need a computer to access my drones, so I can get visuals. But even then, we won't be able to talk to her."

"Maybe Brick will loan you one," I joke. I'm not sure if the stern Alpha is going to help us yet.

I hope so.

I scroll through the file. It's a long transcript of all the audio the tracker picked up. A lot of it is garbled, but some of it is tagged as either "Liora" or Unidentified Speaker."

It's several pages long. I skim the first few paragraphs and get the gist. I use his phone to type,

> Liora's been ordered by the Warden to help prepare the females for purification.

What's purification? Noah fingerspells *purification.*

I love that we're using ASL for covert communication. I can't wait to learn enough to be fluent.

For now, I use his phone to type the message.

> The Warden sends the females to a sacred spring near the Tower to bathe and prepare for the rites. The Seeress usually oversees it.

That's probably when Oma started drugging the acolytes to make them docile.

A phantom pain shoots through me, faint but pulsing through my limbs. Is it regret? Or a warning?

No, I don't have premonitions anymore. This is just my psyche reaching for my gift–and finding nothing.

Maybe I do feel regret.

I bite my lip.

> The lunar eclipse is in two days,

Noah types.

> We're running out of time.

> Plan?

I type.

He shakes his head. He doesn't have a plan.

> Do you think Brick will help us?

> I don't know.

He takes his phone and swipes back to the screen that shows the black map and green glowing lights of the trackers.

I lay my head on his shoulder. I can't do much to help him, but at least I can give him comfort as we watch over his mother and sister, together.

Breakfast is on another tray, delivered to our room. This time, there are four stone-faced guards posted right outside our door. There's more outside our window, patrolling the lawn.

Our reprieve is over.

By mid-morning, Noah is pacing. He's run his fingers through his hair so many times it's standing up. If we were at the cabin, I bet he'd be accessing the drones he left hidden in the treetops on Adalwulf land and flying them all over to see if there's any weakness we can exploit. But he only has his phone.

I'm no help. Instead of visions and headaches, I feel strangely empty. Adrift. It doesn't help that the room smells like sex and anxiety.

We need to get a message to Liora. But how?

Noah's head turns to the door a moment before there's a knock. *Madi,* he signs to me, and I open it.

The human stands outside the door, with even more guards crowded in the hall behind her.

"Good morning," she says while signing. Her fingers move elegantly through the air, like she's casting a spell. "How'd you sleep?"

"Well," Noah says and signs. My cheeks heat a little, remembering that all the wolves present can smell evidence of my claiming.

But then I straighten. I'm proud to bear Noah's mark.

"I thought you might need some clothes, Aster."

I laugh, looking down at Noah's shirt that I've been living in. At least it's better than the tourist trap sweatshirt we bought on the way to the Berkshires. Even with the tense meeting yesterday, the howling moon on it got some funny looks. "That would be nice."

"Noah, you come too," Madi says, and even though she's human, I catch a whiff of dominant alpha in her orange blossom scent.

With a ridiculous number of guards trailing us, Madi takes us to her rooms and gives us a tour of the house along the way.

We pass a stuffy-smelling room with a large portrait of an unsmiling man who looks like Brick.

"That was Bruce Blackthroat. The former Alpha. Brick's father." Madi's voice softens.

I shudder, recalling some of the visions I've had of the man. Like Odin, he was a vicious leader. If he were in charge, I'd definitely be in the dungeon, probably being tortured.

"Let's find you some clothes," Madi offers, beckoning me into a large chamber. Noah lingers in the hallway, letting us have some privacy.

She opens the doors to a large walk-in closet and starts handing me clothes–panties with the tags still on, tank tops, leggings, sweaters.

"The first time I came here, I had no clothes, either," she shares. "I was stranded here during a snowstorm. Trapped with the wolves for Thanksgiving when they didn't want me here."

I hold up one of the sweaters against my body. It's a soft-knit azure with a scoop neck.

"That will look perfect on you."

"Thank you. It must've been hard to get tangled in pack politics as a human."

"I didn't know what they were then. I didn't even know it when I told Brick I quit and stormed out in a blizzard and then found myself surrounded by a pack of snarling wolves."

My eyes widen.

Madi gives a soft laugh. "We had a lot to work through." She glances toward the door. "I imagine you two did, too?"

I bow my head. "Yes. The magic of my Sight was predicated on me remaining unmated. A virgin. I...had to choose between Noah and being Seeress."

Madi tilts her head. "So...you lost your abilities?"

I nod.

Madi pulls me in for a hug. I stumble into her, freezing at first, then letting the human offer her comfort. I'm not used to being shown empathy or compassion, except from Liora. Now this total stranger seems to understand me more than my entire pack.

I change into a pair of leggings and the sweater, and we walk out of the bedroom together.

"I'm grateful you took the chance to warn me," Madi says. She keeps resting her hand on her belly, and I don't think she realizes she's doing it. "You could've just sent a message."

"We couldn't risk that you wouldn't believe me," Noah says. "It was better for us to come in person. Aster and I believe Fate guided us here." But he sighs, and Madi's expression softens.

"You're worried about your mom."

"And my sister. Will Brick help us?"

"I don't know. It's not that he doesn't want to, it's just..."

"He's responsible for the whole pack," I say to let her off the hook. "He doesn't want a war. I understand."

"He's in meetings now with his inner circle. But we'll see him for lunch. In the meantime, is there anything I can do?"

Noah and I glance at each other. There's so much we need help with, I don't even know what to say.

I need access to a computer, Noah signs. He doesn't say anything, which means he doesn't want the guards to overhear.

Madi leads us back into the hall, where the guards trail us to another library-like room. This one has big, beautiful windows overlooking a green lawn.

"This is my favorite reading room," Madi says. "I use it as an office." She holds the door for us but stops her guards from entering. "Noah is helping me with a work project," she says firmly and shuts the door in their faces.

Once the door's shut, she's all business. "Here." She beckons, leading us to a table that holds a desktop. "You can use this."

Noah sits down and immediately starts typing.

Thank you, I sign to her, and she nods.

"I'll be in the next room," she says and signs and leaves to give us privacy. We're lucky she's willing to help us. She probably feels like she owes us.

In fifteen minutes, Noah's activated one of the dormant drones he left hidden in a pine tree near Moon Hollow. I hover over his shoulder, watching him pilot it. We're in luck, Liora is still out in the forest, working in her favorite garden. The screen shows the footage the drone is recording, Noah can't get close because there's a guard standing near her. Which makes sense–security will be tighter since Noah and I snuck in and were almost caught.

"Can you get a message to her?" I murmur.

He shakes his head. He can't move the drone any closer. He told me these drones are state of the art, relaying video and audio to us, but they only work one way.

"Wait." I grab his arm. "Look at the garden." Liora

seems to be tending it, turning the soil as if she's preparing it for planting, but she's spelled out a word with sticks and markings in the dirt. The word *Purify*.

Purify, I spell it out slowly with my clumsy fingers. Of all the messages Liora could send, why would she choose to spell out that word? Is she referring to the purification ritual?

I reach for psychic help before I remember that it's no longer available to me.

Then it comes to me in a flash. "I think I know what she wants us to do."

Sure enough, when we read the audio transcript, we find several passages of Liora speaking about the purification rights.

> You will be cleansed by the light of the moon. The Warden has proclaimed it. I've been given the honor of leading you in the ritual to purify your body, your mind, and your soul. It will only be me, dear one, and another chosen attendant. No one else— certainly no males.

No males means no guards. Liora is making it clear that the purification ritual is our best time to break in and sneak her and Oriana out. She isn't saying anything directly, but that's wise because she and the acolytes are probably being watched.

> And then what?

the unidentified speaker asks. Noah thinks it's his sister, Oriana, but there's no way to be sure.

> Then you will be pure and ready for the
> Alpha Rites. Do not be afraid. Fate will
> guide us.

There are a few more passages of the unidentified speaker sharing their fears.

> I don't want to be chosen.

Liora shushes them.

> It is an honor to be chosen

she proclaims. It's in stark contrast to the way she begged me to help free her daughter when she visited me in the tower, which makes me think she's definitely putting on a show for the guards.

> But do not worry. Fate will reveal your path
> at the time of purification.

I use the computer to type to Noah.

> That's our chance.

> If we can get past the guards, we can get
> Liora and Oriana out.

Noah erases what I've written and types,

> When?

I bite my lip and type:

> Tonight

It has to be tonight. Do we tell Brick?

Noah shakes his head.

The door swings open, and I jump back from the computer as Madi walks in. "Thank you for looking this over, Noah," she murmurs while signing. "This project has been a challenge from the start." She's keeping it vague for the guards.

Noah quickly erases all traces of what we've done from her computer. "Glad I could help," he says.

"Did you have enough time to review everything?"

All done, I sign. My gut is churning. Do we confide in Madi? Or will she take what we share and run straight to Brick? We can't take the chance in case he decides to stop us.

I glance at Noah, but his face is blank.

Madi seems to understand. She inclines her head. "You've been invited to lunch with Brick and I. I will warn you—the Moon Co Bros will all be there."

"Moon Co Bros?" I ask.

To my surprise, Noah grins. It's good to see some of the tension leave his face. "That's what we call Billy, Jake, Vance and Sully. Technically, I was a Moon Co Bro, too." His smile slips a little.

"Once a Moon Co Bro, always a Moon Co Bro," Madi says and signs cheerfully. "Although why you like hanging with those alphaholes, I'll never understand."

"You mated the head alphahole."

Madi snickers. "It was Fate. Can't argue with that, can we?"

Noah agrees and offers me his arm. I take it, needing his touch, grateful for it. For some reason, at the mention of Fate, my insides grew cold.

* * *

Noah

Jake is talking too fast for me to lipread, but it doesn't matter because it's some bullshit story. "So... pants around my ankles...get it on ..the most beautiful dragon shifters I've ever seen,....too excited and blows fire. Poof, there go the bed curtains. I had to scramble to get them free–they were both...if you know what I mean." Jake waggles his brows.

The more Jake talks, the wider Aster's eyes get. My wolf would be annoyed she's so fascinated with the Moon Co Bros, but there's only curiosity in her scent. I remind myself she's been sheltered. And the Moon Co Bros are a lot to take.

"Then the other thinks the first one did it on purpose, and they start fighting. Flames are going everywhere. The bed's toast. And I'm just trying not to get my buns roasted while I pull them apart."

A laugh squeaks out of Aster, and then she shrinks a little because no one else is buying the story enough to laugh. I put my hand on her shoulder to reassure her.

Jake also shoots her a smile. He loves having her in his audience. She's the only one who doesn't realize this story is total bullshit, the rest of us are listening with amused skepticism.

"Finally, the door goes up in flames, and the bouncers come in with a hose. Too late for the room. Everything was in ashes, including my pants. Thaddeus was pissed. He revoked their membership and kicked us all out. But we all went back to the Emerald and had a nice time."

I miss what Billy says, but when I turn to see, his expression is dismissive.

"What actually happened is he tried to make a move on

a dragon shifter and got burned," Vance says. He signs the joke clumsily, but I get the gist.

"Now that I believe." Nickel raises his wine glass to toast Vance. He's the only one drinking wine–we spent the first half of lunch teasing him about acting more French than British. I have a harder time reading his lips because of the British accent. "Dragon shifters are rare. No way there are two female dragons in New York."

"They were male. Twins," Jake says, looking smug.

The rest of the Moon Co Bros snort.

"We can easily fact-check this, you know," Madi says. "I'll just ask Thaddeus."

The smiles slip off people's faces, and they all look at Brick, who has storm clouds in his expression.

Growl, Aster signs to me.

"What?" Madi says and signs, unfazed by her mate's glower. "I liked him."

"He liked you. Too much." Brick captures her hand in both of his and brings it to his mouth to kiss. "No vampires."

"Vampires and wolves don't mix. Even the humans know that." There are chuckles around the table.

"Inside joke," I tell Aster. "It's from a book."

"I can loan them to you if you want," Jake offers. "Do you like to read?"

"I do. I've just never read for fun. Because I was destined to be Seeress, I had to focus on my duties."

The Moon Co Bros' expressions are kind, but the room gets quiet at the reminder of how Aster was raised.

I copy Brick's move and take her hand, holding it close. She squeezes it, and a little tension goes out of me.

It's hard for me to relax right now because my mom and sister are trapped, and I have no idea how to free them. I keep thinking that if we try to sneak back on Adalwulf land

and we're caught, we'll probably be killed, like Moira, the wolf Sully knew. The Warden won't show mercy. It's unthinkable, but I can't stop imagining it.

"The Purification is tonight. I have to get my mother and sister out of there before then. Are you going to let us go?"

Everyone's expression turns serious.

Brick frowns then signs and speaks slowly. "No one is going anywhere until I've had time to consider all the angles."

Chapter Nineteen

We're back in our room in the East Wing. Noah isn't pacing although he has scrubbed his hand through his hair enough that it's standing on end. He stares out the window, down at the line of guards posted on the lawn. I wish he'd say something, but I know what he's thinking. He's calculating how many of them he could fight before they stop him from escaping to save his family.

I shiver, rubbing my arms. Since the confrontation with Brick, there are even more guards posted around our room. I sit on the edge of the bed, wracking my brain to figure out what I can do.

I never had much to offer Noah, and it's becoming clear I'm more of a burden than a mate. I can't really help him. My visions are gone, and I didn't realize how helpless that would make me feel. During the worst moments of my childhood, at least I felt a connection to something beyond. It gave me comfort, made me feel like Fate had a divine plan, and I was being guided. But what did Fate ever give me? My own pack was starving me. My own alpha was threatening me with a fate worse than death: breeding and the future torture of my own children unless I produced credible visions.

But now I don't know what to do. I pick at the bedspread, feeling painfully ordinary. Useless.

A wild thought enters my head. "I could go to them with the moonstone," I say.

I could trade myself–"

No. Noah snaps his index and middle fingers down on his thumb. He crosses the room, signing with furious fingers. "Absolutely not. You will not sacrifice yourself." He bares his fangs, his eyes glittering bright. His wolf is ready to pounce on me just for suggesting it.

"Then what are we going to do?" I whisper.

His expression turns bleak. I can't stand it. I reach for his hand.

There's a knock on the door, and I jump off the bed, miming a knock to Noah to let him know what I heard.

Noah holds up his hand to stop me from answering it. He keeps me behind him as he opens the door–as if he expects whoever's behind it to pounce.

It's Sully. He must be here to bring us back to an audience with Brick. But something's off–he's dressed in black from head to toe. The hall behind him is empty, the guards nowhere to be seen.

"Come with me," he says. "Now."

* * *

Noah

I keep Aster close as we follow Sully down the hall to a small staircase. The guards are suspiciously absent, as if

Sully ordered them gone. He might be helping us–but he might mean to do us harm.

Still, I'm desperate, so I keep quiet as he leads us out a back door to a waiting car. Hope flares in my chest, and I snuff it out. Sully gets in the driver's seat and motions us to get in. I stop Aster from obeying, keeping my arm around her in case I need to protect her.

I wag my index finger from side to side in the sign for *where?*

"I'm taking you to the Adalwulfs. To get your sister and mom."

Why are you helping us? I sign.

Sully looks straight at Aster. "Moira" is all he says.

We get in the backseat of the car. Sully drives off as soon as we shut the door. The car is electric, so it's completely silent as it glides down the long, dark road. The moon is high, almost full, and light plays on our faces as we drive through the forest.

Finally, we're off Blackthroat land, and I let out a sigh. Sully is helping us escape.

Aster asks something–I only catch the second half lip-reading. Something like, "...trouble with Brick?"

I study Sully's face in the rear-view mirror. For a second, I think I see a flicker of a smile on Sully's face. I don't know why he would be smiling, and his expression smooths out quickly. "No one will know that I helped you unless I want them to."

He picks up a container and hands it back to me.

I miss what he says, so I look at Aster, who repeats it, enunciating her lips clearly enough for me.

"This is scent canceling spray." She mimes spraying a can.

Sully meets my gaze in the rearview mirror. "I can get you to the edge of Moon Hollow."

I nod.

"Rest now," I say to Aster, and she curls up beside me. We have a long drive to the Adirondacks.

The rest of the drive we make in silence. Aster dozes beside me. I stare at Sully the whole time, my eyes wolf-bright. Once in a while his gaze connects with mine in the rearview mirror, but he mostly focuses on the road. His whole body is relaxed in the front seat, his eyes glittering in the moonlight but not blazing. His wolf and his man are one.

The moon is high by the time Sully turns off the narrow mountain highway onto a bumpy dirt road. Branches scrape the window as the car bounces over the rough terrain. Aster wakes and Sully slows the car to a stop and turns to face us.

"What is this place?" I ask.

"Technically it's a wildlife preserve owned by the Blackthroat Family Foundation. Brick was able to snatch it up under the Adalwulf's nose. Aiden wasn't happy because the Foundation land is right up against Adalwulf land. After you find your mother and sister, you're going to want to cross that ravine and climb up to the other side." He gives me more details about the terrain—the rock outcroppings that could hide our descent. "There's a cave you can enter. It has a secret tunnel that will hide you."

How do you know about this? I sign.

He signs and speaks back, "Moira told me. She was going to use it." He pauses, swallowing. "My sister was a rebel. She hated Bruce Blackthroat... He was a hard-ass. She had this romantic idea of becoming an Adalwulf and living at Moon Hollow. I don't know where she got it... some wolf must have been sharing propaganda. I lost contact with her. Two years later, I received a message begging for me to rescue her. I came here" –he glances down to the bottom of the ravine– "and found her body. The Warden killed her for trying to escape and left her to rot."

"I'm sorry," Aster says.

Sully's eyes flash green. He looks distant for a moment then shakes his head, as if flicking a painful memory away. "Thank you, Seeress."

Pain flits over Aster's face. "Call me Aster. I'm not the Seeress anymore."

Sully's brow creases in confusion.

I pick up Aster's hand. Fuck. I asked too much of her.

"Mating me made Aster lose her magic," I explain to Sully.

Aster shrinks a bit, and my wolf wants to howl over her pain.

I take my phone out of my pocket and show it to Sully. *I'm leaving this here in case I shift,* I sign.

He nods. *Good luck.*

Thank you. I repeat the sign twice. I don't say or sign anything more, there aren't words or signs to express my gratitude. I can't believe Sully, the head of Blackthroat security, was willing to help us.

It's almost as if Fate is guiding us again.

Sully gets out and guides us into the forest. He hands me a small black pack he's carrying. Inside I find rope, duct tape, and strips of cloth that can be used as gags or blindfolds. There's also a long silver skinning knife in a black leather sheath. I wait until Aster isn't looking to secure it to my belt and cover it with my shirt.

Sully points out the way down into the valley. "This is as far as I can go. I need to stay on Blackthroat land." He doesn't say it, but I understand–if he's caught by the Adal-wulfs, there will be war.

"I'm going to give you a thirty-minute head start, and then I'm going to cause a distraction."

Thank you, I sign again.

"Don't thank me. Get your mother and sister out. Alive."

"We will," Aster makes the *yes* sign and turns toward the path to take the first step towards Adalwulf land.

"Wait." I pull her back. "I want you to go with Sully–"

"No." Moonlight bathes her face, illuminating her fierce expression. She bares her teeth, pointing to herself then me.

My mate is going to stick beside me, for better or worse.

I could order her to stay. It's safer for her. But some-thing in me yields.

"You need me," she says, and that's that. I need her help finding the purification site. Without her, my mission will fail.

I grip her hand tightly as we walk the path that takes us behind enemy lines.

Sully is right, we find the cave and use it to get out. It's a tight squeeze, tighter than the tunnel I used to find Aster. There's a moment when I'm afraid we'll be trapped in the dark, but we make it out.

The land stinks of Adalwulf markings.

We come across a guard post manned by two wolves and hunker down behind a crop of boulders to wait for them to pass. We can smell them. We're downwind, but even if the wind shifts, Sully's scent canceling spray should help us.

The older wolf orders the younger to stay and walks off. I tense, planning to sneak up to the younger and take him out. I move away from Aster, letting my wolf come out enough to turn my fingernails into vicious, curved claws.

I'm about to make my attack when Aster grips my arm and shakes her head. "Don't hurt him," she mouths. Before I can do anything, she picks up a branch and leans out enough to throw it over the guard's heads into the brush behind him. The wolf whirls, tensing at the sound.

And Aster darts away from me, moving too fast for me to stop. She walks right up to the guard, her hands raised. Her back is to me, but she must be speaking because the guard turns again, blanching when he sees her.

My wolf goes nuts. I can't believe the risk she's taking. When I get her back to a safehouse, I'm going to spank her gorgeous ass for taking such a risk. For now, I follow behind, a shadow sneaking around the guard to take him unawares when he's focused on my mate.

* * *

Aster

I rise up and walk forward, showing myself to the guard. When he turns, I recognize him as Benji, a young wolf who used to live in Moon Hollow. He's a lot bigger and broader around the shoulders, but his ears stick out the same way they did when he was a kid. He's just that–a kid the Warden forced into guard duty.

"It's me, Benji," I say. "Aster. The Seeress."

Benji looks at me like I'm a ghost. I wonder what the Warden and Aiden told them about my disappearance, if they told them at all. "I need your help, child," I say, channeling Oma. "Do as I say, and it will be all right."

He hesitates. For a moment, he looks like he's going to trust me, but then he opens his mouth to howl for help. In the next second, a shadow pounces on him, and he's yanked off his feet. Noah gets him into a chokehold, a big hand is clasped around Benji's throat. *No*, I wave my hands to sign when Noah goes to twist his neck. I make the karate chop into my open palm sign for *stop*. "Don't hurt him." I mouth the words clearly, so he can read them.

Noah's eyes are bright as he takes in mine. I feel his rage emanating around him. It's dark and terrible, like the rage of an alpha willing to do anything and kill anyone to get what he wants. It feels like Aiden.

Or not quite. This rage is protective. Noah would do anything and kill anyone for me, but he'll also listen when I ask him not to. "Please spare him," I beg.

With a grunt, Noah puts pressure on Benji's neck until he goes limp, unconscious but still alive.

Noah signs something angrily, his teeth bared, and his eyes bright gold. He's pissed that I risked myself.

He strips Benji out of his jacket, ties him up and uses a cloth to gag him, then drags him into the bushes to hide the body. Benji will be able to get free when he wakes up, which makes me feel better. If he can get free before someone finds him, he can make a choice to keep quiet or be punished for failing at his post.

"We have to move," Noah says. He grabs my hand and together we run with our feet falling into a rhythm. By some miracle, we make it the rest of the way to the tower without being caught. There are a few patrols and guards we have to sneak around—some in wolf form, some in human form, but most of the pack is probably gathered in the throne room listening to Aiden give orders. My heart beats fast from a couple of close calls by the time we get to the purification site.

The dark shape of the tower casts a shadow over the

wooden bathhouse and standing stones our ancestors built around the mountain stream and waterfall. Tingles spread over my body as we approach the sacred ground. The scent of crocuses and daffodils and precious herbs rises in a rich perfume all around us. I swear I can sense the magic. If I still had my gifts, I bet I would receive a vision.

The moon illuminates the many guards thronged around the bathhouse. Their dark shapes are still, perfectly alert. Noah pulls me behind an ancient oak, and I press close to him. I'm not sure what to do. We need to sneak into the bathhouse, to the waterfall beyond, but there are so many guards. Too many for me to distract or for Noah to take out. The only reason they're not pouncing on us is because they can't catch our scent.

What are we going to do?

There's a whistling sound, and a pop like an exploding rocket. The sound makes my wolf cringe and strain to burst out of my skin. I bite back a scream, tasting rust as my fangs graze my tongue. Only Noah holding me tight keeps me from startling and running away.

Far behind us, on the mountain, the red sparks fill the sky and fall with a crackling sound.

Fireworks.

My brain has gone numb. By the bathhouse, the guards in front of us are on their feet signaling to each other. Shouting. Half of them go running off towards the noise. It's back the way we came.

Noah releases me, signaling. It takes me a few times for me to understand what's happening. More fireworks crack and pop in the sky, bathing our faces with red and yellow.

This is the distraction Sully promised us.

It worked. It distracted the guards–for now. But some of those wolves will run straight to Aiden and the Warden, and they'll send every enforcer swarming the borders, cutting off our exit. We have to go now.

Stay here. Noah makes a downward motion with two "y" hands palm down. This time, he's the one who rises and charges the guards. He streaks like a shadow, lightning fast and silent, taking out the three wolves waiting before they register that they're under attack. He pounces so savagely, so quickly, it's over in seconds. Three wolves lie at his feet on the ground.

Energy surges through me–adrenaline so pure and overwhelming, I break into a run. I streak towards him, and we both burst into the bathhouse. Noah hesitates, but I've been here before, so I lead him through the wooden structure to the clearing beyond. This is where the plan gets fuzzy. There's no way to signal Liora without all the girls seeing us. If they haven't been drugged one of them could scream and call for help.

There are candles everywhere and bowls of incense. The smell of pungent herbs is so strong it stings my nose. I breathe through my mouth and search through the smoke. Fireworks still blast in the distance. Water trickles. Ahead of me is the silver plate of the freezing cold pool. There's a group of figures huddled near the waterfall. A bunch of acolytes dressed in skimpy white shifts.

"Liora?" I call, when one of the figures breaks and runs towards me. I recognize her narrow face a second before her face splits into a snarl.

Vera.

Chapter Twenty

After Vera flies at me, her fangs elongating in her rat-like face.

I return her snarl, bracing for her attack, when a white shape flies out of the darkness and slams into Vera, knocking her to the ground a few feet from me.

It's Liora, wearing her white ritual shift. She straddles Vera, pinning the younger wolf and rearing back, raising both hands over her head. She's holding a large rock. Without hesitation, she slams it onto Vera's head, and the downed wolf goes limp. She bludgeons her a second time. Then a third.

By the time I find my voice, Liora is on her feet. "I knew you'd come," she says to me then signals to the acolytes. Two of them cringe back, looking cold in their wet garments. Liora must have sent them into the water to be "purified" already.

"Girls," Liora signs and speaks in a calm voice. "It's time."

What?

One acolyte breaks from the pack. "Seeress?" Oriana says to me.

Pain lances my chest, and I flinch. "Just Aster. We're here to help."

Oriana freezes as Noah approaches us.

"This is your brother," I say. Liora is busy herding the frightened young woman forward.

"We're getting them *all* out. *Now*." Liora's eyes flash bright as she gives us the order. She squares off with Noah, a determined set to her shoulders.

Noah looks like he wants to protest, but he backs down. I don't know how we're going to sneak back to safety with six young women in bright white garments, but Liora isn't going to take no for an answer.

Strength, my wolf whispers. Liora has the strength of a mother. The Warden didn't beat it out of her.

Shift, Liora signals the young women, her hand drawing the shape of a wolf's snout in front of her face. Oriana immediately strips out of the skimpy garment and calls her wolf. Four of the acolytes follow suit, but one sniffles and shakes her head, trembling.

OK, Liora signs. She must have been teaching them sign language, so they could communicate silently. I wish she'd taught it to me growing up, but I'm picking it up fast. She puts her arm around the girl who's having trouble changing into her wolf, comforting her.

She signs to the rest of them to go, or maybe to follow, her two index fingers making an arc toward Noah.

He beckons to them and leads the five female wolves back into the bathhouse.

I bring up the rear, hovering behind Liora and the young girl she's helping. Tingles run down my arms, like mini lightning bolts of adrenaline. I want to run, or fight, or scream, but I make myself hold back and focus on Liora's murmurs to the frightened girl.

"It'll be okay. My son is here. He's here to save you."

"What about the Warden?" the girl warbles.

"Shhh, child, it'll be all right. Fate has another plan for you."

I hope she's right. I have a hard knot in the pit of my belly. The scent of ritual incense clogs my nose, reminding me of all the times I stood with Oma overseeing a rite. It makes me want to puke.

Ahead of me in the gloom, Noah has gathered all the young wolves around him at the bathhouse door. He leans forward enough, so the moonlight gilds his hair. Then he signals us to wait while he scouts ahead.

I crouch with the others in the bathhouse, gritting my teeth. Pressure builds along my sides, like a psychic vise threatening to clamp me and keep me still.

The three guards that Noah took out are in the bathhouse, tied and gagged. He must have taken the time to do that when I was inside, watching Liora deal with Vera. They're starting to rouse and tug on their binds.

Oriana moves from the door as if to sniff one, but Liora waves a hand to get her attention and signals her to stop. The white-gray wolf backs away.

The frightened girl still in human form whimpers, and two of the guards grunt and start wriggling. I wish I had Liora's rock, but I don't know if I'd be brave enough to use it.

Run, my wolf shrieks. It's not like her, she's usually so calm. I'm usually the one freaking out.

Please, I pray. *Please help.* I don't know who I'm praying to. Not the Grandmothers, whom I've turned my back on.

Maybe Fate? *Please. Get us out of here. But most of all, keep him safe. I need him to be okay.*

It feels like a century passes before Noah returns. He signals us to follow his lead, and we do, gratefully. We run from the bathhouse into the woods.

I can't hear anything the forest is unnaturally still. But then–ahead, there are shouts and the sounds of boots stomping in a rhythmic march.

Aiden's been alerted, and he's called up the troops.

I can tell by the tension in Noah's shoulders that our escape route is blocked. Any minute, guards will return to the bathhouse, and they'll find their buddies tied up, and know something's up.

An image flashes into my mind–a memory from the time Noah first came for me. *The tunnel,* I sign to Noah.

The tunnel connected to the Tower. We can go to the Tower and sneak out the tunnel the way I first escaped. We're closer to it than any other escape route. It's not ideal– there'll be guards at the Tower that we'll have to deal with, and if we make it off Adalwulf land, we'll have to continue south on foot, but it's a better plan than trying to go back north the way we came, risking coming across tons of enforcers the whole way. Even if we did get to the ravine and cave, I bet that area and any area near where Sully is setting off fireworks is now crawling with guards.

Whatever we decide, we need to do it now. We can't wait here, or we'll be caught. We have to move.

Noah nods and changes directions. The female wolves follow him, running silently. Liora holds the frightened girl's hand as they both run. The Tower rises above us, a dark shape spotlighted by the almost full moon.

I speed up to catch up with Noah. It feels so good to run flat out, heart and arms pumping, beside my mate, that I look over and smile at him despite the tense circumstances. He meets my gaze, and his lips curl up. We're going to make it.

But the moment we leave the forest and head for the door to the Tower, I feel sick again. All the weakness I felt when I was being starved and imprisoned enters my limbs. I swallow down my bile and the sense that something dreadful is waiting for me and take the lead with Noah at my side.

There are two enforcers guarding the door. Before Noah can rush them, I stride forward.

"Halt," one guard says.

"Let us pass," I say in an imperious tone. "We're under attack. These are the acolytes meant for the Alpha Rites and must be protected at all costs."

The younger guard looks to the older, but neither knows what to do. I'm hoping they don't recognize me, or if they do, they haven't been told that I'm missing.

The frightened girl in Liora's arms lets out a sob, and that convinces the enforcers. They open the heavy wooden door and stand aside for us to file inside.

"Our guard is to come with us," I signal Noah to follow us. "The Warden's orders."

Oriana's wolf bares her teeth at the guards as she enters, but we make it safely inside. The dark depths close around me, and for a moment, I'm ungrounded, suspended in a black void, not knowing where I am or who I'm with.

Then I blink, and I'm watching Noah look for the secret door that leads to the tunnel.

"What are we doing back here?" the girl sniffles. Liora signs something to her while saying, "All will be well, child.

I go to help Noah open the door. It creaks a little, and I wince, hoping the guards don't hear.

"Let us sing to the moon to guide us," Liora says, and as one, the girls in wolf form throw back their heads and howl. The sound bounces off the stone walls, filling the space with an eerie melancholy. It's beautiful.

Noah and I open the door, and Liora gives another signal. The wolves all fall silent.

"And now let us meditate in peace and rest," Liora says loudly, for the guard's benefit. I never knew she was so crafty. I must be staring at her, wide-eyed, because she winks at me.

Despite the hammering of my heart against my ribs, the corners of my lips curve up.

Then Noah takes my hand, and we descend into the tunnel, leading the wolves together.

But something's wrong. The minute the darkness closes around me, I'm back, floating in that void. It's not a vision–I don't have those anymore. But it's disorienting.

I squeeze Noah's hand and breath in his grounding scent. I can do this.

But the pressure clamping me is back and rising. There are voices whispering in my ears.

I push through, making myself put one foot in front of the other, but it's like I'm being dragged out of my body. The whispers are getting louder.

When Noah and I get to the end of the tunnel, there's a knot of enforcers waiting for us.

Aiden and the Warden found the tunnel. But of course, they did. After my disappearance, they would've gone over every inch of the place and, once they found it, posted guards at what they'd consider a vulnerable point. In my fear, I forget.

The only thing that saves us is the element of surprise. The enforcers aren't facing the tunnel entrance–they're not expecting anyone to emerge from it. As soon as Noah and I step out, we see them and bolt, the young wolves on our heels.

I can smell the forest ahead, the end of Adalwulf land, and it smells like freedom.

But with a shout, the enforcers realize what's happening and give chase. The young wolves scatter.

Liora is struggling with the most frightened acolyte. With a shriek, the little one rips her hand from Liora and runs back into the tunnel, the way we came.

Liora goes to chase her, and I shout her name. She can't save the girl, and if she stays, she'll be caught and killed, like Moira. The Warden won't tolerate this sort of insubordination.

We have to get out.

"Stop," the enforcers cry. Three of them chase after the acolytes. Two of them run towards us.

One of the enforcers blows a whistle, calling in more reinforcements. Halfway through the blast, the white and grey wolf that's Oriana leaps onto him, snarling. She's not a huge wolf, but she's big enough and heavy enough to knock the man back a step. He snarls back, grabbing at her.

Then Noah is there, thrusting his arm towards the man's throat. His fingernails must have turned to sharp wolf claws because blood spurts and the man falls back. Oriana leaps clear, blood staining her fur.

"Run," Noah orders, pointing, and she turns and flees towards the border. With luck, the others will follow her.

The other two enforcers turn on Noah. He faces off with one, but when another tries to leap up behind, I lose it.

My wolf breaks from my skin, ripping at my clothes. I don't think, I just act, and before I know it, I've got an enforcer on the ground, and I'm tearing at his back. I taste blood, and then Oriana is there, slitting his throat from behind with a four-claw slash.

I rise to all fours just as Noah takes out another enforcer. Liora runs to help him, and Noah points to the border of the land.

"Go," Noah orders, using an Alpha command. "Now."

In the grip of the Change, Liora falls to her knees. She casts off her shift just before she changes into a wolf–a white and grey one that matches her daughter. In wolf form, she streaks away.

I hear whistles in the woods. The enforcers calling in reinforcements. In another minute, this will be all over.

I can only hope that Oriana and the others make it out.

Suddenly, I'm in another world. The full moon is gone, and there's only darkness, and a hundred wolves surrounding us. They have glowing red eyes. What did Aiden do to them to make them have red eyes? They're also bigger, stronger, faster than any wolves I've ever seen.

And they have no aura. They're soulless. When I feel into their energy, it's a violent, empty, hungry void. A nothingness.

I can hear someone shouting my name. Calling me back.

Noah.

He's here with me. I sense him. "No," I mumble and try to wrench away. I need him to leave me. I need him to go, to save himself.

The vision changes. I'm at the Cradle, watching Aiden move towards the altar with a knife in his hand. Noah is bound there, tied down with silver rope that cuts into his skin, bloodies it.

My arms are bound, and I can't move. The Warden is

holding me back. I'm screaming as Aiden stands over Noah, blocking my view, and his arm strikes down.

I know the moment Noah dies. I feel it. It's like I'm being ripped in two. Pain wracks my body, and I'm shaking so hard, I don't know how I'm still conscious.

I don't want to watch, but I can't look away as Aiden steps back, lifting a bloody chunk of meat. Noah's heart. Aiden tore it from his body, and now he's crowing, his blond hair black with blood, as he throws his head back and swallows the organ whole. The Warden and all the red-eyed wolves start howling, but the sound cuts out.

I'm staring into Noah's eyes, but he's gone, gone, and he'll never return. He'll never hold me again, or love me, or protect me.

And it's my fault. I did this. I turned away from my fate, and that's the reason my mate is dead.

At the foot of the altar lies another body. Liora, in human form, her sightless eyes staring into the black sky. And I have to watch as Oriana is led, stumbling as if drugged, to the altar to be "claimed" in the Alpha Rites.

NO, I shout in my mind.

It can't happen. I won't let it happen.

But the vision continues, more images flowing into my mind's eye in a horrible fast-forward cascade. Madi sobbing over a tiny grave. Aiden ordering red-eyed wolves to advance and kill a crowd of humans. Thick, oily smoke boiling from the rubble of New York City.

It's coming, the Grandmothers inform me sadly. It's not even a shock to hear their voices–it feels inevitable. *Only you can stop this. But you must take your place.*

I see myself as Seeress, with the tiara on my head. Calling on my powers to cleanse the land.

Take your place, the Grandmothers urge. *It's the only way.*

And then I'm back in reality. "Aster! Aster?"

I'm in the forest with Noah. He's holding me–he must have carried me here. There's no one around us, but I hear whistles in the distance. The enforcers are coming, and Aiden and the Warden will probably be with them.

I want to cling to him, but the taint of my vision coats me. I don't know why I had a vision; they're supposed to be gone. I'm supposed to be free!

Take your place.

I don't want to! But...I can't be the reason Noah is killed. I can't stand for him to touch me, knowing that I might cause his death. And I know if he stays with me now, he will be caught, and so will his mother and sister. He needs to go and lead them out, it's their only chance. I know it like I know my own name

I can't have him here. It hurts, but losing him will hurt worse.

"You need to leave." I face him, so he can see my lips clearly as I sign, *GO.*

"Aster–" his arms tighten around me, and I thrash, wrenching myself free. I must look crazy, and maybe I am, but I have to do this. I have to do this even though my eyes sting with tears, and my heart is cracking, bleeding poison.

"You need to leave now. Go with your sister and mother."

"I'm not leaving you."

I say the first thing that comes to mind, what will get him to go away. "I'm not your mate. I can't be your mate. I want nothing to do with you. I belong here. You must set me free." It's all lies, poison, but I make myself believe it, so it smells a little true. It helps when the poison floods my body, numbing me from fingers to toes. I let the coldness take me and say, "I helped you get your mother and sister out. My debt to Liora is paid. But now I must go back to my calling. The Grandmothers spoke. I belong here." *Go with them,* I plead silently. *Go and be happy and live.*

"Aster–" He reaches for me.

I slash my hands down. "No! I don't want you as my mate. If you touch me, I will scream."

His hand falls, his expression broken.

I back away, and then I have to turn.

I can't look at him anymore, or he'll see the tears running down my face.

Chapter Twenty-One

*N**oah*

The scent of male wolves closes in on me. If I don't run now, no one will get out.

My wolf doesn't want to leave my mate, though. Searing pain lances through the center of my heart, leaving that organ nothing more than a bloodied scrap.

I force myself to think of my mission. Of Liora. And Oriana, the sister I just met.

I shift, tearing through my clothing and letting it drop in shreds as I race after the women. To my left, further in the trees, there's one acolyte wolf torn to the ground by enforcer wolves.

Fuck.

A quick glance over my shoulder shows another one captured further back.

I force some speed into my legs, tearing across the forest floor on four paws, following the scent of my mother and sister until I overtake them and one other acolyte.

They're the only ones who got out.

Fuck. It's a shit show.

Aster....

I lost Aster.

Forever.

I still don't even understand what happened. All I know is that my wolf wants to stop and howl until he's hoarse.

I force myself to keep running, leading the she-wolves off Adalwulf land to the other side of the highway and into the forest. From there, I keep parallel to the highway, running in a little stream to hide our scents.

We race through the water for miles before I deem it safe enough to come out then head another five miles north to the cabin where I first brought Aster.

Fate, no. I can't even think about her.

She...left me.

She fucking abandoned me just like Liora. Chose remaining with the Moonborn over being my mate.

She betrayed me.

I feel the metal bars of a cage slam down around my chest, locking down all emotion. All capacity for connection. All trust.

I will trust no female again.

Not as long as I live.

I shift and unlock the cabin door with a key I'd hidden, flicking on the lights and ushering the she-wolves into the small space.

I don't know if it's safe here, but the women are exhausted, and we need to regroup.

I lead them in and yank on a pair of sweats.

The she-wolf I don't know lowers her head and tucks her tail in fear.

Come, I sign. *You can wear my clothes.* I toss pieces of my clothing on the bed then leave them there to shift in privacy.

The image of Aster wearing my flannel shirt crowds into my mind, nearly dropping me to my knees. My eyes and nose burn with the pain of it.

But I'm the alpha wolf here. I have to provide for those weaker than I am. Mechanically, I go through the motions of building a fire and pulling food out of the refrigerator.

Liora emerges from the bedroom. *Just we four got out?* she signs. Her eyes look haunted. She knows what happens when an acolyte tries to escape.

My anger with her returns in full force. She abandoned me for the Moonborn, the same as Aster.

Aster chose to stay, I sign.

Liora narrows her eyes and shakes her head in obvious disbelief. *No,* she signs. *I don't believe it.*

Truth, I sign.

Liora shakes her head. *But she's your mate. I smelled your mark on her. She can no longer be Seeress.*

My lips twist into a bitter frown. *It wasn't true. She didn't lose her Sight after I claimed her.*

How do you know?

She had a vision.

When?

My stomach rattles like I swallowed rocks that have sunk to the bottom. *Before she told me she belonged with the Moonborn. Just like you.*

Liora stares at me then reaches for my arm.

I jerk back, not wanting her touch.

Noah...my son. Sorrow fills my mother's face. Her eyes are wet with tears. *Aster's vision must have told her to stay. Maybe it was the only way to get us out. She wouldn't abandon you. Just like I didn't abandon you. She sacrificed herself.*

I pick up the toaster from the kitchen counter and hurl

it against the cabin wall so hard it crumples from the impact.

Sudden movement from the living room snags my gaze, and I see Oriana, who must've jumped in shock. Her mouth is open as if she screamed.

Choosing Moonborn over me was not a sacrifice. It was a choice. Own up to it, I sign and stalk outside, slamming the door behind me.

* * *

Aster

Noah's gone.

I betrayed him.

I did it to save his life, but the look on his face tore me to shreds. There's no more Aster. I died when I told Noah I didn't want him as my mate. When I crushed his heart and all hope.

All around me sound the whistles and howls of enforcer wolves. They surround me. Their boots trample the daffodils, the crocuses, destroying the grove where I broke Noah's heart. And my own. A full phalanx of them drag two weeping acolytes back to Adalwulf land. Soon Aiden will be here with the Warden, and I will learn my fate.

It doesn't matter what happens to me. All that matters is that Noah will survive. Along with his mother and sister.

Go. Live. Be happy. Be free.

The largest enforcers crowd around me, their auras grey streaked with black. These are Aiden's chosen Alpha Force. There's a red sheen to their eyes, but they're not fully soulless, not yet. One of them grabs my arm, holding me still. Another barks something at him, and he lets go as if burned.

The Alpha Force wolves glare down at me, crowding close but not daring to touch me.

I still have power and authority here. I need to use it.

I don't care what happens to me, but I need to do something about the captured acolytes. They don't deserve to die. And I need to do all I can to protect Noah and his family. I can only hope they run fast and far, escaping this place forever.

"I am the Seeress. I have returned to you. All will be well." I have to fucking sell this, but my voice sounds hollow, imperious. Soulless.

I sound like Oma.

My wolf whines, wanting to go to Noah. Not understanding what we've done. *Fierce,* I tell her. *Strong. Protect mate.* Her power flows into me, stiffening my spine. In the recesses of my mind, I hear the Grandmothers whispering. I'm angry with them, though, so when I feel the visions ready to burst on me, I don't allow them through. I use my newfound strength to keep them at bay. Maybe I'll let them in when I'm alone. Safe.

Except, I won't be safe. Without Noah, I'll never be safe again. The thought makes my knees buckle, but somehow, I stay upright. It helps that Noah's scent still clings to me. The mark on my neck throbs, reminding me why I'm doing this.

I smell the Warden's mold-like scent before his order rings out, "Stay back from her. She's dangerous."

The Alpha Force doesn't move. They answer only to Aiden–Aiden made sure of that.

The Warden grinds his teeth, but there's nothing he can do. He glares at me, and I keep my face serene.

I'm no longer Aster. There's nothing left of my old self. I died when I rejected my mate.

I am the Seeress. My pack can kill me, imprison me, torture, and try to use me—it doesn't matter. They can't hurt me. Aster is dead.

The Seeress is all that remains.

So when Aiden appears, striding through the ranks of his red-eyed wolves, I feel nothing. Triumph glitters in his eyes.

"Take her to the dungeon," he says.

* * *

Noah

I prowl through the woods around the cabin in my bare feet for an hour, patrolling it like a sentry guard. Trying to cool off, so I can make a plan.

I can't think about Aster or Liora.

What's done is done. They both made choices I disagree with.

But I'd known I was asking a lot of Aster to mate me. Asking her to give up her magic. Her visions. The powerful position she holds with the Adalwulfs. She's basically their alpha female since Aiden is unmated.

And she explained to me the lure of the Moonborn. Their magical connection to nature and all that.

I guess what we had wasn't enough to sway her to leave it all.

I force the shattering pain back into the cage, stuffing it as far as it will go.

I need to forget about her and think.

We can't stay here—it's not safe.

As much as I hate to ask anyone for help, I need to contact Sully, at least to get my phone and rented car back.

I catch the scent of Oriana outside the cabin and stalk back to make sure she's not exposing herself.

She lifts her hand to her forehead in the sign for *hi*.

I stop. The cage around my chest rocks with fresh emotion. The enormity of the fact that I have a sister who I am just meeting for the first time hits me.

Fresh sorrow wells around something else–a protectiveness. She's family. My pack. A female wolf I would defend with my life even though I know nothing about her.

Thank you for rescuing us, she signs. She appears one part afraid, one part in wonder. Like I'm some knight in shining armor who swooped in to change her fate.

I suppose I am.

You're my sister, I sign. *I would not let them harm you.*

She runs to me, shocking me with a tight hug. Her scent is familiar and grounding. Like my wolf recognizes we're related. That she's safe. My arms band around her, and I hug her back.

She pulls away, looking awkward. *Will you come inside? My–our–mother made French fries for everyone.*

French toast? I sign back with a faint smile. The signs are similar and easily confused.

Oriana blushes and corrects the sign.

The last thing I want to do is come inside and eat, but I do need to get us the fuck out of here. It's time to stop wallowing and take some action.

I nod and follow her in. Ignoring the females at the table, I go to my computer and send a message to Sully with the location of the cabin. Then I message Nan, letting her know I got Liora and Oriana out, and I'd like to send them to her in Kentucky.

Hell, maybe I'll go too.

I need to be as far away from Aster and everything that reminds me of her as I can.

My heart will never heal. I don't care about that. I don't need anyone.

But I do know that staying in New York may drive me to madness.

* * *

Aster

The dungeon is a lot like the Tower, except for the stink of suffering. Old blood, rotting bones. Odin kept his dissidents down here, letting them starve to death if he didn't torture them first.

It's built under the throne room, which is fitting. All Aiden's power and authority comes from suffering and an abuse of power. Wicked to the core.

My cell is mostly clean, other than a large bloodstain by the door. It's a solid room with no windows, built of sturdy grey stone.

None of the Alpha Force harmed me. They also haven't given me food or water, but I'm fine with that. They can beat me, starve me, and I will welcome the pain gladly. It won't hurt as much as betraying my beautiful mate.

The visions haven't descended. Not yet. As soon as the door clanged behind me, I welcomed them, welcomed the void, the obliteration of myself, but the Grandmothers were silent.

Not that I want them to talk to me. I'm pissed at them. I used to think they were wise, all-knowing ones, but maybe that's not true. Maybe they're just vengeful spirits playing puppet master and cackling when they make us dance.

Fuck that.

There is a ghost hovering in the cell with me. A shifter in wolf form, scratching at the door, whimpering to get out. In life, the poor creature was tortured–I can tell because the ghost wolf has no eyes. I extend my hand and let the transparent apparition sniff me. Warm energy flows out of my hand into the spirit, a little light and love that will help ease the ghost's suffering. The ghost wolf settles on the floor at my feet.

I don't often see ghosts or spirits. I wonder if that's a new dimension to my Sight. I don't know why it's back, or why it came back right when I was about to escape with my love.

But I supposed it's Fate. I had to make a choice to free Noah or watch him be killed.

I made my choice. I'd make it again.

I only hope one day he understands.

The ghost wolf at my feet sighs. He's a giant, twice as big as my wolf. Larger than Noah's, too–possibly the biggest wolf I've ever seen. Certainly the biggest ghost wolf I've ever seen. He must have had a strong will and a lot of life energy to cling to this realm so strongly. And also unfinished business. I wonder who he was, but don't say anything to him. Talking to him will pull him more to this realm, and I want him to continue his transition to the beyond if his soul so chooses.

But if I had to name him... Hugh? He looks like a Hugh.

The giant wolf's ears prick up, and he hauls himself to his feet. He doesn't bare his teeth or growl but stands between me and the door facing it.

A second later, footsteps ring out on the flagstones in the hall. I strain to hear, but there's no rustling of other prisoners, no moaning. I must be in an isolated area. Aiden doesn't want me close to other prisoners. He thinks I'm more powerful than I am.

Or maybe I'm the one who's confused. I was trained to be Seeress all my life. I walk beyond the veil. I am powerful; maybe it's time I acted like it.

My strength isn't in teeth and claws; it's different. It's more.

What would Oma do? No, what would Aster do? What would a shifter loved by a mate like Noah do?

The thought gives me strength when the door swings open, and Aiden walks in.

The room fills with his Alpha power. But I remain seated on the floor, relaxed in my meditation pose. The ghost wolf, Hugh, bristles. He stands as if ready to block Aiden from me, and even though he's not corporeal, it feels nice to have a protector.

Aiden glares down at me. He doesn't look great. His black suit and blond hair are immaculate, but his face is thinner, the shadows under his eyes, darker.

"Seeress," he sneers down at me. I taste his aura, but it's the same, a turbulent black storm with the occasional flash of red lighting. There's a red tint to the black storm. I wonder if he's dosing himself with whatever poison he's giving the Alpha Forces. If he has, it hasn't turned his eyes red...yet.

Between us, Hugh growls. The sound makes me smile.

Shock flashes over Aiden's face. He hides it immediately, probably because any human emotion was beaten out of him by the brute of his father.

I need to remember that whatever was done to me, Aiden knew worse torture and from a younger age.

And he's not even the true Alpha. Noah is. I can drop

that bombshell at any time, make the Warden complicit, and ensure all our deaths.

"It's so good to have you back with us," Aiden continues.

"Sarcasm is the lowest form of wit," I retort. I read that in a book somewhere. "And it doesn't become you. You're the Alpha, Aiden. Act like it."

His eyes flash silver at my chiding tone. I really do sound like Oma.

"Tell me why I shouldn't have you killed."

I shrug. "If Fate wants me dead, I will die. But I have visions yet to see."

"You're a traitor to this pack."

More power gathers in me. It feels like...Noah's alpha power. Was this what Oma siphoned from Odin?

"You See so little it might as well be nothing." Aiden might rip out my tongue for this, but fuck it. I'm going to keep lecturing him, Oma-style. It's too much fun. "I am the Seeress. I walk beyond the veil. You cannot order me around like one of your Soulless."

He blinks at the word Soulless.

"That's what your Alpha Forces are, aren't they? Soulless. You've poisoned them to make them more powerful, more compliant." I sniff. "I thought you might be better than your father, but I was wrong."

"I am nothing like my father," Aiden's voice rings out, painfully loud. Hugh's fur stands on end, and the ghost wolf lets out a sharp bark.

Aiden doesn't like being compared to his father? Interesting. I can use that to steer his actions toward good. Or use it to attack him. Either way, he revealed something about himself, and I have a weapon to use against him. And he knows it because he goes cold again.

"I allowed myself to be taken," I say. I'm telling the truth; I wanted to go with Noah. "And in doing so, learned much about the enemy pack." Also true but not because I planned to betray Noah. Because I planned to stay with him.

"You betrayed us."

"I betrayed *him*," I swallow down the pain. "And then I returned."

Aiden can't deny I allowed myself to be taken by his Alpha Force. I rejected Noah and sent him away. "It was a test of Fate, and I passed." I spread my hands as if to say, *and now I'm here.*

He has to believe me when I say it was all part of Fate's plan. What does he know about Fate's plan, anyway?

I hold all the power here. And if he kills me, then I die knowing I protected my love until my last breath.

Let death come, I tell my wolf. In front of me, Hugh whines. Lightning is flickering along his ghostly form, and I can see the clear markings of his fur—midnight black with some white hairs around his face. He still doesn't have eyes, but in the empty sockets, there's a bright amber glow.

"It all went according to plan," I say. I hold the certainty in my heart to make my words true. Because it did all go according to plan—Fate's plan. I got out with Noah. And when the time came, I made my choice to save him.

Now I will use whatever power I have left to stop Aiden and the Warden. Save the acolytes. Do what I can to guide my pack from injustice to justice, from war to peace.

"Now we will host the Alpha Rites, and I will give myself over to the power. And I will give you a vision that will guide you for ages."

"What makes you think I would let you out of this cell?" Aiden's eyes are flashing silver. His wolf is going wild. Right in front of him, Hugh is bristling like he's ready to pounce. Maybe Aiden's wolf senses the ghost wolf?

"I will have a vision whether I am in the Cradle or not," I shrug. "If you are afraid of my power, Alpha, then by all means, keep me under lock and key. The full moon brings me power no matter what. I walk the veil even if my body is chained."

"You will be chained, then. Your body will suffer silver bonds until I free you from them."

"Do what you will. If that's what it takes for you to feel safe, then so be it." I smile as I taunt him. Silver chains will burn wherever they touch my skin, but whatevs. I've survived pain and discomfort many times before. "But never forget, Alpha, that I do not live to serve you. I live to serve this pack, and I seek the wisdom beyond the veil, so I might lead us all according to Fate's plan. One day, you and I will die. But the pack will still remain." And I will guide the pack towards good, I vow. I sense the Grandmothers nodding and whispering their approval.

Just let Noah live, I tell them. *Keep him safe, watch over him. I will give myself over to you, but if you put him in danger, I will slit my own throat. That is the price of my sacrifice.*

The whispers fall silent. The grandmothers know I'm not bluffing. I'm ready to die.

That'll teach them to manipulate me.

"One more thing, Alpha," I let my voice boom in the small cell. "No harm shall fall on the three acolytes in your care. They are innocent. They were led astray, but I allowed it. It was a test of Fate to see if they are worthy of bearing an Alpha. They are not, but Fate still requires them for its plan."

"Insubordination must be punished."

"Then punish them like wayward pups. They are mere children. They can be rehabilitated. Send them to Moon Hollow to tend the gardens, meditate, and pray. In a few years, they will be tested again. If they are not worthy then, do as you will." Before then, I will find a way to free them, if I have to die doing it.

I have nothing more to lose.

"I should kill them and make an example of them."

"If you do, a curse will fall on this pack, a curse so great not even a thousand Alpha rites will lift it," I decree. There's a roll of psychic thunder. Hugh plants his haunches on the blood-stained stone floor, throws back his huge head and howls.

There's no sound, but Aiden must sense something because he goes still, watching me as if I'm an adder, waiting to strike.

"I will spare the acolytes, if you tell me who killed Vera."

"It doesn't matter. Fate was done with her," I say. I hold out my hand and Hugh trots over to me to sniff my fingers and take a little more power. Light pulses from my fingertips, gilding his fur. Every pulse makes his form less translucent. I wonder if he'll eventually absorb so much that he'll be corporeal.

After a moment, Hugh curls his giant body at my feet and relaxes, letting out a sigh. I close my eyes, letting peace flow through me.

I can feel Aiden seething by the door but continue to ignore him. He doesn't matter. I've said what I need to say.

Almost. Before I let myself drift into the void, I give him one last message. "Vera got what was coming to her. Whoever sows death, reaps it. You'd do well to remember that."

Chapter Twenty-Two

oah

We pile out of Sully's SUV in front of the Blackthroat mansion. The three she-wolves with me are wearing my shirts as dresses, with no footwear or even pants to cover up. They vibrate with tension. The stench of their fear fills my nostrils.

The war between the Blackthroats and Adalwulfs has been so bad that wolves are afraid to step on the opposing pack's land, even when brought by invitation of a pack member.

Brick and Madi come outside to meet us. Brick wears a snarl, but before he can say anything, Madi speaks.

"Come in," she welcomes us, throwing open the door and gesturing.

To me, she signs, *Aster, where?*

I shake my head, and her eyes round in dismay.

I give her an abbreviated hug while keeping my gaze on Brick, whose air is dangerous.

"Alpha," I say, attempting to show respect, even though I've done nothing but disrespect him and his pack all along.

Guilt weighs against the gratitude I feel that showing up here is even still an option.

"Not your alpha." He bares his teeth.

"We beg sanctuary. This is my mother, Liora, and my sister, Oriana. And Sophie, another acolyte set to be bred."

Horror registers on Madi's face, and she beckons them in.

"Liz, please find clothing for our guests," Madi says to the servant I recognize from the meal we had.

Liz's eyes flash amber, like she wants to fight them, and her lips close in a thin line, but she inclines her head. "Of course, Luna."

She leads the females away, and Sully and I follow Brick and Madi to Brick's office.

Brick turns on Sully. "You helped them."

Sully averts his gaze and shows his throat, but his words surprise me. "You knew I would."

Brick gives him a frown, but that seems to be the end of his rebuke because he looks at me. "What happened to your mate?"

The word *mate* momentarily rocks me on my feet. My breath knocks out of me. The cage threatens to open and let loose the violent storm of emotion I've compressed inside.

"She chose the Adalwulfs," I say.

Madi's eyes widen. "What do you mean? What happened?"

I don't want to remember it. If I remember it, everything will come out of the cage.

I don't want to think about Aster ever again.

It's too hard for me to speak right now. The grief soaks me. I sign without words, not caring if they understand it all. *We were being chased through the woods. Liora wanted to get all of the acolytes out, but we lost some of them. The rest of them shifted to run.*

I stop. The rest is too painful.

Brick and Madi stare at me.

What? Madi opens her palms, shrugging.

I suck in a ragged breath.

Fuck, it hurts.

Aster had a vision.

The vision was important. That's what changed everything.

She thought she'd lost her Sight mating me. I force a swallow. *She believed she had to remain a virgin.*

Madi makes the barfing sign, and I realize the misogyny tied up with that notion. It was probably all a lie to keep her devoted to an alpha who wasn't going to mate her. Sort of how Catholic nuns wear wedding rings as "brides of Christ."

A wave of sickness washes over me, and the floor seems to shift beneath my feet.

My poor mate. Manipulated...

No. I can't think of that. She made her choice. My hands clench into fists at my sides. *She had a vision, and then she said she had to stay.* I need to get through this conversation, so we can move on to practicalities. Getting safely out of New York. Figuring out what will happen to Sophie, the other girl we rescued. Maybe the Blackthroats will take her in if she doesn't want to come with us.

"What was the vision?" Brick asks.

Fuck! Can we not drop this?

I shake my head. *I don't know.*

Her visions are usually warnings? Madi signs. *Like the one with me and Vera?*

"Vera is dead," I speak out loud to tell Brick, hoping we can shift topics. "Madi is safe."

Brick's eyes glow amber, and he flashes his teeth. "Good."

"But are they warnings, Noah?" Madi persists. "Did she get a warning that she needed to stay back, so you could get out?"

That thought makes me want to tear the office apart with my claws.

Liora suggested something similar.

I shake my head in frustration. *She said she couldn't be my mate.*

"But was that to make you leave her?" Madi just keeps poking at my wound. The cage is rattling now. Vibrating from the intensity of holding everything down on lock.

I want to storm out of the office. Leave this fucking conversation. But the insult to Brick and his mate would be too great. I'd never make it out the door.

I can't speak or sign.

"Maybe she knew she had to stay back to buy you time to get your mom and sister out," Madi suggests.

I feel like I'm bleeding from every pore.

Brick walks over to me, a look of sympathy in his gaze. I must not be masking my instability as well as I'd hoped. He drops a hand on my shoulder. "Would you do anything to save your mate if she were under threat?"

It's like my gut has been punched so hard my stomach is stuck under my ribs. I manage a nod.

"Even hurt her to make her leave and get to safety?"

My vision flickers. Suddenly, I hear the chatter of a thousand voices in my head. Whispers twining in and over each other—too many for me to understand any of them.

Goosebumps stand up on my arms and crawl across the back of my neck.

Is this...who Aster called the Grandmothers? Are they speaking to me now?

Excruciating pain lances through my head. This must be how Aster feels. Maybe now that we're mated, there's a thread to connect the magic between us.

Like the alpha bond.

The one she's supposed to complete with Aiden.

"My mate," I croak, dropping to my knees. I clutch my head, trying to make the blinding pain stop.

I suddenly see Aster, my beautiful starlight. She's in a filthy prison cell. Aiden is screaming something at her, but she seems unperturbed.

Then, just like the dreams I used to have with her, she looks right at me. Like she sees me, *seeing her.*

I love you, she signs.

Suddenly the clamoring stops. The pain lifts. My eyes fly open as it all becomes clear.

My mate needs me, and I've been acting like a fucking man-child with my head stuck up my ass.

I look up at Brick and do the one thing I've resisted my entire life.

"Alpha," I say. "I need your help."

Chapter Twenty-Three

N*oah*

"The only way I would declare war on my enemy would be to aid a member of my own pack."

My heart thuds against my breastbone.

I can't decide if he's telling me no and throwing it in my face that I played this all wrong, or if he's demanding my fealty.

I hope it's the latter.

"I am yours." I show my throat.

He makes me suffer, staring down at me for a long moment before he offers me a hand and tugs me to stand. "Welcome to the pack." He pulls me in for a grim bro-hug, thumping my back once before releasing me.

Madi stands on tiptoe to pull me in for a hug, too. "I'll get the team to strategize," she signs and says when we pull apart, going to the door.

"In the dining room." Brick ushers me out. "We'll need food. This is going to take some brainpower."

A few minutes later, Nickel, Sully, Vance, Billy, Brick, and Madi gather around the giant table in the elegant Blackthroat living room.

"Our newest pack member requires our assistance," Brick announces, attempting to sign as he speaks. "His mate has been taken by our enemy."

I expect one of them to say something about how my mate *is* the enemy, but no one does. Nor does anyone seem to begrudge my late admittance to their pack.

For the second time tonight, a mixture of guilt and gratitude close my throat.

What happened? Billy signs.

He was the first to learn ASL to communicate with me. Madi mastered it in college–no doubt along with several other languages. I got the sense that Billy's competitive side didn't like her knowing something he didn't. The two of them had a rough start, mainly because Billy hated humans. Brick nearly shut him out of the pack for rejecting Madi. Then he had to get over his bias fast when Fate smacked *him* with a human mate.

I explain our near capture and how Aster turned back. "Aster is their prisoner. The Adalwulfs plan to bind her to their alpha during a Blood Bonding ritual under the lunar eclipse tomorrow," I explain. "It supposedly creates a psychic connection with Aiden, so she receives visions for the highest good of the pack. Aiden wanted the moonstone tiara I stole from the museum for the ritual."

The housekeepers bustle in with platters of cold cuts, cheese, olives, and bread.

"Should we invite the Moonborn females to this conversation?" Sully asks Blackthroat. "They've been living there. They might have insight."

Brick nods, and Sully gets up, returning a few moments later with Liora, Oriana, and Sophie.

I get up and pace behind the table, my wolf too wound up to sit. "My accomplice has the moonstone tiara. We were planning to return it to the Mayan people. I could offer to trade it for Aster."

"That won't work. They want the tiara for Aster to wear," Liora points out. "But they might allow you to trade it for Violet, Lupe, and June. The young ones who didn't get out will be sentenced to death... or sacrificed in the Alpha Rites."

"Then it's settled," Brick says. "Call your accomplice and get the tiara."

What if Aster meant it when she said she didn't want to be your mate? Oriana signs.

I give her a tight smile. *Aster just shared a vision with me.*

Oriana's eyes widen.

She's waiting for me to come for her.

* * *

Noah

The morning of the lunar eclipse, the sky is streaked red and purple. There's a heaviness to the air, and in my mind, I sense vibrations like thunder. It's not the weather, it's a psychic sense.

I try to reach for Aster and get nothing. I reach for calm and try to send it her way. I doubt it's working, but it makes me feel better.

After breakfast, Catherine Adalwulf, Brick's mom, takes my mother and sister out for a walk in the Blackthroat gardens. There are guard wolves everywhere, and that's the only thing that keeps me from escorting them.

I gather with Brick, Madi, and the pack's top wolves in the dining room. Everyone looks serious and stressed. The tension turns the air into mud. We're working on the plan for tonight.

"Noah," Madi waves to get my attention and signs, "Your friend is here."

"What's up, party people?" Esme walks in with her arms spread like she's ready to hug all of us. She's wearing a worn Pink Floyd t-shirt with her usual leather jacket and skin tight black jeans.

I greet her with a hug. "Nice shirt."

"I know, right? Dark Side of the Moon. Get it? Because of the lunar eclipse."

Is this the thief? Brick asks, signing clumsily.

Esme gives him a winning smile. "Don't worry, Alpha. I'm off duty." She tosses me a small leather pouch. I peer inside, and the tiara sparkles at me.

"Don't let it out," Esme instructs. "It's not happy about being hidden away. It wants to come out and wreak havoc."

Madi's eyes go wide. "How do you know?"

I've got a bit of clairtangency. Esme signs fluidly. *Runs in my family.*

"Who's your family?" Billy asks.

"Montaigu. You may have heard of us. We're famous. Well, infamous. Is Nicholas Twylton-Wickham Cavendish the Seventh here?"

Nickel steps forward.

"It's possible my great-great-grand uncle stole a Tudor brooch from your ancestors at the turn of the last century. Sorry about that." She whirls away from Nickel and rubs her hands together, looking excited. "So what's the plan, man?"

"We want you, as a neutral party, to make contact with the Adalwulfs," Brick says and signs, looking grim. "Offer them the deal: the tiara in exchange for their three virgin sacrifices. Tell them your witch cult wants them for a sacrifice of your own or something."

"Okay, sure." Esme wriggles her fingers and then holds up my cellphone. She must have picked my pocket during the hug. "Oh, not this one." She winks and tosses it back with a quick, "Sorry. Habit."

It's fine, I sign back. And it is–I'm used to it.

Brick gives her the number, and she makes the call to Aiden.

Esme turns her back, pacing as she speaks, so I can't read her lips, but Madi interprets for me. *I wish to speak to your alpha,* she signs. *Well, give him a message. I have something he wants. Ancient Mayan. Sparkly moonstones.*

Tell your alpha to call this number if he wants to make a trade. She pivots and grins at me as she ends the call with a dramatic punch of her finger.

The room falls silent as we wait.

"How long do you think it will take?" Madi says and signs.

"Not long," Brick says.

"Is anyone bored yet? I can do tricks." Esme pulls a deck of ancient looking Tarot cards from her pocket and spreads them in her hands. "Pick a card, any card," she offers to Nickel.

Pass, he signs.

She pivots and offers it to Madi, who seems more willing to play along. Madi plucks a card that shows a stone tower getting struck by lightning and set on fire.

"Hmm, the Tower, very interesting. Looks like some old structures are coming down."

"Hey British, are you a duke? A werewolf duke?" Esme cocks a hip, looking Nickel up and down.

Jake leans in, grinning. "As a matter of fact, his family wants him to marry an heiress, so he's eligible to inherit the title."

"Duke?" Esme's dark eyes sparkle.

"Viscount." Nickel looks unamused.

Esme snaps her fingers. "That's right, British, I have something for you." She shows her empty palm and then with some sleight of hand, the Tower card appears. "Oops not that." She tucks it away and points to Nickel. "Check your right pocket."

He does and pulls out an ornate gold brooch with a big red stone in the middle.

"There's your brooch. If anyone asks, you found it in some furs stored in a wardrobe. Must have gotten lost."

Nickel stares at the brooch, looking stunned.

"You're welcome." Esme turns away. Her gaze snaps to her phone, and she brings it to her ear.

"Alpha!" A brilliant smile lights her face. "I knew you'd call." She holds the phone away from her ear, wincing, like he's yelling at her.

Her lips are blocked by the phone, so I can only partially read them, but Madi interprets again. *Here's my offer: the tiara in exchange for all the young virgins you plan to sacrifice tonight during the lunar eclipse. I have a better use for them.*

Esme holds the phone away from her ear again. *Five o'clock tonight at the gate to your property. Be there or be square.* She gives another dramatic punch of her finger to end the call. "Done." She grins at me. "What's the endgame?"

You get the acolytes to safety while I free Aster, my mate, I sign.

"We just need some sleight of hand. Maybe we run a Maltese Falcon. Or a Bohemian Rhapsody." Esme frowns.

I shake my head. *I have a better plan,* I sign.

Chapter Twenty-Four

I snarl at the searing pain of my fur and skin burning beneath a silver choke chain. My hackles are raised, shoulders hunched as Esme drags me forward on a leash. My paws skid in the soft earth. Saliva drips from my bared teeth as I growl. My vision blurs from the toxic proximity of the silver to my eyes.

I scent hordes of male Adawulfs and beneath it, the scent of a female. Not Aster, though.

The iron gates to the Adalwulf property swing open where fifty Adalwulf soldiers flank their alpha and the Warden in battle formation.

One young she-wolf dressed in a gossamer slip huddles behind the men.

My wolf is too debilitated from the silver assault to read lips, but I feel the blast of Aiden's ragey energy as he confronts Esme. Something like, "...fuck are you?" He points at me. "And who is he?"

She yanks on the chain, dragging me up to heel. I snarl

and toss my head, fighting the cruel lead. Esme beckons the acolyte forward. I catch her lips forming the word "others?"

Aiden snaps a hand out to grasp Esme's throat, but instantly drops her, shaking his reddened palm.

Silver dust. That's probably what's smarting my eyes.

His soldiers lunge forward, but he holds a hand up to stop them, more wary now.

Esme's unperturbed, shaking her head with a smirk. I blink hard to focus on her face, so I can follow the conversation. "Give me the girl." She beckons the acolyte forward again.

"Give me the tiara." Aiden shows his teeth.

Esme pulls it out from the pouch tied to her belt loop and drops it on her own head. "Girl first. Then you get your prize."

The wolves shove the terrified girl forward.

Esme takes the tiara off and tosses it like she's tossing a frisbee for a dog. A grouping of soldiers all lunge to catch it and pass it to the Warden, who examines it, then nods.

"I brought you another offering." Esme pulls up on the leash, dragging me up on my paws to choke my breath. I wheeze, my eyes bulging.

Aiden looks at me with disdain. "He's not mine."

"No, but this is the wolf who marked your Seeress." Her smile is maniacal.

The Warden and Aiden slo-mo turn as one to take me in.

I show my teeth and lunge at them, and Esme yanks me back. The silver choke-chain cuts into my flesh.

"What do you want?" Aiden asks.

I try to read her lips. "...gift to you. ...show...faith. My coven seeks a partnership...your pack."

"...steal from us...good faith?" The Warden shows his teeth at her.

I don't know what he says, but Aiden blasts him with Alpha Command, and the Warden shuts his mouth.

"What coven?" Aiden demands.

"The Montaigus."

Aiden stares at her a moment longer then reaches for the leather handle of my leash. "Give him to me."

I dig my paws into the dirt and make him drag me, like I don't want to be taken to their dungeon. Like I'm not hoping to be brought right to my mate.

Like this wasn't my plan all along.

* * *

Aster

My cell door clangs open, and Hugh leaps to his feet, snarling.

I take my sweet time opening my eyes.

"Get up," the Warden rasps. He's in white ceremonial robes. His raccoon face paint is fresh, with the added emphasis of lines and dots on his forehead and cheeks. "It's time."

I don't make any move to rise. "What about the acolytes?"

"They have been found unworthy. They will be punished and kept in confinement until the next Alpha Rite."

Phew. At least I saved them, for now.

I told Aiden nothing about where I've been and why. Only that I've been following the guidance of the Grand-mothers, which I know unnerved him. It's one thing to believe one of your key pack members has gone rogue. A rogue member can be tortured. Punished. Starved and forced into submission.

It's another thing to believe the Grandmothers are working against you, the supposed alpha of the pack.

I've been meditating, cultivating stillness. I've made it clear to the Grandmothers I won't be doing anything that puts my mate in danger, but I am open to their advice and help. I can feel them considering this. They haven't said anything yet, but I feel the rumbling of psychic thunder, the heaviness to the spring air. Tonight's lunar eclipse will be a massive portal for power.

I only wish I knew what to do with it.

I stand, keeping my face serene.

Come, I sign to Hugh.

The ghost wolf stands at my heel.

Talk to me, Grandmothers, I demand. They owe me their guidance.

Perhaps they were demanding only my sacrifice to pack. For me to get up on the altar and be alpha bonded to Aiden. Or worse, bred by the alphas of the pack. Maybe that was the reason they warned me what would happen if I left with Noah. To ensure my compliance. Now that they have it, they have no need to guide me anymore.

But it doesn't matter what happens to me. All that matters is that Noah and his family are safe.

But why guide Noah to rescue me from the tower? Was it just for me to help him get his mother and sister out?

It seems so cruel to bring my mate to me only to rip both our hearts out when I leave him.

I gasp.

What if they brought us together so that Noah–the true alpha born of the Alpha Rites–would be the one to breed me?

That thought brings tears to my eyes.

Could there be life growing inside me already? I put a hand to my belly, but of course I don't feel anything there. It's too early. And I might not be pregnant at all.

A bittersweet pain spears me. Part of me hopes beyond all hope that I am already pregnant with Noah's pup. But raising a child without him, raising a future alpha of this twisted pack, pitches me into an ocean of hopelessness.

Really, Grandmothers? Am I just to be bred and denied my mate's companionship like Catherine Adalwulf endured with Bruce Blackthroat? Destined to murder her own mate to ensure the safety of the pack?

Disgust stirs in an oily lump in my gut.

I step out of the cell and into the hall, and I get a whiff of a familiar scent. Shock ripples through my body.

No.

Please, Grandmothers, no, I pray because I have no one else to turn to.

Why is my mate here?

Hugh presses against me, and I'm grateful for his ghostly reassurance even though it feels like a cold hand pressing against my leg, chilling me. I fight to keep my voice even. "Is someone else here?"

The Warden gives me a cruel smile. "Yes. A new prisoner. One you know. Rather intimately, I believe."

Trembling starts in my legs, traveling up through my trunk, straight to my teeth. I bite down to keep them from chattering.

"Tonight, your punishment for defiling your body will be to watch the male who took your virginity bleed out at your feet."

My heart stops. I can't breathe. Can't suck air into my vibrating lungs.

Noah.

No!

He was supposed to be safe, with his family. Why is he here?

I school my face, so I don't look horrified. The Warden is watching my face closely, gloating a little. I need to remain calm, so I can figure out how to get Noah out of this.

My heart pounds in my chest. I want to be sick. He wasn't supposed to be here!

He'll never leave us, my wolf whispers. *Mate.*

I let her calm surround me, even as my brain scrambles to search for a solution. At least I know he's still alive.

"You proved yourself to be unworthy of your calling," the Warden is saying. He's like a buzzing mosquito, and with all his war paint on, he looks like a clown.

"The Grandmothers have orchestrated it all," I say and stare him down. My eyes burn, but I am the Seeress. Guided by the Grandmothers. The Warden is nothing but a pale poser clawing for scraps of the magic I wield.

Finally, he looks away. He snarls, but I don't flinch. I just won that dominance game, and now I'm going to win the war.

When we arrive at the Celestial Cradle, the red moon has risen. I feel the power along the ley lines running through the Cradle, and also the sense of hollowed ground. But I also feel the taint of what Oma, Odin, and the Warden have wrought in this land, the violence and bloodshed. The Earth is unconcerned with death because death is part of life. Even the Grandmothers agree on that.

If death is what's in store for me, I am willing to die tonight.

But there's no way I will allow them to kill my mate.

* * *

Noah

I stayed in wolf form the entire time they tortured me. I had hoped to be taken to the dungeon where I would escape, find Aster, and get the fuck out of here.

Unfortunately, I've had at least six wolves on me at all times, including Aiden and the Warden.

Aiden used all the Alpha Command he could wield, but I refused to shift. Even when they nearly choked the life out of me with the silver choke collar. I do pretend to be hurt worse than I am, making a show of hanging my head and staggering on my paws.

I had Esme use real silver because I knew they would never buy that I was her prisoner unless they saw real suffering.

I don't give a fuck about the pain. It's nothing compared to the anguish of losing my mate. I was an idiot to let her sacrifice herself for me, but it won't happen again.

This time, I'm doing the sacrificing.

One of the links of the choke collar has a catch. All I have to do is shift to human form and unlatch it to get myself free, but when I read the Warden's lips about sacrificing me in front of Aster, I decide to bide my time and wait until then. As soon as I have eyes on my mate, I trust I will know what to do.

It's a weak plan, but it's all I've got. Getting myself battered isn't ideal, but I'm trusting my wolf will pull out all the reserves of energy and power for Aster.

They drag me out, bloody and beaten. The hallway is filled with red-eyed wolves, lurking in man form. There's something off about them. I can sense a red tinge to the air around them—maybe their auras?

They lead me to the forest.

The Warden walks in front of me. Two red-eyed enforcers drag me in chains behind him. A crowd of hundreds of wolves in human form part as we come through. I smell excitement, anticipation, fear, wonder. Some horror. This pack is used to violent spectacles. A part of them probably craves it—as long as they're not the ones suffering.

Through my paws on the earth, I sense the pulse of a steady beat. A drum, perhaps. The ritual has begun.

I peer through the blood dripping in my eyes to the black obsidian altar nestled at the base of the Celestial Cradle.

A surge of electricity runs through my body and every bit of fur that's not matted with blood or silver dust on me stands on end.

My mate.

My beautiful mate stands like some ethereal goddess on the altar. Aster appears unharmed, dressed in a filmy white robe with the moonstone tiara on her head. Power and magic emanate from her.

For a horrible moment, I wonder if I was wrong to come. If she did, indeed, mean to take her rightful place by Aiden's side and forsake me as her mate.

The Warden climbs up beside Aster and points at her feet. The enforcers heave me up on the cold stone.

The Warden addresses the throng. I don't watch his lips. Instead, I stare up at Aster, my heart balanced on the tip of an ice pick.

She doesn't look at me. Her face is a serene mask. I don't even scent fear on her. I just feel power vibrating from her.

Something cold shimmers beside her. If I narrow my lids, I can make out the edges of a large wolf guarding her.

A spirit, perhaps? One of the Grandmothers?

A soft energy blankets me. My pain disappears. Wounds close–even beneath the silver chain. Whether Aster is feeding energy into me or just being near her is healing, I can't be sure. I still don't know for certain what Aster wants.

Either way, the moment is now. I need to figure out if Aster wants saving and start fighting my way out of here if I'm going to survive.

Except I'm realizing my plan is total shit. I'm surrounded by hundreds of enemy wolves. I don't see how we're going to get out of this alive. Esme and Sully worked out an escape route for us but even if Aster wants saving, it's the two of us against maybe five hundred wolves.

But I plan to go down fighting. They sure as fuck won't be binding my mate to another male today.

The moon begins to disappear behind a dark swathe of clouds.

The Warden produces a long curved obsidian blade with a jagged edge. He grasps my scruff to lift my hanging head and bare my throat. "Time to atone for your sins, Seeress."

* * *

Aster

Oh fate, Noah.

Grandmothers, no!

I flick my hand to signal Hugh, and the ghost wolf charges. He's incorporeal, but when his ghostly form leaps through the Warden, the man staggers back a step. His face under his absurd face paint leaches of all color.

The power of the eclipse pours into me, activating the

moonstone in the tiara and cycling through every energy center in my body.

Noah seizes the moment, sinking his teeth into the Warden's hand and snapping his head to send the knife flying.

The ghost wolf lands easily on the ground behind the Warden, shaking like he just got wet.

The Warden doubles over, the whites of his eyes flashing. He literally doesn't know what hit him.

With lightning speed, Noah shifts and somehow swiftly unlatches the cruel silver collar.

He grabs my hand, and I gasp at the power that surges between our hands.

The Alpha Bonding.

The rite I was supposed to complete with Aiden under the eclipse is happening now. *With Noah.*

Because *he's* the true Adalwulf alpha.

The first-born pup from the Alpha Rites years ago.

This is why the Grandmothers orchestrated his appearance here in the Celestial Cradle at this exact moment. It's why they brought us together to fall in love and mate. Why they then wrenched us apart to experience the anguish of losing each other. We each had to follow our personal journeys to get here. Had to know heartbreak and feel a love so pure we would sacrifice our own peace and sanctity, or even our own lives to save one another.

They played us both like puppets, so Noah would risk everything to show up to rescue me here in this moment.

Magic pours into me from Noah. Alpha power. A deep sense of calm. The steely spine of leadership. Our powers mingle, weaving his ferocity with my Sight. I cling to him like he's a lifeline. Because he is. He is my hope and my salvation, and when I'm with him, I feel like I can do anything.

The Warden, Aiden, and all his enforcers freeze, staring at us. Immobilized.

The magic pulses between us, following the cadence of the beating drums. A golden light surrounds us. I turn my face up to the eclipse to receive the blessing of the Moon Goddess. The moonstone tiara channels a bolt of power straight through my body and into Noah's.

The dais we stand upon cracks in half, just as the moon reemerges, bathing Noah in light.

He's in exactly the position Oma described to the Warden when she shared her vision of the pup with no ears, straddling two halves of the broken dais.

Suddenly, I know what to do.

"This wolf is your true alpha!" I lift our joined hands in victory, like he's a boxer who's just won a fight. "It's time for the truth to come out." I shout over the pounding drums. The wind whips my hair, and I raise my free hand, commanding attention as only a Seeress can. "The last Seeress prophesied this moment."

"Kill them!" Aiden snaps.

His enforcers don't move, seemingly frightened or mesmerized by the magic I wield.

I go on. "Aiden was never the true alpha chosen by the Grandmothers. He was not the first born after the Alpha Rites" I let the wind carry my voice to the edges of the land. I don't need to shout, though, because every wolf but Noah can hear what I'm saying. There are gasps and murmurs as I proclaim to Aiden, "You're not the true alpha of the pack."

Chapter Twenty-Five

ster

The drumbeat stops. No one else makes a sound. They're all processing what I just told them. Aiden's eyes blaze, but he remains still, his face a ferocious mask.

"The Warden and the last Seeress developed the Alpha Rites to choose the next alpha because Odin could not produce an heir." I point at the Warden, whose mouth is open as if he's being strangled. His clown makeup makes his angry face look ridiculous. "The Grandmothers marked the next alpha as the first-born pup after the Alpha Rites. Odin believed that pup was Aiden, but it was not. Liora's son, Noah, was the first-born."

"Lies," the Warden shouts. The sound is lost in the rippling roar of all the wolves present, clamouring for the truth. "She's lying!" His voice cracks. Anyone looking at his expression would see his fear as he takes in Noah, as if for the first time.

He's been looking for the wolf with no ears for years and still didn't recognize he was Noah.

"I am the Seeress." I grip Noah's hand for strength. "I walk beyond the veil. Listen to my words or suffer the consequences."

"Oma wanted to kill the first-born pup because he was born without hearing, but Liora sneaked him out, and the Warden looked the other way."

"Seize them," Aiden orders his red-eyed wolves, flicking his hands towards the Warden and us. The enforcers secure the Warden but stop short of the dais when Noah growls. Hugh stands between us and them, his teeth bared and tail lashing his legs. The enforcers can't see him, but they must feel something strange and dangerous because they stop in their tracks.

"Stop!" Noah's voice carries the timbre of Alpha Command, and the enforcers freeze. "I didn't come for your pack. I don't want to be alpha. I just want to leave with my mate." His eyes search mine, as if looking for my agreement.

Of course, he would doubt me after what I told him when we parted.

I nod.

His eyes shine. He turns back to Aiden. "Let her go, and you'll never see us again."

"I *am* the chosen Alpha," Aiden snarls at me. "I am Odin's son." He has to save face in front of the pack.

I face him, speaking more softly. "He tried to make you as cruel as him, but you get to choose." The crowd's murmurs die away until there's silence in the Cradle. I say to all of them, "We all get to choose. If you choose cruelty, then life will not be kind to you. But it doesn't have to be that way. You can choose to make this pack better."

No one makes a sound. Noah's moved to my side, still holding my hand. Supporting me, as he always does. I can feel the power of the tiara pulsing around us. It feels like a prowling animal, ready to strike.

Please let them listen to me. Please allow my mate to live.

"The Adalwulfs will reign now and for all time, with me as their Alpha." Aiden fixes his eyes on Noah. "Fate has delivered me a solution. Once I sacrifice the true Alpha, then I will be next in line."

NO! Power surges through me in a rushing tide. It's white hot and so intense, my eyes water and my teeth ache. A vision rises up in me, straight from the Grandmothers. A Seeing of our pack's future if Aiden leads us where he wants to go.

Show them, the Grandmothers whisper. They're all talking at once, their voices adding to the vision, making it unstoppable.

I'm caught in the psychic tsunami, but Noah's arms around me keep my feet on the ground. The mark on my shoulder spreads warmth through me, helping me find which way is up and which way is down.

Deliver the vision, child. Now!

My own eyes flash bright when I snarl at Aiden, "You wanted a vision? I'll give it to you." I touch my free hand to the tiara, feeling the burn. "Take it. Take it all."

I push the vision towards Aiden and the entire pack. Images of violence and war, our pack lands ravaged, mothers crying over slain pups, red-eyed wolves every-where. Aiden commanding an army of red-eyed enforcers, his own eyes glowing black like a demon's. New York City in flames.

Aiden stiffens and jerks, his eyes fixed on the unseen. It's like lightning struck. Not from the moon, or the sky, but from my own mind, intensified by the tiara. Wolf after wolf convulses, their minds' eyes filled with the horrible images.

The entire pack jerks in unconscious movements, the way I do when in the grip of vision.

I howl, letting the power rush through me. I hold the vision, and Noah holds me, and our Alpha Bond sends power pulsing through the entire pack in a surge so strong it sends Aiden and the Warden to their knees.

My teeth grind together. The only thing keeping me upright is Noah's strong body at my back. I sag into him, letting him hold me.

I got you, he speaks into my mind. His voice is warm and gentle, a relief after the vision scoured my insides. I feel like I just gave birth.

I did it. I let my vision into the world.

It's done.

It's just begun, child.

The wind whips around the Cradle. Pups cry and grown wolves moan.

The only sound is a clacking sound overhead.

The wind whipping around us is from the blades of a black helicopter, descending upon us.

"That's our ride," Noah says.

That does it. I go limp, letting him lift me in his arms. I've got no more energy. I'm done.

Something descends from the belly of the chopper, falling through the air in what feels like slow motion.

It's a long rope ladder. At the top, a slight figure clambers down a few rungs and waves. "Hi, friends!" she calls. She balances with one hand and foot on the ladder, completely at ease. "Looks like you're having a great creepy ritual and all, but it's time to skedaddle. Hang on and we'll pull you up!"

The chopper dips lower until the ladder drags on the ground near the dais.

"Hang on," Noah orders. His muscles flex as he leaps down and rushes towards the chopper.

There's a blur, and a wolf appears between us and our escape.

Aiden. And he has a knife in his hands. He howls, raising the blade, aiming for Noah's throat.

Hugh leaps between us and the blade.

A final surge of lightning flashes from the tiara. I cry out, directing the flow of power as best I can. It blasts in a smooth channel right into Hugh, making his eye sockets blaze bright with amber fire.

The ghost wolf leaps, whirls in midair, and turns on Aiden. I expect him to run through the alpha like he did the Warden, but when his paws hit Aiden's chest, I hear a thump. He crashes into Aiden as a fully corporeal form. Taken by surprise, Aiden tries to fight, but Hugh's already knocked him to the ground. The former ghost wolf opens his jaws and vomits up a ball of blue light straight into Aiden's face.

Aiden's body starts to convulse.

Noah doesn't hesitate, he runs for the ladder. I cling to his neck, so he can free his arms and climb up a few rungs.

"Stop them!" the Warden shouts. He frees himself from the red-eyed wolves and starts to run towards us.

A dark-hooded figure leaps from the crowd and attacks the Warden. Tucked against Noah, I can't see what happens, but in the end, the Warden goes flying into a flock of enforcers, who clamp their arms around him.

The hood falls away from the shadowy figure's head, revealing Sully. Somehow, he must have infiltrated the pack in time for the ritual. "For Moira," he snarls at the Warden. "Next time, I won't miss."

He makes a beeline towards the ladder, leaping atop the

dais and grabbing onto the lowest rung of the ladder just before it swings out of reach. This makes the ladder swing, which makes my stomach swoop. I duck my head, focusing on Noah's strong arms around me. He's got me, he'll never let go.

Above our head, Esme cackles and whoops as the chopper lifts us higher and higher to freedom.

The wind buffets the heck out of me and Noah, whipping my hair over my face. I peek through the strands, sucking in cold air to fight the fear of being suspended on a flimsy rope ladder several hundred feet above the ground.

Below us, the Celestial Cradle glows with the golden light of the torches lit for the ceremony. It gets smaller and smaller as the helicopter gains height, until the wolves look like scurrying ants and the torches are mere spots of light.

And then we're speeding away over the dark forest, leaving behind the pack lands that were my home for so long.

But no longer. I've given up my role as Adalwulf Seeress, forever. I've left my pack, my birthright, behind. That life is over, and this is goodbye.

"You all right?" Noah murmurs in my ear. I cling more tightly to him, and he gives me a reassuring squeeze. I press my face to his bare chest, inhaling his woodsy scent until calm rushes through me. Whatever my destiny, whatever happens next, I'll face it with Noah.

"You lovebirds okay?" Esme shouts.

"We're okay," I shout back. *We're okay,* I mouth again to Noah. He grins, and my mating mark throbs, reminding me I'm his. Reminding me that whenever I'm with him, I'm home.

Chapter Twenty-Six

Noah

I sit behind Aster in a hot bath, leaning back against the marble and slowly dragging a warm washcloth up her thigh. After our dramatic exit by helicopter from the Adalwulf estate, our pilots–three rowdy young werebear mercs Sully brought in–landed the bird at The Blackthroat estate where I carried Aster straight to the en suite bath in our room.

Getting her naked, holding her, keeping our bodies connected skin-to-skin felt like a necessity. Even now, having her in my arms, knowing she truly is mine, the sense of near desperation clings to me.

I still don't understand everything that happened. Even up on that cracked dais, I didn't know whether she'd orchestrated the whole thing to manipulate me into leading her pack, or whether she was just trying to keep us both alive.

I thank the sweet Moon Goddess for the moment she agreed to leave with me, and I could be sure she was the female I thought she was. That what we have together is real. That she loves me and wants to be my mate.

I pick her up and turn her to straddle me, so I can read her lips.

"Aster. Starshine. You nearly killed me when you said you didn't want me as your mate." I sign and speak so that she can learn ASL.

Tears spring to her eyes. "I know." She cups my cheek. "I had to make you leave. I hated hurting you, but I knew it was the only way."

"Why? What did you see?"

I had a vision–" she chokes up. I feel her pain as acutely as if it's my own.

"What was it?"

"Your death. The Grandmothers forced me to go back." A tear streaks her cheek, but she laughs as she wipes it away. "They pulled all the strings, and we both were their puppets. They crowned you as the Adalwulf Alpha and completed the Alpha Bond of Seeress to Alpha. I guess they want you and me to lead the pack."

I stare at her, fully digesting her words. My heart pounds against my chest. "And you were still willing to leave with me?"

Fresh tears spill down her cheeks. "Of course. I don't want to be Seeress anymore. I don't want anything to do with the Adalwulf Pack. All I want is you."

I grasp the back of her head, pulling her mouth to mine. I stroke my lips across hers softly, savoring the sweetness of the moment. She kisses me back, her tongue slipping between my lips.

I love you, starshine, I pull back and sign.

I love you forever, she signs back, moving in for another kiss. My cock lengthens, and she wiggles her hips, rubbing over it.

I groan, my hands moving to her waist. She reaches

between her legs to grasp my cock, rising up and attempting to lower herself onto it. The water in the bath makes it too slick. She giggles when I slip out.

I laugh and reach behind me to pull out the plug, letting the water drain below our hips. Lifting Aster by the waist, I guide her onto my cock. Aster's pouty lips part, and she slowly undulates, taking me deeper, then moving back. She's a goddess, glorious and ethereal. Magical.

And she's all mine.

I grip her hips, urging her deeper. Faster. She bounces over my cock, her breasts dancing, her lovely blonde hair cascading in waves around her slender shoulders. Our mingled breath quickens into panting. I flick my tongue over her nipple as it dances in front of my face, squeeze and knead her lush ass.

"Come for me, starshine." I bring the pad of my thumb to her clit, and she screams. The vibration goes straight to my dick. My balls draw up tight as Aster's inner thighs clamp around my waist, and the tight walls of her channel convulse.

I grip her ass and arch my back as I come, too. My middle finger slides down between the cleft of her ass, pressing against her anus. I feel the vibration of her shriek bounce off the walls of the bathroom as I fill her with my cum.

"Oh Fate. Oh Fate. Oh sweet Moon Goddess," Aster pants, rocking her hips to ring out the last aftershocks of her beautiful orgasm.

I wait until she's complete, then lift her off me and climb out of the tub, wrapping her in a fluffy towel.

I'm not finished with you, I sign, sweeping her up into my arms and carrying her to the bed.

After a second glorious round of sex, I hold her nestled against my body and peer down at her lovely flushed face.

"So, how long have you known?" I sign and speak.

She copies my signs–my brilliant mate, learning ASL so quickly. *Know what?*

"That I was the 'true alpha'? Or did you make that up?"

No, she signs. "When I was a child, I overheard the Warden and Oma talking. She told the Warden he needed to find and kill the deaf wolf pup swapped with Aiden at birth. She'd had a vision of "a wolf with no ears" standing on the cracked dais with the Adalwulf mantle over his shoulders." Aster looks up at me. "When I learned you were Liora's son, born of my pack, I knew you had to be the wolf from her prophecy."

"Because there can't be that many deaf wolves born into the pack?"

"You're the only one I know of."

"Why didn't you tell me?"

A frown appears between her brows. "I don't know. I was still deciding what it all meant–to me, for you, for all of us."

I nod. "That makes sense. You hadn't chosen to mate me yet."

Aster smiles and trails her fingertips along the back of my neck. "My wolf had. I knew you were my destiny–I'd been dreaming about you for so long. I was just a little slow to sort it out." She gives me a slow slide of her lips across mine.

My wolf rumbles with contentment. Having her orange blossom scent in my nostrils and her body beneath mine soothes away the remaining franticness of almost losing her.

"I honestly didn't feel it all come together until the

moment we alpha bonded, and the dais cracked. That's when I realized it was straight out of Oma's prophecy."

I brush her hair back from her lovely face. "You really don't care about leaving your pack?"

Aster smiles. "You're my pack. You're the only pack that matters to me."

"I pledged myself to the Blackthroat pack to get their help rescuing you." I study Aster's face. I don't know how she'll take that news. I know she doesn't trust the Black-throats. She grew up hearing terrible stories about them.

She gasps, her eyes warm. "You're no longer a lone wolf! I'm so glad. You were keeping yourself away from others to your own harm."

"You're right. I...my whole life was spent ensuring I was self-sufficient, so I could infiltrate the Moonborn. I worked my ass off to get an Ivy League education and a job on Wall Street. I mastered total control over my wolf side to never need a pack. But I was willing to throw all of it away for you, starshine."

A wicked grin stretches her lips. "Aiden will hate that he lost his Seeress to the Blackthroats. My magic was the one thing they had that the Blackthroats didn't."

"But what about the Grandmothers? Will they hate it?"

Aster swallows. "I don't know. Part of me wondered..."

What? I sign.

"Maybe they're already planning for the next generation."

I stare at her, trying to decode her words. Finally, it hits me. "Are you pregnant?"

A mysterious look comes over her face. "It's still so early. But...I think so."

Triumph–the triumph I should've felt the moment I grabbed the ladder swinging from the helicopter and lifted off with my mate—surges through me. Pure joy. Victory. Celebration.

I leap off the bed and swing Aster around. She giggles hysterically as I throw her in the air and catch her.

"A pup. Fate, a pup! Nan will be so happy. And my mother...."

It's the first time I've called Liora *mother*, but it feels like she should be included in this celebration. And Oriana. My sister. Our future pup's aunt.

"Let's wait a bit until I'm sure," Aster pleads.

I drop kisses all across her face. Her neck. Her breastbone. "Of course."

I fall back on the bed and pull her on top of me. "So you're moving in with me? You'll live in the city?"

For a moment, a flicker of trepidation crosses her face. She's never known anything but isolation in a cult. She's never held a job. I don't know if she's even been to school.

"I know it will be a big adjustment to live in the city. If Brick gives me my job back, I'll have plenty of money. We could look for a property out of the city. Maybe in New Jersey. Somewhere with a little land, so you don't go nuts."

Aster's eyes go soft again. "I'll be okay. As long as I have you, everything will be fine. We'll figure it out. You're my mate. You're all I need."

"You're all I need, starshine. You're everything to me. I'm sorry I doubted you."

"No. I needed you to doubt me. But thank you for coming for me, anyway."

Always, I sign.

Chapter Twenty-Seven

ster

Brick and Madi threw a big bonfire to welcome us home. Smell of charcoal, charred cedar, and roasting meat. My mouth waters at the platters of pork, beef, chicken, and even venison weighing down each table.

Three of the Blackthroat's friends, werebear triplets named Hutch, Bern, and Canyon flew the helicopter and helped rescue us. They are part of some shifter ops merc team somehow connected to Brick. Apparently, they requested payment in bacon, which is why there are six whole hogs roasting on a spit–two for each of them.

"Mmm, meat," Esme hums. She tugs her hair out of its ponytail and fluffs it until it falls down her back in a silky, curly mass. Instantly, all male attention zeroes in on her, but she seems oblivious. "Anyone up for a hot dog eating contest?"

Across the lawn, the three triplets raise their hands.

Noah snorts. "You're human. You can't out-eat a shifter."

"Watch me."

I sidle up to her and offer her the tiara. Before I let it go, it buzzes against my hand as if excited to greet her. "This isn't mine."

Esme produces a black velvet bag from somewhere and carefully enfolds the tiara inside. "I know, I know. I'm going to get you back to where you belong," she whispers to it and tells us, "I'll make sure *Museo Maya* finds this on their doorstep soon."

All around us, Blackthroat wolves settle in for the meal. Oriana and Liora are seated at the table with the alpha couple and Catherine. It looks like Jake and Nickel and the rest of the Moon Co Bros are entertaining them. There's room at the table for Noah and me and Esme, too.

The gang's all here, except for one. Sully is nowhere to be seen. I want to thank him for all his help, but I suspect he needs some alone time. He seems like he's still grieving Moira, and his vendetta against the Warden has just begun.

I wonder what's happening to Aiden and the Warden. If I were Aiden, I would use this moment to check the Warden's power. But something happened to Aiden when the ghost wolf leaped on him.

I nudge Noah so he'll look at me to read my lips. "Did you see what happened to Hugh?"

"Who?"

"Hugh. The ghost wolf."

"He attacked Aiden and became real again."

"Ghost wolf?" Esme asks, leaning in close. "Was he hot?"

Noah chuckles at Esme's ridiculous question.

"Kind of?" I describe Hugh's wolf and then what happened at the end. "He sort of spat something at Aiden. It looked like a ball of light."

"Interesting," Esme murmurs. "I didn't see it, but my best guess is Hugh died with a beef against Aiden's lineage, and his life force was so strong, his soul was able to hang around. And then the eclipse or maybe the tiara helped him take physical form again."

"That was my guess, too," I say. "But what did he do to Aiden? And if he's back on the physical plane, what does that mean?"

"I can look into that." She accepts a plate of ribs from Liz and rubs her hands together in anticipation.

The barbecue is delicious. I stuff my wolf so full of meat I bet she never feels starved again.

Brick gets up and comes over.

"Alpha," Noah says.

"Yes. We need to make things official," Brick says to Noah.

"I'd like that, Alpha." Noah tilts his head slightly, showing his neck in a sign of respect.

"I want to join too," I say.

"Excellent. We're honored to have both of you. The next run will be at the full moon, and the full induction to the pack will happen then."

Noah accepts fist bumps and backslaps from Jake, Nickel, and the rest of the Moon Co Bros. *One of us,* Billy signs, and it warms my heart seeing Noah stepping into community.

Liora also watches her son with his new packmates with a small, relieved smile. The lines have fallen from her face, and she looks as serene as I remember her being during my childhood.

"You also have pack protection," Brick tells her. "You and Oriana and Sophie."

"Thank you, Alpha," Liora says. "But I think it's time I

returned home. To Kentucky. Oriana wants to meet her Nan, and all her second cousins."

"Sophie would like to stay," Oriana says and signs. Beside her, Sophie blushes and ducks her head.

Catherine leans in, putting her hand on Sophie's shoulder. "You can stay with me. I'd love the company. That is, if you allow it, Alpha."

"I'll allow it if it's what you want, Sophie," Brick says.

"Oh yes, please," Sophie says eagerly. I can imagine it's heartening to have such an elegant older wolf take an interest in your well-being. As a former Adalwulf defector, Catherine is the perfect person to help her adjust to her new pack. "Thank you, Alpha."

"Don't thank me, thank my mother. And mind what she says. Speaking of which, Noah," Brick glares at my mate. Noah doesn't flinch. "I'd like to offer you your job back. On the condition that you submit to punishment for the stunt you pulled at the museum."

"Excuse me, that heist was perfect," Esme mutters, making everyone but Brick and Noah grin–although Noah wouldn't have heard her. I pick up a piece of cornbread and munch on it to hide my smile.

"I accept your offer, Alpha. Thank you."

"Ugh, I was hoping you'd say no, so I could poach you," Madi says as she signs, "I'll make you an offer you can't refuse."

"Maybe I like being a Moon Co Bro." Noah sits back and rests his arm around me.

Madi groans. "Noooooo, not you, too. That office has way too much testosterone." She wrinkles her nose at Brick, who grins back. Brick looks more relaxed than I've ever seen him before, with his arm around his mate's shoulders. Every once in a while, he drops a kiss on her shoulder. Right now, he's resting a hand on her belly as she says, "Aster, as soon as we get back to the city, I'll introduce you to my friend Aubrey, Billy's mate. We can have a ladies' night out. Esme, you're invited too."

"Sweet! I'm in." Esme says.

"Excellent," Madi says. "We can show Aster all the best spots in the city."

"Will you work at Moon Co, too?" Oriana asks me.

Suddenly everyone is looking at me. "I don't know," I gulp, feeling my cheeks heat. "My skills aren't really in the tech field."

"I know of a psychic who runs an investment firm," Jake says. "I'll introduce you if you think stock market stuff might be your thing."

I don't really know what "stock market stuff" would entail, but that's okay. I'll ask Noah later. "I haven't thought about what I want to do. I guess I've just never had a choice before."

"No rush. Take your time," Noah says, and I nod, relaxing against his arm. It's nice knowing no matter what I decide, my mate will support me.

"My family's always looking for help at our antique shop," Esme says. "You'd be good at handling the artefacts, even the feisty ones. But honestly, they're a nightmare to work with. My family, not the artefacts. Forget I said anything."

"But you'd end up with some great stories," Noah says.

"That is true," Esme says, and at everyone's prompting, launches into some of the most fur-raising stories I've ever heard. That goads Jake to tell another weredragon story, and then Nickel shares about his ancestors' exploits involving the royals of England and several other European countries.

By the end, everyone's lying, but we're all laughing too hard to care.

I eat and eat and eat until I can't eat anymore, and then I just sit back, surrounded by my mate and newfound friends and family, and just take it all in. I can see myself doing this for years, no decades to come. And that's not a vision or a premonition. It's just a fact.

"Thank you," I whisper to the Grandmothers. I don't know if I trust them fully, but I do know it's a great gift to hear them. I'll call on them for advice and consider what they say, but from now on, my life and my choices are my own.

And I choose Noah.

By the time the sun's setting, Esme and the triplets are the only ones still eating.

Finally, Esme tosses the bones onto the empty platter. "All's well that ends well," Esme smacks her lips and belches. The three werebear triplets' heads rear up and swivel towards her as one. Their eyes light shifter bright with excitement.

Then they start trying to out-burp her, and the next few minutes turn into a belching contest.

Esme wins.

Epilogue

oah

I park my rental car in front of my apartment in Brooklyn Heights and lead Aster, Liora, and Oriana up to my quiet two-bedroom. I've lived beneath my means since working at Moon Co, despite the generous salary Brick pays me as a member of the executive team because I never knew how long it would last. I have money saved if Aster wants to buy or build a house somewhere with more land.

We enter the building and walk up the stairs. As we approach the door, Liora freezes, catching the scent of a she-wolf.

Nan.

I video-called her from the Berkshires to let her know I succeeded in getting Liora and Oriana out, and they wished to go to live with her in Kentucky. She found the first flight out, insisting on accompanying them back. *Oriana's never been on a plane, and your mom hasn't mingled with humans in thirty years. There's no way I'm letting them fly out here alone,* she'd signed.

I touch my mother's back to reassure her as I unlock the door.

Nan comes flying out of my kitchen, where apparently she was deep-cleaning my cupboards.

Liora stands frozen in the doorway, rooted to the ground.

Nan throws her arms wide. "Come here, my baby. I'm so glad to see you." She rushes toward Liora, who bursts into tears and falls into her arms.

Our grandmother, I sign to Oriana, who also tears up. *She gives the best hugs.*

I tuck Aster by my side as we let them have their reunion.

Liora finally lifts her head from Nan's shoulder, wiping her eyes. "This is your granddaughter, Oriana."

"Come here, child." Nan envelops Oriana in a hug, then pulls back and surveys her. "Oh, aren't you beautiful? I'll bet you're as smart as your brother, too." She glances at me and starts signing as she speaks. "And strong."

Liora reaches for my hand. "Thank you for raising my son." She's still crying.

Nan comes over to me. "He's turned out to be such a fine boy," she says and signs then hugs me.

Liora wipes her face and also signs as she speaks. "He did, better than I could've imagined."

Nan envelops Aster in a hug. "Welcome to the family, my dear Aster." She looks at me and signs, *Beautiful. What a prize.*

I know, I sign back. *I'm beyond lucky.*

"Can we tell them?" I ask Aster.

This morning she told me that the Grandmothers had shown her that she is, indeed, pregnant with a boy pup.

She smiles and nods.

Nan gasps, already guessing at our news. Liora catches on, eyes wide and hopeful. "No..."

Oriana looks confused.

I wrap my arms around Aster from behind, drinking her scent in. *Aster's pregnant*, I sign.

Judging by my mom's wide-open mouth, she's screaming. Nan, Liora, and Oriana all pile in for a group hug, and we laugh as our bodies jostle together in the joyful pile of love.

I'm so happy, Liora signs. *So happy for both of you.*

Me too, Oriana signs. *I'm going to be an aunt.*

I'm going to be a great-grandmother! Nan signs.

By afternoon, Nan, Oriana, and Liora are on a plane. It feels like a sudden rupture to let them go, but we all agreed that staying in New York and delaying their transition to their new life would just make things harder. Aster and I promised to visit next month.

I take Aster shopping to start her new wardrobe, and as we walk back to my building, she stops in front of a yoga studio, looking through the glass at a class taking place.

"I want to try yoga," she says.

"Yes." I pull her against me. "Anything you want to try, you should. There are so many things you haven't had the opportunity to taste. I think you could just spend the next year trying new things. Finding out what lights you up."

She lifts her beautiful face to mine. "Well, maybe not the *whole* next year..." She smiles.

My brows drop in confusion.

"Maybe just nine months." Her smile grows wider.

A fresh explosion of happiness bursts inside me. "That's

right. You'll be very busy in nine months. *We'll* be busy." I hold her close, swaying slightly on my feet, slow-dancing with her in the middle of the sidewalk. "You're going to be the most amazing mother."

She lifts her light blue eyes to mine, and I see a streak of uncertainty. "Will I? I never even had a mother. I was raised by a cult."

"I know you'll be perfect. Your love will guide you."

She searches my face, as if she's not sure whether to believe me.

"Your love saved me, Aster. I'm not the same wolf as I was before we met. Because of you, I've found my family and my pack. You showed me the importance of connection. You made me realize what's important."

Her pretty lips part on a breath, and I lean down to slide mine over hers.

"You're perfect, Aster. You will guide our family with your beautiful heart and your powerful magic."

Her eyes grow bright with tears.

"I can't wait to walk through life with you at my side. It feels like I just started living."

She reaches up on tiptoe and loops her arms around my neck, kissing me back. She says something against my lips that I can't quite read, but I feel certain that her sentiment was that she feels that way, too.

* * *

Day and night, he sits on his throne. No fire, no luxury, just the shadows passing over the cold flagstones.

No Seeress, either. He lost her. Not that she was any use to him before. Her disobedience led to betrayal.

He will do anything to make sure it will never happen

again. Aiden Adalwulf doesn't lose. Failure is weakness, and weakness is death. He learned that lesson over and over in this very throne room.

The sound of marching boots heralds the arrival of his wolves. The doors slam open, and Brutus leads a squadron of enforcers to stand before Aiden's throne. Half are human, and half are in wolf form. Every one of them has a red sheen to their eyes.

"Alpha." Brutus stands at attention, fixing his gaze to the wall beyond Aiden to give his report. "We've collected the strongest pups from our vassals, as ordered. The pups are secured in the barracks. Dr. Osborne has administered sedatives. Training starts tomorrow."

Finally, something's gone right. "Did the vassals behave?"

"They were honored to have their pups chosen to become part of the pack's elite forces. The few who would reject the honor are now in custody, slated to be re-educated."

"Excellent." Aiden's methods of re-educating disloyal wolves was more gentle than his father, but far more effective. And long-lasting. As the Warden and any wolf who dared question the purity of Aiden's bloodline after the Blood Moon were finding out.

"Osborne is considering testing a strain of *Lupercalium* on the pups," Brutus says. "He asks permission to select fifteen of the strongest pups–"

"No." Aiden's voice echoes through the massive room. "Give it to the weakest."

Brutus tilts his head slightly, showing the barest sliver of his throat in obedience. If he has any moral qualms about testing a drug on the pack's youngest and most vulnerable, he says nothing. Perhaps he realizes what the drug will do. It will either kill them or make them stronger.

Aiden knows that this is kindness. He's giving them a chance to be stronger. His father would've just killed them.

In this world, the weak die, and the strong survive. Aiden is the strongest of all. He cannot be weak.

He clenches his fist and lets the pain wrack his body. It hurts like his bones are being pried apart, but no sound escapes from behind his clenched teeth.

Brutus lifts his head, sniffing the air as if he's caught a strange smell. There's no scent but the stench of fear and iron. Aiden had the throne room scrubbed when he became Alpha, but the scents of the violence of the past still linger in this place.

At times, Aiden thinks he can hear the moaning of past prisoners. The begging of the condemned. It's distant, like it's coming from the dungeons, but that's impossible. The Warden is in a soundproof room to better hide his tortured screams. The rest of the wolves in the dungeons have had their tongues cut out, for daring to ask questions about the wolf with no ears. They're lucky Aiden allows them to live.

Brutus sniffs the air again. Automatically scenting for weakness.

"Is that all?" Aiden snarls, ready for this audience to be over. Brutus' eyes flare red, as if his wolf is ready to do violence, but the light dies as quickly as it came.

"There's one more message from the doctor: The humans have been procured. Operation Romulus is ready to expand."

"Tell Osborne to get on with it." Aiden's already assigned a squadron of enforcers to the lab to assist with the experiments and keep an eye on the scheming doctor.

"Trust no one. And lockdown our borders. No one gets in or out."

"It will be done, Alpha." Brutus tips his head to the right to signal submission, then straightens and thumps his fist against his chest. "Romulus rules."

"Romulus rules," the rest of the enforcers shout, striking their chest with a fist.

The echoes of their shout linger long after they've stomped away. But all too soon, the silence advances. The longer the shadows in the corner grow, the more the ghostly whispers rise.

Stupid pup. Stupid and weak.

The voice sounds like Odin. His father.

But Odin is long dead. A ghost.

And ghosts aren't real. Right?

It's probably just the wind. Yes, that's it. The wind, moaning around the corners, fading into a plaintive whine that sounds like a young pup crying for his mother.

His mother is dead too, murdered by Odin. There's no help coming for that crying pup.

No, the pup isn't real. It's just the wind.

He has to remember that. It's been hard, though, ever since the shadow wolf attacked him that night. The night he lost the Seeress and gained a curse.

But when he turns his arm over and stares at the black poison spreading through his veins, he remembers. And he goes back to his plotting, his plans.

It's only a matter of time until the poison spreads up his arm, and to his heart. He's in a race against death.

He will win.

And when he does... he will make the Adalwulf pack whole. One leader, one mandate. Operation Romulus will be realized, not just for his pack but for all packs. And one day, the whole world.

And his enemies?

They will live long enough to know that he is the greatest wolf who ever lived. The Alpha of all Alphas. He will allow them to grovel before him, and then he will slit their throats and let their blood be the wellspring from which a new race is born.

Romulus Rules.

And soon the whole world will know.

* * *

Thank you so much for reading Big Bad Betrayal!

For a special bonus epilogue where you can meet Brick and Madi's baby, Sabrina Joy, click here.

If you enjoyed this book, we would so appreciate your reviews and recommendations.

Want More? Order
Alpha's Claim

The werebears from Bad Bear Mountain are back, starting with Darius, the Wall Street Viking who boxes with Brick at the gym. We've included Chapter One below.

Order their story now!

. . .

Chapter One - Alpha's Claim

Paloma

The moment the deadbolt to my bedroom door clicks into place, I dash for the closet.

Black clothes, so I won't be seen against the building at night. Flexible toe socks, so my toes can grip the rough-hewn stone of the mansion.

I quickly strip out of my "work" dress and into my escape gear.

I have an estimated three to eight minutes until they figure out how to get power back up, and in that time, I need to be out to the balcony, down the wall, and into the ocean where the security cameras won't pick me up and thermoscans won't see my heat signature.

"You got this, you got this, you got this," I whisper-chant to myself as my trembling fingers draw the lock-picking tools out of the pouch. I'd stowed them in the pocket of these black yoga pants weeks ago after I caught the gardener's thirteen-year-old son picking a lock to the garage during one of my rare unguarded moments in the garden. He'd told me he hadn't meant any harm and was just practicing his lock-picking skills. He'd shown me the instruction book and tool kit he ordered online. I said I would keep it between us, but I had to confiscate his instruction book and tools.

I drop to my knees in front of the French doors to the balcony.

Slipping the slender tension wrench into the lock, I apply pressure to its plug. Then I slide in the pin. I close my eyes to concentrate. I've practiced this at least a hundred times. I already know how to find and set each pin, one at a time, until the lock fully disengages. With a little more pressure on the tension wrench, I turn the plug.

Click.

This is as far as I've ever gotten. I couldn't open the doors before because the electronic monitor at the top would notify Thom's security team that a door had been breached. Now, with the power cut to the property, I have a moment.

I let out an exhale, stow the tools in my pocket, and use both hands to pull the doors open.

They don't budge.

I scan the door frame. Did I miss something? A second lock? A physical bar or barrier? I don't see anything.

"Come on," I growl in an undertone. I pull harder.

It's not moving.

"*Juepucha,*" I mutter. "Come on, you bitch." I yank with all my strength. The doors fly open, and a gust of ocean breeze fills the room, making the curtains flap.

Yes!

My days as the girl in the tower are over. I slip out and silently shut the doors behind me.

You've heard the stories about girls in towers, right? Some of them are supposedly fair maidens. Some princesses. Some have long hair that can be used as a climbing rope to save them.

Me? I guess I'm a mage of sorts. I can see the future of a company, just by looking at its numbers.

Hence, my usefulness as a day trader.

I am also technically a maiden if that means virgin. The jury's out on the fair part. Does that mean good-looking or pale-skinned? I was never sure. Whatever. I'm Latinx, so I identify as BIPOC if you were wondering.

I throw a leg over the carved marble railing that brackets the balcony to straddle it, then the other, balancing my weight on the one-inch ledge that rims the outside.

Don't look down, I whisper.

My particular fairytale lacks the trellis for me to climb down, but metal wires run horizontally along the building to support the ivy. I lean out, wrap my toes around one of them, and test it with my weight. It holds.

Holding my breath, I transfer one hand to another wire. It cuts into my hands but serves. I leave the safety of the ledge and feel with my free foot for a wire below. It's farther than I expect, but I eventually catch it. Then I realize some of the ivy boughs might be thick enough to hold me.

That works better. I scale down, seeking the wires with my feet but sliding my hands along the thicker ivy cords. I'm three floors up, a distance that feels far higher and longer to scale now that I'm doing it. And I've already wasted too much time.

The lights could come back on any second now.

One of the branches I'm holding is too thin, and it breaks. I plunge downward, my fingers grasping for something else to hold and finally catching. My skin is torn, and my fingers burn, but I barely notice. All my focus is on getting down.

I jump before I should, jarring my ankle and smacking my knee on the earth below. But it doesn't matter–I'm out. I take off running for the ocean as fast as I can.

I've been training for this, too. Every day, I race on my treadmill that faces the ocean, whispering to my body that the day will come when we can make a break for it. My illness was a small setback, but the medicine seems to be working.

I wasn't ready for it to be tonight. I wanted to locate Wren and make a plan to get her to safety before I escaped. I also need to figure out how to access the medicine keeping me alive. Last time I tried to escape, I collapsed before I could get far. But I'm feeling stronger now and don't have a choice. I'm out of time.

Thom let me in on his disgusting plan tonight at dinner.

Tomorrow night, he arranged to auction me off to the highest bidder. It's not enough that I make him billions. He must sell me to one of his buddies to cement a merger. His twisted version of an arranged marriage.

Sorry, no.

Not happening.

This time, my escape plan will work. It has to.

The mansion's lights come back on in a sudden blaze.

Dammit.

Run, run, run. I put my head down and sprint as fast as I can. My feet hit sand.

An alarm goes off. It will still take them time to realize I'm gone, hopefully. So long as–

"Hold it right there!" A male voice shouts.

No! I've been spotted.

I could still make it. I'll hide in the water. I reach the water and run in, diving into the cold water before it's deep enough, so it's more of a belly flop. I adjust my hands on the rocks below to propel me into the deeper water.

I don't look behind me. I don't want to see how close they are. Whether they're coming for me. I squeeze my eyes closed and paddle hard, forgetting that I may not survive the ocean even if I'm not caught.

But I am caught.

A strong arm loops around my neck and shoves my head under, holding me down.

I struggle, kicking out, using my elbows, trying to duck out of his grasp. I need to take a breath.

Is this guy trying to kill me?

Clearly he doesn't know that I'm the golden goose.

Everything's muffled by the sound of water around me, but I hear shouts above. Lights blaze in the periphery of my vision. I'm starting to pass out.

And then I'm up. Held by my hair above water.

"What are you doing?" Thom rages from the shore.

"I'm sorry, Mr. Thompson. I thought she was an intruder."

"*Get my daughter back to shore.*"

His *daughter*. Every time he calls me that I want to barf.

Two men grab me by the arms and drag me forward, out of the ocean, onto the beach where Thom slaps me hard across the face.

I figure this is my one chance. If there's any man who works for Thom who has any conscience at all, I need to alert him. If he doesn't disobey now, maybe he'll raise a flag with the authorities.

"Let me go!" I scream. "You can't auction me off. I'm not your property! You can't keep me prisoner here forever!"

A needle jabs into the meaty part of my arm before I even see it coming. I stare into the eyes of the man who delivered it and detect a sadistic gleam of pleasure in them right before my vision goes dark and my legs forget how to hold me.

. . .

\#

Darius

Billionaires have a certain sort of smell. Not just clean human skin, but the extra bouquet of expensive skin care products, rare perfumes, richer food.

That's what my bear thinks, anyway. After years living in Manhattan, my poor animal's nose has attuned to all sorts of city smells. It's a relief to helicopter to the Hamptons for the weekend. I step onto the tarmac and breathe my first clean lungful in months. The air tastes sweet with a tang of salt. Across a half-mile of manicured lawn, sunlight flashes on the wind-whipped sea.

The richer you are, the more land you can afford. My host, Thom Thompson, owns a massive estate on the water between wildlife preserves.

Woods, my bear points out. *Let me out!* He wants to strip off my human skin and lumber into the wild. Keeping him caged in has been the hardest part about living in Manhattan. These woods are nothing like the wilderness of Bad Bear Mountain, where I grew up, but it's enough to remind me of what I'm missing now that I've made New York City my home.

Later, I tell him. I can't go romping around in a pine forest. I'm not here to relax. I'm here to network.

I check my collar and shoot my cuffs. I'm in my best off-hours blazer, designed to look casual while still perfectly tailored. My loafers are handmade in a small village outside of Milan. I'm groomed head to toe to fit in with the humans

I'll be rubbing elbows with all weekend, the one percent of the one percent.

My one unruly feature is my thick blond hair. I get it cut every week, but I swear my bear makes it grow faster to spite me. The wind tousles it as I stride from the helicopter.

"This way, sir." An estate staff member in a navy blue uniform takes my suitcase and guides me towards a mansion that would make Great Gatsby turn green. I brace myself, expecting the place to smell old, like oiled wood and ancient horsehair furniture, but the inside is modern.

The owner and the man who invited me is waiting in the foyer to greet all his guests. "Darius, welcome."

"Mr. Thompson," I shake his hand, careful not to use too much pressure. A firm handshake from a bear shifter would crush a human's bones.

"Please, call me Thom," he says in a reedy voice. He's casually dressed in an outfit that costs more than a new car.

"Thanks for inviting me."

"Of course, my boy." Thom and I have met a handful of times, but he's the sort who fancies himself a mentor. He makes a show of taking younger men under his wing, giving himself credit for their success, and discarding them the second they fall from grace. "I'm sure you'll find this weekend instructive." He doesn't let me get a word in, so I settle for murmuring my appreciation as he continues. "Farpoint has several pools and tennis courts. And the golf course. I hope we'll be able to get a few rounds in tomorrow. They tell me it might rain." He frowns as if the weather is an employee who needs a reprimand. Wealth can insulate a person from any inconvenience, but nature is nature.

"I'm just happy to be out of the city."

"Yes, I'm so glad you could come to my humble abode." The *humble abode* he's talking about has almost thirty bedrooms. It's over hundred thousand square feet, not including the guest and pool houses. "Nester will show you to your room, but don't linger. Cocktails will be served here until six, and then we will sit down for dinner."

More guests arrive, so I thank him and move on, following Nester up two flights of stairs and down a long hallway to a room with windows that overlook the ocean.

Let me out.

My bear is still clamoring to get outside, into the woods.

I placate him by opening the windows to clear the smell of billionaire. I throw each of them open and breathe in the ocean air. A breeze ruffles my hair. I swear it grows another centimeter as I stand there. I swipe my hand through it and sigh. I have to go back downstairs.

I'm here to work, and the work takes place over cocktails and dinner.

I head down to the reception room where a waiter takes my drink order, and I carry my whiskey on the rocks over to the fireplace.

There's a massive oil painting of Thom over the mantel. He's in a striking pose, with a younger woman seated by his side. My eyes are immediately drawn to her perfect oval face. Dark hair, dark eyes, plump lips. The woman's skin is a few shades darker than Thom's pasty complexion.

She's the most stunning woman I've ever seen. The painter must have been a little in love with her. She's too beautiful to be real.

I did my research on the host before coming here and didn't find any evidence that Thom was ever married. The woman is probably his partner, but she's young enough to be his daughter. She doesn't look old enough to be out of college, but I've met plenty of men who prefer trophy wives in their twenties.

No, my bear makes his displeasure known. I ignore him. He's been increasingly unhappy with everyone and everything. Living in the city around so many people is hard on him. I work over a hundred hours a week. Now that my business has its legs under it, I need to be better about taking the weekends off to let my bear out.

Next weekend, I promise him. Until then, I'll squash him down.

The grand receiving room fills with people. There are a few older men who look like Thom plus a fresh crop of frat boy-types with weak chins, strong cologne, and expensive watches bought with Daddy's money. The room reeks of entitlement.

These are the people I'm supposed to schmooze with all weekend. For most people, a few days lounging in a mansion with the ultra rich would be a dream come true but not for me. There's nothing relaxing about glad-handing humans all day and convincing them to invest in my company.

But I didn't build Mountain Top Investments from nothing without sacrifice. Thom Thompson owns the most successful hedge fund in the world. I'm here to learn his secrets and see if he was serious about partnering with my investment firm for a real estate deal.

I toss back my drink and prepare to wade into the fray. Before I do, the scent of hothouse flowers catches my attention. It's coming from the nearby hall. I wander that way and stop short at the sight of a woman descending the grand staircase. She's short and curvy with pillowy lips and shining hair.

It's the woman from the painting. I was wrong. The painter didn't exaggerate the flawless balance of her features. She is fifty times as stunning in real life.

She descends slowly, scanning the room. She's dressed in a modest white dress that makes her golden skin glow. Halfway down, she catches me staring, and her lovely dark eyes are narrow with a glare. Her scent blooms for me, orchids and gardenias, with a bitter undertone.

My chest rumbles as my bear tries to voice his opinions. He's as transfixed as I am but unhappy with the rotten edge of her scent. I step back, grunting to cover my bear's growl, and rub my breastbone to settle him.

The woman reaches the bottom step, and two hulking men in black suits and clear earpieces step forward to flank her. Her head bows, and she heads the direction they point. Two more men fall into step behind them.

Something about the way her bodyguards hover upsets my bear.

No.

He's never been so vocal. For a moment he wrestles me for control, and only years of subduing him allow me to keep the upper hand.

What the fuck is happening?

I dart through the doorway, keeping the woman in my sights. This settles my bear. She's standing beside Thompson now, silent and pouting. They had a tiff, perhaps. Her sugar daddy didn't give her the Mercedes she wanted.

When we all head to the dining room for dinner, the bodyguards surround her again. One of them holds the chair out for her, like he's a combination bodyguard / butler, and she sinks into the seat opposite the head of the table.

Something makes me slide into the seat beside her, and she gives me another cold look. She smells wrong–like poison. Is she sick? Up close, I note the dark circles under her eyes. They're not enough to diminish her beauty but could be a sign of poor sleep. Perhaps a headache. That would explain the bad temper.

Thompson stands at the head of the table and clears his throat. "Thank you all for coming." He paces around the table, like he's our school master teaching us a lesson. "This will be a weekend to remember."

Everyone murmurs their assent.

He stops behind the young woman's chair. "And I'm so pleased to present my daughter, Paloma, to you all." He places a hand on her shoulder.

Daughter. My research didn't turn up the fact that Thom had any children. He must have worked hard to keep that information under the radar.

I study Paloma's face for any hint that she might be related to Thom but can't find any. Her mother must have been a rare beauty with dominant genes.

"She's been working hard at her trader position with Thompson Capital, but I was able to convince her to take some time off," Thom continues. "She's done great things at the firm, and I'm so proud of her." There's a smattering of applause.

Paloma doesn't appear moved by his praise. If anything, it seems to deaden her.

Thompson picks up his daughter's hand and kisses it. Her expression never changes. She stares straight ahead as if in silent protest.

If Thompson notices her attitude, he doesn't seem to care. "By the end of the weekend, I might have another announcement regarding a merger of a more personal variety."

More applause, this time louder, with an eager edge. A few of the older businessmen lean in and whisper something to their younger counterparts. "...bidding...tomorrow night…" I hear one say. My shifter hearing is sharp enough to pick up on the words, but they make no sense.

What did Thompson mean by a merger of a more personal variety? Something's going on.

Thompson proposes a toast to his daughter. We all raise our glasses. Paloma doesn't move to take her glass, and one of the bodyguards leans over her and prods her arm.

That's when I notice the purple marks marring her skin between shoulder and elbow. They look like someone grabbed her arm and gripped hard. She lifts her wine glass, and her dress sleeve falls away, revealing more bruises.

My bear rears up. He's going crazy, wanting to burst from my skin. Damn, after all these years living in New York City, I thought I'd learned to suppress that wildness. I blink at my plate, hoping to hide any brightness in my eyes. My fangs sharpen, and I grit my teeth, forcing my bear to retreat. *Stay back*, I tell him.

I force myself to focus on eating, but it's a struggle not to watch Paloma. Three courses in, I dare to look back at her. She's sitting with that hardened look on her beautiful face. If I hadn't seen the bruises, I might think her haughty.

But now I think it's a result of abuse.

Her head bodyguard leans forward again. "Eat," he orders her. She subtly shakes her head, but he reaches over her and cuts her steak like she's a child. He forks a piece of meat and holds it in front of her lips.

A muscle clenches in her jaw. "No," she mutters. "I'm not hungry."

"*Stop*." There's bear in my growl. My outburst attracts the table's attention. Thom and his conversation partners go silent. I half rise out of my chair before I know what's going on. I face off with the bodyguard. "The lady said no."

"It's getting late. Perhaps you're tired," Thom says to his

daughter. He doesn't wait for her to respond. "Take her to her room." He gestures to her bodyguards. They draw back her chair and take her limp arm to guide her away.

My alarm bells are ringing. No one seems to think this is odd, but I am weirded out by the whole interaction between Thom's brooding daughter and her controlling bodyguards.

Something rotten is going on in this mansion, and I intend to figure out what.

Order Alpha's Claim now!

Want FREE books?

Receive a slew of free Renee Rose books: Go to **http://subscribepage.com/alphastemp** to sign up for Renee Rose's newsletter and receive free books. In addition to the free stories and bonus material, you will also get special pricing, exclusive previews and news of new releases.

Did you know you can buy direct from Renee Rose? Get signed books, special editions, and heavily discounted bundles. Use this coupon for an additional 10% discount on your entire order - READER10

Or go here

https://shop.reneeroseromance.com/discount/READER10

Download a free Lee Savino book from www.leesavino.com

Other Titles by Renee Rose

Paranormal

Werewolves of Wall Street

Big Bad Boss: Midnight

Big Bad Boss: Moon Mad

Big Bad Boss: Marked

Big Bad Boss: Mated

Big Bad Bully

Big Bad Betrayal

Wolf Ridge High Series

Alpha Bully

Alpha Knight

Step Alpha

Alpha King

Alpha Varsity

Bad Boy Alphas Series

Alpha's Temptation

Alpha's Danger

Alpha's Prize

Alpha's Challenge

Alpha's Obsession

Alpha's Desire

Alpha's War

Alpha's Mission

Alpha's Bane

Alpha's Secret

Alpha's Prey

Alpha's Sun

Shifter Ops

Alpha's Moon

Alpha's Vow

Alpha's Revenge

Alpha's Fire

Alpha's Rescue

Alpha's Command

Bad Boy Bears

Alpha's Claim

Alpha's Mate

Alpha Doms Series

The Alpha's Hunger

The Alpha's Promise

The Alpha's Punishment

The Alpha's Protection (Dirty Daddies)

Two Marks Series

Untamed

Tempted

Desired

Enticed

Wolf Ranch Series

Rough

Wild

Feral

Savage

Fierce

Ruthless

Primal

Rugged

Ravenous

Dangerous

Other Paranormal

Claimed by the Storm

Contemporary

Chicago Bratva

"Prelude" in Black Light: Roulette War

The Director

The Fixer

"Owned" in Black Light: Roulette Rematch

The Enforcer

The Soldier

The Hacker

The Bookie

The Cleaner

The Player

The Gatekeeper

Vegas Underground Mafia Romance

King of Diamonds

Mafia Daddy

Jack of Spades

Ace of Hearts

Joker's Wild

His Queen of Clubs

Dead Man's Hand

Wild Card

Chicago Sin

Den of Sins

Rooted in Sin

Made Men Series

Don't Tease Me

Don't Tempt Me

Don't Make Me

Alpha Mountain

Hero

Rebel

Warrior

Master Me Series

Her Royal Master

Yes, Doctor

Her Russian Master

Her Marine Master

Her Fire Master

Her Hollywood Master

Her Stepbrother Master

Yacht Kings

Revenge

Double Doms Series

Theirs to Punish

Theirs to Protect

Holiday Feel-Good

Scoring with Santa

Saved

Other Contemporary

Black Light: Valentine Roulette

Black Light: Roulette Redux

Black Light: Celebrity Roulette

Black Light: Roulette War

Black Light: Roulette Rematch

Punishing Portia (written as Darling Adams)

The Professor's Girl

Safe in his Arms

Sci-Fi

Zandian Masters Series

His Human Slave

His Human Prisoner

Training His Human

His Human Rebel

His Human Vessel

His Mate and Master

Zandian Pet

Their Zandian Mate

His Human Possession

Zandian Brides

Night of the Zandians

Bought by the Zandians

Mastered by the Zandians

Zandian Lights

Kept by the Zandian

Claimed by the Zandian

Stolen by the Zandian

Rescued by the Zandian

Other Sci-Fi

The Hand of Vengeance

Her Alien Masters

Also by Lee Savino

Paranormal romance

<u>The Berserker Saga</u> and <u>Berserker Brides</u> (menage werewolves)

These fierce warriors will stop at nothing to claim their mates.

<u>Draekons (Dragons in Exile) with Lili Zander</u> (menage alien dragons)

Crashed spaceship. Prison planet. Two big, hulking, bronzed aliens who turn into dragons. The best part? The dragons insist I'm their mate.

<u>Bad Boy Alphas with Renee Rose (bad boy werewolves)</u>

Never ever date a werewolf.

<u>Tsenturion Masters with Golden Angel</u>

Who knew my e-reader was a portal to another galaxy? Now I'm stuck with a fierce alien commander who wants to claim me as his own.

Contemporary Romance

<u>Royal Bad Boy</u>

I'm not falling in love with my arrogant, annoying, sex god boss. Nope. No way.

<u>Royally Fake Fiancé</u>

The Duke of New Arcadia has an image problem only a fiancé can fix. And I'm the lucky lady he's chosen to play Cinderella.

<u>Beauty & The Lumberjacks</u>

After this logging season, I'm giving up sex. For...reasons.

<u>Her Marine Daddy</u>

My hot Marine hero wants me to call him daddy...

<u>Her Dueling Daddies</u>

Two daddies are better than one.

<u>Innocence: dark mafia romance with Stasia Black</u>

I'm the king of the criminal underworld. I always get what I want. And she is my obsession.

<u>Beauty's Beast: a dark romance with Stasia Black</u>

Years ago, Daphne's father stole from me. Now it's time for her to pay her family's debt...with her body.

About Renee Rose

USA TODAY BESTSELLING AUTHOR RENEE ROSE loves a dominant, dirty-talking alpha hero! She's sold over two million copies of steamy romance with varying levels of kink. Her books have been featured in USA Today's *Happily Ever After* and *Popsugar*. Named Eroticon USA's Next Top Erotic Author in 2013, she has also won *Spunky and Sassy's* Favorite Sci-Fi and Anthology author, *The Romance Reviews* Best Historical Romance, and has hit the *USA Today* list fifteen times with her Bad Boy Alphas, Chicago Bratva, and Wolf Ranch series.

Renee loves to connect with readers!
www.reneeroseromance.com
reneeroseauthor@gmail.com

facebook.com/reneeroseromance

instagram.com/reneeroseromance

bookbub.com/authors/renee-rose

goodreads.com/ReneeRose

About Lee Savino

Lee Savino is a USA today bestselling author, mom and chocoholic.

Warning: Do not read her Berserker series, or you will be addicted to the huge, dominant warriors who will stop at nothing to claim their mates.

I repeat: Do. Not. Read. The Berserker Saga.

Download a free book from www.leesavino.com (don't read that either. Too much hot, sexy lovin').